About the author

Edward-Alan Scott was born in America in
1946. Since then he has lived and worked
around the world in education and as a
novelist.
His first book, *Project Dracula*, was
published in 1971 when Scott was working in
Ireland as medical officer at an exclusive
boys' school. Leaving Ireland to research
Mayday 747, he virtually lived at Heathrow
Airport gathering material for the novel.
The depth of his research is typical of his
meticulous approach to any literary project:
every fact is checked in painstaking fashion
to ensure total accuracy and authenticity.

Mayday 747

ALAN SCOTT

SPHERE BOOKS LIMITED
30/32 Gray's Inn Road, London WC1X 8JL

First published in Great Britain in 1973 by Sphere Books Ltd
Copyright © Edward-Alan Scott 1972
Reprinted June 1973
Reprinted September 1973

TRADE
MARK

Set in Intertype Plantin

Printed in Great Britain by
Hazell Watson & Viney Ltd
Aylesbury, Bucks

ISBN 0 7221 7687 2

For Edwin W. Ebel

MAYDAY 747

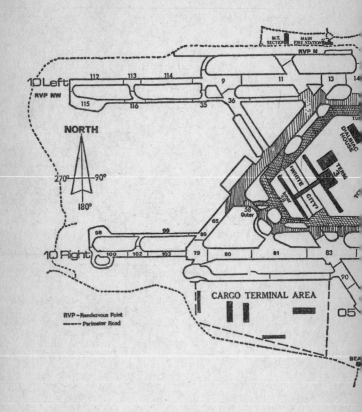

M.T. SECTION

MAIN FIRE STATION

RVP N

10 Left

RVP NW

112   113   114   9   11   13   14

115   116   35   36

D'ALBIAC HOUSE

TURN

WHITE CITY?   TERM 3

NORTH

270°   90°

180°

Inner   WHITE CITY

58 Outer

98   99   65   89

100   102   103   79   80   81   83

10 Right

90

CARGO TERMINAL AREA

05

RVP — Rendezvous Point
----- Perimeter Road

BEA

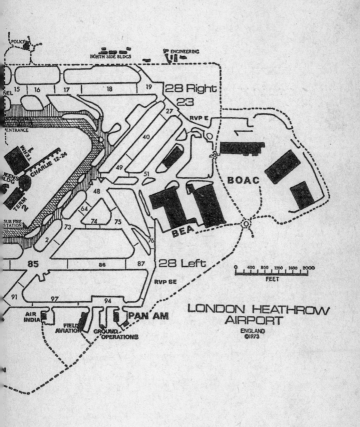

LONDON HEATHROW
AIRPORT
ENGLAND
©1973

It was one of those dull overcast mornings that has always been a curious phenomena of the British summer. The sun was there all right because you could notice a dim glow behind the sticky hot cloud bank that hung like a shroud over London's Heathrow Airport, but on the ground the air was tense and close.

On an average day weather at Heathrow was something to be ignored – one lived with the rains and blustery cross winds, or thought oneself lucky if the sun shone bright and clear. Weather was regarded with the same disdain as a fickle woman and on this particular July morning the closeness of the air was as noticeable as the perfume on a French whore. Kevin Blake, one of the Chief Officers in Engineering Section, had been sweating out two and a half hours over AGNIS without much success. AGNIS was taking the day off in the docking stands known as Charlie where Aer Lingus and BEA had a monopoly on the parking bays. AGNIS – Azimuth Guidance Nose In System – was another of Britain's competitive efforts in aviation and until now she had proved a labour saving boon to the industry. The automatic docking system was based on the also-British invention of Visual Approach Slope Indicators which guided inbound aircraft on to the runway thresholds using a specifically calibrated series of lights which told a pilot whether or not he was 'on the beam' for a normal landing. Using the same principle, AGNIS did away with the traditional batmen who directed planes into the docking bays, but this morning the batmen from Marshalling Section were back because AGNIS wasn't co-operating.

AGNIS had little enough to do at the worst of times and Blake was damned if he could trace the electrical fault which had put the system out of action. There were three lights in a small black box – two red bars and a green bar in the middle all of which stood vertically. When a Captain had swung the nose of his airplane into the bay, he would line himself up with the green bar. If he saw either of the red lights, he knew he was parking out of alignment. It was a simple system and effective. But the even numbered stands – Stands 12 through 24 – were inoperative AGNIS-wise, Blake was frustrated because he knew it was a minor fault, and Engineering were having their troubles finding it.

The stands known as Charlie also had another problem. A Gulfstream Two Executive Jet belonging to American Plastics Inc. had gone down on her port landing gear at the entrance and was partially blocking all aircraft movements into and out of the stands. While extra men from Marshalling Section juggled in and outbound planes around the crippled jet, Field Aviation Services and TWA Ground Support had been called in to help replace the two tyres which had left their tread on Runway Zero Five. That was two and a half hours ago, and the nine o'clock rush hour was in full swing.

Nine storeys above all this in Aerodrome Control, Mark Meyer, the Approach Controller, was bringing in planes which had been knitted into the ILS approach pattern from the stacks at Bovingdon and Epsom. When the Gulfstream Two had radioed that she could no longer taxi under her own power without grinding the hell out of her undercarriage, Meyer had called up Ground Operations for a search of Zero Five. It was quite common for a jet to lose a tread – sometimes both on one gear as aircraft tyres were re-treaded several times – but Meyer wasn't going to clear Air Traffic for a landing on Zero Five if there was a bloody great hunk of rubber sitting on the centre-line.

James 'Buff' Congdon had inspected the runway after Meyer phoned him. As expected, part of the tyre was still there along with an aluminium alloy wheel rim that was broken into a dozen pieces and scattered over eight hundred feet. It wasn't only the tyres that had gone on the Gulfstream.

Congdon made one sweep down Zero Five in the Yellow land rover, picking up the pieces as he went. He drove back to the threshold of Two Three – Zero Five's reciprocal – and once again made a careful sweep, his eyes accustomed to spotting the smallest item likely to cause offence to landing aircraft. Satisfied, he turned off Block Seventy Three and drove up the taxiway until he was at the turn off point for Charlie.

Kevin Blake noticed him arrive from his vantage point on one of the AGNIS lights and, fed up with the unco-operative system, he slid down the ladder and ducked beneath EI-ASH, an Aer Lingus 737.

'You in charge of this?' Congdon said to the back of a pair of white overalls bearing red TWA insignia.

The overalls stood up from the port gear of the Gulfstream and turned around. 'Only until someone else wants to help.'

The head on the overalls was sweating profusely, and he wiped his forehead with a grubby oily hand.

'Here's your tyre back,' Congdon began, hauling a still warm hunk of rubber from the land rover. 'And I got the pieces of your wheel rim.'

The TWA man scratched his head. 'Wheel rim? She didn't lose any wheel rim.'

Congdon figured he'd deny it. They all did. He had a table in Ground Operations covered with bits and pieces of un-claimed aircraft parts. There were fuel caps from the wings, nuts, bolts, screws, shattered runway lights, razor blades, Boe-ing hub caps, pillows, oxygen masks and three bright yellow BOAC Do-Not-Remove-From-Aircraft Press Bags waiting collection. All found during the every-three-hours examination of the runways the Ground Operations Unit of the British Airports Authority carried out.

The TWA man looked at the pieces of wheel rim on the left hand seat. 'No,' he said, shaking his head. 'This plane's got her rims. See for yourself.'

Congdon knelt down and examined the battered gear. TWA was right.

'Look, mate,' he began wearily. 'We only act as agents for this company. We were told she lost her treads and to get her jacked up and fixed and out of here damn quick. And that's what we're trying to do, O.K.?'

Congdon looked up at the overcast. It was goddam oppres-sive. 'O.K. So it isn't your rim. So what plane took off without a wheel rim.'

The TWA man had gone back to his job. 'I don't know and I don't particularly give a damn. I was supposed to clock off three hours ago and I don't get overtime for this.'

Kevin Blake had made his way over and was grinning. It was good to know that someone else was having problems. 'Morn-ing, Buff,' he said. 'Been collecting again?'

Congdon turned from the undercarriage and tossed the pieces of rim on to the seat. 'Some bloody fool's taken off on Zero Five or Two Three and lost a wheel rim. They'll sure as hell know about it when they try to land.'

'What kind of plane?'

Congdon shrugged. 'You want to fit the pieces together, you can tell me. I better inform the Tower.'

Blake fondled the pieces of aluminium alloy as Congdon jumped into his seat and snatched the microphone. 'Tower this is Checker.'

'Checker, go ahead,' replied Jim Ramaley from Aerodrome Control.

'Runway Zero Five checked and clear. Bits of the tyre laying about and a wheel rim. But the rim isn't off the Gulfstream. You might want to look back on your departures since 0600 and notify whoever took off on Two Three that they might be in for a surprise when they land.'

'Roger, Checker. Any idea what kind of airplane that rim was off of?'

'Negative. I can get one of the lads to piece it together, but by that time whoever it was will have landed.'

'Roger. Thanks very much.'

Congdon replaced the microphone and sighed.

'It's one of those mornings, eh?' Kevin smiled.

'Not bloody half. Do you know we're still trying to get that goddam crane?'

Kevin raised his eyebrows.

'There's some bloody crane – you know, a bird type crane – that's got loose from one of the local zoos and Ted's been out every six hours with that damned net of his trying to snare it.'

'Likes the airport, does he?'

'Has done for the last week. If it were me, I'd have a go with a twelve bore and be done with the bloody thing. You can guess what would happen if a bird that big got sucked into some jet that's coming in.'

Blake whistled. 'Well, I better get back to my own troubles. We've got a short somewhere and AGNIS is out.'

Congdon started the land rover. He pulled out a pair of dark glasses from the dashboard. The overcast was getting worse and making everything a dull grey. At least the sun glasses offered some contrast.

Jim Ramaley handed the report from Congdon over to Rob Anderson and told him to issue a statement to all the airlines that someone had lost a rim. For the moment Aerodrome Control was too busy to start checking through all departures on Two Three.

The designation of runways at Heathrow was the same as at any airport anywhere in the world. Though the actual configuration of the landing strips might vary from a single runway to two or more parallel runways with intersecting diagonal strips, the numerical identification of the threshold of any runway was the magnetic bearing of the touchdown area in relation to an ordinary compass. Heathrow had three runways, two parallels with one shorter strip which ran from the threshold of Two Eight Right to a point some two thousand feet down Two Eight Left. If an aircraft was landing on this shorter strip, he would be told by the Tower that he was clear to land on Two Three which would mean he would approach towards the threshold nearest Two Eight Right. If the aircraft was approaching from the opposite magnetic direction due to a change in the wind, he would use the same runway, but the Tower would inform him to land on Zero Five – the opposite end of Two Three. The two twelve thousand foot parallel runways at Heathrow were designated Two Eight if approaching from the East, and One Zero if coming in from the West. An easterly wind meant that planes would land and take off on the Tens – technically, One Zeros – and a westerly reversed the procedure such that planes used the Two Eights. If the Tens were in use as they were today, the easterly wind also meant that Zero Five would be used for landings and take offs rather than Two Three which was used only with the Two Eights. It was all a question of reciprocals, the Tens being the opposite bearing from the Two Eights, and Zero Five being the reciprocal of Two Three. Easterly winds demanded the use of the Tens and Zero Five, westerlies called for the Two Eights and Two Three.

Ted Thurnblad was sitting in one of the Ground Operation's land rovers known as Seagull at the end of One Zero Right. Ted was the bird catching specialist among the Ground

Ops team of twenty-one men. Because birds posed a hazard to aircraft, he had to either catch them or scare them off whenever a particularly large number congregated around the airfield. He used a flare gun to frighten them after blaring out tape recorded bird calls over the loudspeakers on top of Seagull. But this morning Ted was out for big game: the crane that someone from Mechanical Transport Section had spotted hovering around the runway presently in use for take offs. To catch the crane, Turnblad had an enormous net which he could fire from a cannon-like mortar which had been borrowed from the RSPCA unit at the airport. He was grinning at the thought of snaring a Trident or Boeing 737 instead, but the £250 reward out for the crane confined his intentions which might have been lucky for the airlines. It was a frustrating job to search the immediate area for a patch of white feathers when jets were blasting currents of hot kerosene-fumed air in his direction and the longer he stood by his cannon ready to fire the net, the less inclined he was to bring the crane down alive. He retreated to the front seat of Seagull when a 747 Jumbo Jet lined up on Ten Right waiting for permission from the Tower to begin her roll.

Ted parked in the loop at the end of the runway and he was well clear of the exhaust blast of departing aircraft. But he knew the Jumbo had a habit of blowing its exhaust downwards and away from the rear of the plane so he knew he was in for a hell of a heating. With four engines each big enough to drive a bus through and each throwing out nearly fifty thousand pounds of thrust to lift the three hundred tons of monster airplane, Ted wished he was a bit farther away. He figured it must be like standing under a Saturn Five moon rocket sitting where he was, and if a 747 could blow its smaller brother, the 707, on to its back if it was too close behind, he wondered if Seagull would keep its four wheels firmly on the loop. He also wondered why the hell a peaceful bird like a crane would choose such a noisy turbulent area to spend the morning.

The ground trembled slightly and Ted braced himself. He saw the jellied hot air build up behind the 747's engines and almost at once the inside of Seagull reeked of kerosene. The vibrations increased as the roar grew into thunder, the two hundred and thirty foot fuselage began to move forward, and the five thousand five hundred square feet of wing area lumbered along – the whole lot riding on eighteen giant wheels divided between five bogies. The exhaust swirled around Seagull tossing up pebbles and dust from the grass verge. Seagull rocked slightly resigned to stay just where she was, and in a moment the Jumbo was six thousand feet away and picking up enough speed to lift her nose off the centreline. Another thousand feet and the monster had become airborne, creeping into the skies like a timid child, unsure but unwilling to retreat. Thurnblad shook his head, half admiring, half hating this creature of the new era.

Unconsciously, he scanned the runway surface. He considered the mess the 747's were making of the runways and taxiways – the bits of concrete they were churning up as they ambled along to their holding point for rolling, and how the weight of the 747's was just too much for the present runways. Engineering had completed a strengthening of the East bore of the airport entrance tunnel which ran under One Zero Left, but the West bore was still unfinished. All it needed was a bad landing by one Jumbo and that could finish it. The runways were designed to hold 250,000 pounds and the Jumbos were three times that weight when fully loaded.

But the crane was still his immediate problem. Thurnblad raised his binoculars and searched the dirty porridge grey above him. The time was 10.15 a.m.

The seventy miles of roads within the airport boundary were – strictly speaking – private. The general public was allowed access to certain areas where they could watch the movements of aircraft at Heathrow, but signs clearly stating 'Authorised Vehicles Only' failed to keep plane spotters and the casual onlooker away from the more choice viewing areas. The favourite places, of course, were at the extreme ends of each of the three runways where the shattering thunder of low flying jets offered some masochistic thrill. Despite the bold warning signs that clearly advised all vehicular traffic to keep moving, there were a number of cars parked on the grass verges of Two Eight Right and – further along the perimeter road – Two Eight Left. And this was causing havoc in Approach Control.

Bill Auer was Chief Training Officer for Air Traffic Control at Heathrow. It was his task to keep an eye on everyone concerned with bringing aircraft into the biggest and busiest airport in the world, and to get the same aircraft out again with the least fuss. He had been with ATC at Heathrow for seven years. He was married with three children, two boys and a girl. At the moment he was sipping coffee in his office and trying to forget the gloom outside. The weekend was coming up and he had promised to take his sixteen-year-old son out on the car parks and teach him the elements of motorcycling before the boy turned seventeen and could be legally let loose on the general public. Auer was trying to equate motorcycling with flying. *If you're going too slow on a motorcycle, and you take a hard camber, it might be the same as a stall in an airplane. The result was the same. You hit the ground. Maintain speed and heading . . .*

The phone on his desk rang. Auer put his coffee down.

'Chief Training Officer,' he said.

'It's Edwards here, sir. I think we've got motor traffic blocking the ILS radar again. I'm getting some bad readings on my screen.'

Auer frowned. 'O.K., Hugh. I'll get the police to scare them away.' He rang off and swore. Those damned sightseers again. Little did they know they could bring a bloody great jet down on top of them any second. He picked up another phone and dialled the tower. 'Hello, Mark? Are you picking up any interference on the touchdown indicator – at the ILS boundary?'

'Not too much, but Jim just did a visual check of Two Eight Left and there's some traffic out there all right.'

'Thanks much,' Auer said quickly, banged down the receiver and dialled the airport police. Normally he thought himself to be more forgiving than he felt at the moment, but he hoped that just for once the police would scare the living hell out of these spectators. There were highly sensitive localisers where today's crowd had chosen to park their cars, and the metal from the cars could affect the beams which fed a landing aircraft with critical information on its final approach attitude. In this case the cars parked on the verges around Two Eight Right might be messing up the signals on the localiser positions at the end of the runway for the landings on Ten

Left. If the signs weren't there to warn spectators clear of the sensitive area, they might be forgiven for turning an international airport into a parking lot, but how often had these same people been warned to keep away from the thresholds of the runways, Auer wondered. It wasn't enough that Heathrow provided the viewing balconies on top of Queen's Building for the million-odd spectators who flocked to watch the aircraft arrive and depart each year. There were special car parks for spectators, and special bus tours which took plane spotters and other enthusiasts all around the airfield. If all this wasn't enough, then the airport was willing to turn a blind eye to the hundreds of youngsters who clung to the miles of fences guarding the runways along the perimeter road. During the summer holidays the number of plane spotters marching across Heathrow in all directions looked like something out of the Children's Crusades, and still the Authorities chose to ignore them provided they obeyed the simple warning notices which politely, but firmly, instructed pedestrians and vehicles to keep clear of the few hundred-foot threshold boundaries – six of them in all. If their presence didn't pose a threat to the localisers – which it did and they didn't seem to care about – then they were risking severe injury to their hearing when the decibels from the aircraft swooping in fifty feet above them reached a level far greater than the human ear can tolerate.

Auer repeated again to himself that all this wasn't enough. The Queen's Building, the car parks and tour buses, the leniency of the airport regarding trespassers and the warning signs – it wasn't enough that some people had to park their cars in restricted areas and botch up the ILS system which could kill a planeload of passengers if a discrepancy on the localiser wasn't picked up quickly in Approach Control. But that was another sore point which he chose to ignore for the moment as the Desk Sergeant answered his call to the police station.

Emergencies at Heathrow come under three categories: local standby, full emergency and AGI or, aircraft ground incident. The latter two call for a turn out of the airport fire service, the police and medical unit, Motor Transport Section and possibly Engineering. It could also mean the call up of local fire brigades who would meet at pre-arranged rendezvous points. Everything from the moment an emergency was declared was carefully, meticulously worked out and explained in the Emergency Procedure Manual. Anyone involved in an emergency knew exactly what his or her duty was and could report for that duty not later than three minutes from the instant an incident was declared. Practice drills were frequent. At night the airport fire service often drilled in total darkness. The driver of the lead tender was blindfolded and the highly delicate azimuth radar in Aerodrome Control pinpointed his every position enabling a Controller to direct the lead tender to an incident in zero zero conditions. It was a strict precaution but a necessary one. No one really knew that the driver of that tender was barrelling around the runways and taxiways without sight and totally reliant on the tower who instructed him to turn right or left or come to a stop. The driver knew the intricate roadways and taxiways of Heathrow blindfolded – literally.

But the immediate emergency had occurred in daylight, and there was only one person involved. Twelve-year-old Timothy Provost's head was trapped between the guard rails on top of the Queen's Building.

Jim Harrison, Chief Fire Officer, had arrived on the scene in the domestic tender and parked outside Queen's Building while another rescue tender had circled around the apron, past the still inoperative Gulfstream, into the stands known as Charlie. Timothy Provost was not frightened – just suffocating from the dozens of spectators who had known just what to do, and in doing it had nearly decapitated him.

'What do you think, Sean?' Harrison asked with a smile. 'Chop off his head or the railing?'

Sean Cahill knelt down by the boy and held his head up for him. 'It's a damned nice face, Jim. I'd hate to just cut it off.'

'All right,' he sighed. 'You better get the hydraulic ram.'

Cahill pushed his way through the crowd and disappeared down the stairs.

'What's your name?' Harrison asked quietly.

'Timothy,' the boy replied. 'I'm sorry about all this. I mean – I didn't mean to.'

'No, of course you didn't. But how did you do it?'

Timothy tried to turn his head. 'My telescope. It dropped on to the stands and I tried to see just where. The only way I could look was through the railing.'

'The stands, eh? You know a lot of airport jargon. Your father work here?'

'Yes, Sir,' the boy replied. 'He's with BEA.'

'Is he flying?'

'Briefing, Sir.'

'Well,' Harrison said, rising, 'I guess someone better tell him his son is trapped on top of the Queen's Building.'

Kevin Blake had noticed the fire service arrive from his position above the AGNIS light in Stand 12. He had also seen Timothy's head firmly wedged between the railings above and he wondered just how Harrison was going to organise this one. He returned to his work, sorting out a handful of cables when he spotted Ron Michelson and Bill Jeffreys pushing through the spectators on the Queen's Building with what appeared to be a tool box and several odd bits of steel pipes.

'Oi,' Blake called out to the apron tender. 'How're you going to get him out?'

One of the sub-station firemen glanced up and saw Blake leaning out over the AGNIS beam. 'Looks like they're using the ram to me,' he shouted back.

Blake swung his leg over AGNIS, climbed down the ladder and made his way across the stand to the tender. 'Just what does that do?'

'You watch,' replied the fireman. 'It makes short work of those railings.'

Michelson and Jeffreys had unloaded their equipment and were sorting out odd bits of piping which they wedged horizontally between the two railings trapping Timothy's head.

'That ram'll shift eight tons,' the fireman explained to Blake. 'They can use it to push things apart like those railings, or to lift. It's better than acetylene torches for jobs like that 'cause it won't do any real damage. Once they get the lad out they'll just bend the rails back into place.'

Blake grinned. Obviously the boy's old man had arrived from somewhere and was having a good laugh. Between Michelson and Jeffreys and the old man, Blake couldn't see

Timothy, but he could just spot the rails beginning to separate under the pressure of the hydraulic ram. He shook his head. There wasn't a thing that could happen at Heathrow that some section couldn't handle. He grinned at the fireman. 'And I bet you were expecting a full-scale emergency.'

The fireman looked up at Blake who had hoisted himself on to the bonnet of the tender for a better view. 'This is just fine with me. I'd only like to know how the devil these kids can get their heads through those railings, but never get them out. This is the third one this month.'

Blake jumped down from the bonnet. 'You're doing a fine job,' he smiled. 'And when your young friend up there is freed, you come over to that AGNIS beam and give me a hand.'

'You get your head stuck in it and we'll do the same for you. And I wouldn't keep smoking up there if I were you. You'll have this whole ruddy place going up in smoke with all these fumes about.'

Blake returned to his work, and from time to time stopped to wipe the sweat from his forehead and see just how far the fire service had got in freeing the plane spotter. He wondered why he never got an easy job.

At exactly 1100 hours Timothy was freed and his telescope found, albeit a bit battered. He was taken to the Medical Centre and treated for minor abrasions to his neck. The fire service stood down and returned to their station on the North Side of the Airport.

There were other emergencies that occurred at Heathrow from time to time which even the Fire Service were at a loss to deal with. As Harrison reflected over past incidents that he had been called to remedy, the one which stuck in his mind was Operation Birdnest which had threatened the temporary loss of a two million pound VC10. At the time the incident arose Harrison had been responsible for documenting how the Fire Service dealt with each airport emergency and his report was circulated among the fire services located at other British airports. It had been a difficult decision to include Operation Birdnest in one of the Incident Accounts and, in the end, Harrison had given in and, with the assistance of Frank Bradley, the Senior Officer of the airport RSPCA, prepared a detailed account of how a VC10 was saved from imminent disability.

The VC10 had belonged to BOAC and had been parked in the maintenance area for a major overhaul. The four turbine engines at the rear of the aircraft were serviced first, but while the rest of the plane was being overhauled someone had left an engine cover off the exhaust end of number two. It was spring and a pair of starlings declared squatters' rights among the exhaust jets of number two before anyone could spot the nest. By the time the VC10 was ready for service and the engine covers removed, the two starlings had not only constructed their spring residence but were in the process of raising a family. A simple solution would have been to start up the engines which would have resulted in instant eviction of the unwanted tenants. But BOAC was at this time promising to take good care of anyone who travelled with them, or so they advertised all over the world, and since it was obvious that these two starlings had discerning taste in choosing an airline, a solution other than roasting the family alive had to be found. The Heathrow Fire Service was called in.

Harrison had dealt with every conceivable type of aircraft incident in his twenty-eight years as an airport fireman, but this was something new. The Emergency Procedure Manual prided itself on covering any aircraft contingency, but within its comprehensive directives was nothing that offered a solution to the eviction of aircraft squatters. The Manual did say that no aircraft could undertake to manoeuvre on Heathrow's stands, aprons, taxiways or runways with passengers aboard, unless each passenger was suitably strapped into his seat and briefed by cabin staff on emergency procedure, and this had to be interpreted to include stowaways – in this case, a family of starlings. So the RSPCA was called in and, in co-operation with the Fire Service and BOAC, the nest was carefully removed, the family relocated to a nesting area more suited to the smaller aviators, and the VC10 was able to enter service again. With the world jet industry spending over £450 per second, Harrison had to give BOAC credit for not simply blasting the birds to kingdom come rather than holding up a jet airliner whose every minute out of service was costing money.

In terms of emergency categorisation Operation Birdnest was listed under Aircraft Ground Incident, BOAC Maintenance Area, Aircraft Registration Number G-AVBD, VC10. Nature of Incident: illegal tenancy resulting from immobility of aircraft contrary to aircraft manoeuvring procedures.

David Coburn, Chief Officer in Motor Transport Section, looked up briefly as the siren went. Nobody was scrambling for the emergency vehicles and he figured it was another bomb threat. Every day now for the past few months his section had been called out on bomb disposal duty. Luckily, just about every call had proved a false alarm. But he was taking no chances with his men, and Coburn – along with his Salvage Officer – had designed a bomb carrying vehicle tailor-made to the job.

His assessment that the siren heralded another bomb call was correct, and he heard the disposal vehicle pull out of the garage area. The landrover growled under the weight of the armour cylinder fitted on to its tail and at the armour plating that protected the driver. It would be another unclaimed suitcase, he decided. Another innocent piece of baggage which might carry enough explosive to rip apart half of one of the Terminals. But, usually, it wasn't just any Terminal – it was Terminal One where BEA and Aer Lingus hung out. The IRA had threatened this sort of thing, and to date they had made it hell for Motor Transport by sending over luggage which would never be claimed once it reached Heathrow. But they hadn't laden the suitcases with bombs. Not yet, anyway. Coburn wondered how much longer his boys would be safe. After so many false alarms – suitcases filled with rocks, or old clothing – it wouldn't be too much longer before they grew careless. And then it might be the real thing.

The Arab situation wasn't much better. After the massacre at Lod Airport in Tel Aviv, Security at Heathrow had been stepped up and the Metropolitan Police had been drafted in to assist the British Airport Authority Constabulary's three-hundred-strong force. Everyone who didn't have a valid ticket was under suspicion, and the crowds that gathered on top of the multi-storey car parks were under close surveillance. So far, the crowds were the usual tight fisted spectators who would rather avoid paying ten pence to watch the air traffic from the Queen's Building.

The police security at Heathrow had been stepped up not only with local Metropolitan Division constables, but with men from the Special Branch. The airport was taking a tough hand in protecting not only the passengers, but the overall welfare of everyone who worked for the airlines, the ground support sections, ATC and anyone else who had the right to be within the airport boundary. Anyone who didn't share this right, or who was out to cause trouble, faced the dark blue and black Hillmans which patrolled the inner and outer roadways. These particular policemen were special. They didn't bother with niceties. They carried ·38 revolvers, tucked neatly in their waistbands, and they would not hesitate to use them. Then there were the extra police dogs brought in at night, and, although the BAA had their own guard dogs, they were meek compared to the ferocity of the Metropolitan's canine force. These two extra precautions, armed police officers trained and willing to shoot to kill and guard dogs equally willing to immobilise any suspicious character, gave some greater security to Heathrow during the threat of IRA and Arab hostilities, and the ever-present threat of a hi-jacking. And, as if these men and dogs were not sufficient, Securicor Guards had also been employed by the Airport Authority to relieve police constables in Aerodrome Control. Despite the warning signs advising the public that the Tower was strictly off limits, people thronged into the building with hopes to visit the Tower – just to have a look. In the Tower and on the airport roads, in the car parks, on the stands and in the Terminals, there was an army of uniformed and plain clothes policemen, all of whom were ready to pounce at the slightest provocation. And, surprisingly enough, arriving and departing passengers never really noticed or questioned why there were so many police about. To them, like most of the world, violence was something too common to worry about and, besides, they had planes to catch or relatives waiting.

So, Terminal Three, the long-haul departures and arrival building, was under constant supervision. It would be here that an incident was most likely to occur. And with the recon-

25

struction programme in full swing, Terminal Three Departure Building was a mess. The new docking area for the Jumbos – known as White City – had called for the take-over of a long disused runway which ran diagonally to, and intersected with, the main runway. But the docking area meant that each 747 would disgorge three hundred passengers, and with four and five jumbos frequently arriving in quick succession – and departing in similar fashion – the Terminal had to be redesigned to cope with an average of six thousand passengers an hour. As the motto of Heathrow explained, 'Alterations as usual during business hours'.

But Heathrow had been lucky. So far. Even with all the construction work the safety record for the year had been good, with the exception of one tragedy which wasn't really the airport's fault. The plane had taken off normally, and it was either pilot error or instrument error or some vague avionic error that might never be discovered which caused a Trident One to split up in a field two miles from the airport with a loss of 118 lives.

Usually, there was at least one bad incident each year. Coburn, who had been thinking about all this in the seclusion of his office, hoped it was their one and only. He would be more than happy to give Ireland back to the Irish if it would stop the IRA from sending over false bomb scares, and he wished the goddam Arabs would confine their hostilities to the Middle East and leave innocent countries alone. For the Arabs had threatened Heathrow as they had threatened every other airport that accepted Israeli flights, and Coburn knew it was going to be a long, tense summer. He knew that every time the siren went, it could mean another shoot out – a hijacking or some lunatic threatening to blow up an airplane. Coburn recalled what Alan Manley, the Chief Officer in Air Traffic Control, had written in the BAA magazine. 'The gradual realisation that the old happy days where everything in civil aviation was done on trust are on the way out.' That was written maybe six months ago, he remembered, and with the summer spate of hi-jackings in America, the 'old happy days' were not 'on the way out' – they were just plain bloody gone. There was even the question of moving the El Al ticket and check-in counters away from those of the Arab airlines and when it came to having to consider such ludicrous recommendations as these, Coburn was beginning to feel that civil aviation was facing a completely new era. The problems ahead for the fellow that replaced him in ten years' time would be about as big as the wide body jets Boeing, Lockheed and Douglas were building. Coburn was glad he would finish his career with Heathrow before the new era was too much upon him. It would be something for younger men to tackle.

Gavin Bartlett, Chief Engineer for BranAir Charter Inc., an American firm with office space in Queen's Building, was studying a list of stolen merchandise. The six Boeing 707s and two DC8s that BranAir ran from London and New York to various parts of the world were suffering a serious loss from souvenir-happy passengers. It appeared that the seventies had introduced a far more sophisticated air traveller who was prepared to take the risk of stripping aircraft naked, more especially since a recent best selling novel had informed the general public that airlines were reluctant to prosecute stowaways or pilferers for fear of bad publicity. The unfortunate thing was that the novel was absolutely correct – it had been correct in too many sensitive areas of airline management. At the moment Bartlett's list included silverware, pillows, blankets, cups and saucers, monogrammed magazine binders, plastic drinking glasses, 'Do Not Remove' safety instruction cards, stereo headsets for in-flight entertainment, and minor implements from the galleys such as coffee pots, pitchers and similar. He couldn't believe that the list revealed a passenger who had actually managed to remove a liferaft and was perfectly prepared to walk off the aircraft with the raft tucked under his arm. And another paragraph explained how a fifteen-year-old boy unclipped an emergency oxygen cylinder and mask from the overhead rack and was caught only after Customs had detected a strange bulge in his jacket in a place the male species wasn't known to bulge. Upon further examination the youth was discovered to have stuffed into his flight bag and clothing no less than six plastic bottles of complimentary BranAir after-shave and cologne, four dozen packets of WashN'Dry paper face cloths, two 'under your armrest' ash trays and – to the boy's credit – every conceivable

27

give-away item the 'pocket in the seat in front of you' contained. Only the lad had also helped himself to ten other pockets. When questioned by BranAir, the report went on to explain, the boy was quoted as saying he wanted to start his own airline and freely admitted to having collected just about everything except for the actual plane. Bartlett wondered how long it would be before passengers like this boy were carrying off toilet doors, sink fittings, a set of tourist class seats and, if the aircraft were allowed to sit on the ground long enough, maybe even one of the engines. If passengers weren't satisfied with building up their collection slowly Bartlett knew they could always hi-jack one of BranAir's planes and ask the Captain to set it down in their back garden. At least it would render BranAir's insurance claims easier to make.

At the end of the report which Bartlett was studying was attached a circular which had been sent round to all sixty-three airlines which Heathrow catered to. It mentioned a new item that passengers had added to their 'shopping list' when on board commercial airliners. To anyone involved in civil aviation this new item was on the *strictly taboo* list, and however forgiving the various airlines were in dealing with pilfering passengers, the circular encouraged the toughest possible measures to ensure that passengers refrained from stealing life jackets. Bartlett nodded unconsciously as he read. He admitted it was a likely souvenir. Each jacket came complete with self-inflating CO_2 device, a flashlight, an indicating light affixed to the collar and a whistle. Stowed beneath each seat (as the sign in front of each passenger said) the life preserver was easily removed in flight and easily hidden beneath an overcoat or inside hand luggage. Several of the major airlines had been taking heavy losses in replacing these jackets and it wasn't at every turn around point that the theft was noticed. Commercial aircraft are cleaned, fuelled and fitted out for the next flight in sixty minutes – and there just isn't the time to inspect each seat and replace every missing life jacket. But IATA regulations demanded that there be a jacket for every passenger, and an airline could be heavily penalised if an inspector ever found that someone was going to be short of a yellow life preserver.

Bartlett was more concerned for the passengers than he

28

cared for IATA regulations. He cursed the passengers who removed an important article that could easily mean life or death. And he was going to make damn sure that any passenger caught stealing a life jacket was prosecuted. Bad press be damned. No one in civil aviation blamed the Ada Quonsett derring-doers – hijackers were the worry of the day – but financial losses of the nature airlines faced from pilfering was growing into a serious problem.

In Terminal Three Police Constable 38 had taken up his post opposite the baggage claim area. Unaffected by the sticky gloom outdoors, PC 38 was happy to be back on the job. He had been called out for special duty twenty minutes before when ATC had informed the Constabulary that a charter flight carrying American university students was on approach. There hadn't been one charter flight in from the States that PC 38 hadn't witnessed arrive – though his interest was more in the baggage than in the passengers.

Rusty, as he was known in familiar circles, began his tour of inspection as soon as the baggage appeared. Piece by piece he carefully studied the luggage, pretty much unnoticed by the passengers eager to claim their goods and be done with Customs formalities. It was when the last few pieces appeared that Rusty found something. Without hesitating, he rolled on to his back, stuck his feet in the air, and panted. That was the sign. Rusty's handler seized the luggage, and seized the two passengers who were about to claim their bags.

'I'm sorry, gentlemen,' PC Adams began, addressing the two American students. 'Would you mind bringing your bags to the Customs counter?'

Martin Batchelder looked up at PC Adams, down at PC 38, and directly at the Americans. 'Are these your bags, gentlemen?'

'Yea,' replied one sourly. 'They're ours.'

'Are you carrying any alcohol, cigarettes or tobacco, gifts or any other article liable for duty?'

The one American looked at the other. Both shook their heads.

'Are you carrying any prescription drugs or any drug that is likely to contravene the laws of this country?'

Both shook their heads.

'Are you travelling together?' Batchelder asked, opening the first suitcase, a tattered black bag with several peace signs and 'Jesus Saves' stickers peeling off.

'We're brothers,' replied the sour one.

Batchelder already knew that one of the suitcases probably contained drugs. Which suitcase and which type of drug he didn't know. If it was cannabis, it was usually a bulky parcel. Pills were always hidden in rolled up socks. Heroin and LSD were more carefully concealed. He had seen Rusty single out this black bag, however, and the labrador hadn't made a mistake yet. Rusty could sniff out anything but LSD. He had a keener nose than the Alsatians they had tried. Being a hunting dog, he could be trained to smell out anything that was smellable. Unfortunately LSD is as odourless as it is tasteless.

These two Americans were real fools, Batchelder thought as his hand squeezed a pair of socks. And for a two-week charter holiday. They couldn't last a fortnight without using some kind of drug. He removed the socks.

The Americans were visibly shaking when they saw the pair of blue socks in Batchelder's hand. He watched their eyes as he slowly opened them. When he had laid both socks out flat, he lifted them and shook them over the counter. Eight capsules fell out, the bottom half of each capsule black and the top half clear.

'Are either of you dieting?' Batchelder asked.

'No, Sir,' the older of the two replied sullenly.

'Do you know what these are?' Batchelder continued.

'Dexamphetamine spansules,' the older admitted quietly.

Batchelder looked up at PC Adams. 'I'm afraid I shall have to ask you two gentlemen to accompany this officer to the police station.'

Strangely and without a word, the two American students gave in. Batchelder smiled inwardly. It wasn't that he liked catching people out. Not unless they were carrying something really dangerous like heroin or LSD. He was not an unrealistic man and had, himself, used amphetamines when the shift work grew too exhausting. But the sheer idiocy of these two young American students humoured him. If they had only put the capsules in a bottle and declared them as a prescription drug . . .

Batchelder knew that the two-week holiday for the two Americans was suddenly over.

The Number One Director in Approach Control was having a busy morning. Aircraft were coming in on the Airways system from Amber One and Two, Red One and Green One, and the stacks at Bovingdon, Ongar, Epsom and Biggin were building up. Having cleared the jumbos, 707's, Tridents and 737's to three thousand feet, he was busy getting the other aircraft on the downwind leg and knitting them from left to right on to their finals for Runway One Zero Left. The Landing Director took over from the knitting pattern and established the planes on to the localiser with a closing heading of forty degrees or less. The rest was up to the Captain who would intercept the glide path after he was established on the localiser beam.

Every arriving aircraft was jotted down on to a strip of paper which recorded an aircraft's change in flight level on descent, and closed circuit television relayed this information direct to West Drayton Area Control who were responsible for fitting aircraft into the stacks. As one aircraft left the bottom of the stack for his downwind leg, West Drayton cleared another to take up its position at the top of the stack.

The traffic stack at Ongar had now reached capacity and planes were being switched to a heading of two six zero for Bovingdon. From three thousand feet the planes would drop to two thousand for an intercept on the localiser and at six and a half miles from touchdown, the planes established themselves on the glidepath. Both these final ILS procedures guided the aircraft right down to the threshold and it was up to the Captain to keep himself 'on the beam' all the way in.

Because the French and Germans were reluctant to carry too much air traffic on their congested air routes, Departure Control at Heathrow was now facing delays. Only so many planes could take off in the direction of France – otherwise a serious air congestion would build up over Europe. Rome had also been issuing new restrictions, and this only served to confuse the heavy departure scheduling in Radar Control. A plane could not be ordered to start its engines if the Captain faced

31

a thirty minute wait sitting in his stand or trundling slowly up the taxiway, so precise departure schedules had to be continually up-dated. If the passengers were lucky, they would be held in the departure lounge until the delay was over, but it never worked out as easily as that. More customary was for everyone to board, strap themselves in and then sit it out until Departure Control was able to instruct the pilot to start his engines and begin taxiing. At the worst of times, passengers sweated out forty minutes in a fasten-seat-belt No-Smoking environment, wondering what the hell was wrong.

But, despite the air traffic, the atmosphere in Approach Control was relaxed. There were enough men and enough radar screens to give each incoming aircraft personal consideration. David Wilcox was content to sit back in his chair, puffing his pipe and catch up on *Aviation News* with his feet propped up on the control console. Every few minutes he gave a cursory glance at one of the two screens in front of him, requested a squawk for an airplane's identification and when he was satisfied that the three bleeps appearing on the radar screen were in the correct position he went back to his reading.

David Wilcox was not the only Approach Controller who was satisfied enough with the pictures appearing on the ten and fifty centimetre radar screens to feel he could catch up on *Aviation News*. John McKeon and Sean Phelps were equally relaxed if not slightly more attentive as inbound flights were passed along from the stacks and their progress relayed to Aerodrome Control above. It was easy to spot an aircraft passing the outer marker at four miles from touchdown and clearing the inner marker at two thousand feet. The whole operation of introducing an arriving aircraft to its flight level in one of the stacks, releasing it to a lower flight level until it could be taken over by Approach Control, and then observing its correct heading until the Captain had more or less taken control of the final landing proceedures, was carried out in such an orderly and pre-determined sequence that unless some aircraft missed its cue and either dropped to the wrong flight level or was sailing in on the wrong heading, there was little to do in Approach Control. Any deviation would be spotted instantly by the controllers who were so accustomed to what is the correct approach that the slightest error would be as recognizable as if the plane had disappeared altogether.

Above Approach Control in the green glassed-in Tower the men who made final checks on all incoming and departing aircraft were having it slightly rougher than their co-ordinators downstairs. Once down, an aircraft had to be guided to its docking bay, and, unlike American airports, every airline at Heathrow shared bays with other airlines. To get a plane from its touchdown to full stop, then direct it along the maze of taxiways and aprons to its allocated bay without it marching across a taxiway junction where departing aircraft might be headed was a tricky business. There was no margin for miscalculations. Jumbo jets had to be given special clearance: a smaller aircraft lining up behind a 747 could be blown straight back to the stands if too near the exhaust, whereas a number of 707's and 737's could line up behind each other in close comfort. With twenty miles of runways, taxiways and aprons to keep track of, everyone in Aerodrome Control had to maintain a careful track of who was moving around and where.

Yet, sometimes even the constant vigilance of the Tower was not enough to prevent minor incidents on the ground and it hadn't been too long ago that one such minor accident occurred. A 707 had been instructed by Departure Control to turn off Block 99 and hold at the stop bar at Block 102 where he was to wait for clearance to take up his position on ten right for his roll. Behind him was a 747 and either the 707 hadn't pulled far enough into the taxiway, or the 747 had proceeded down 99 too quickly, but, before either Captain had realised what had happened, the port wing of the 747 had removed the 707's tail. Immediately, the Tower declared an Aircraft Ground Incident and the Fire Service turned out promptly. But the only information the Tower could give was the registration and airline of the two aircraft involved who had, by this time, taken their own corrective action. There was a long line up of other aircraft waiting to take off so the 707 had entered the runway at Block 102 and was slowly trundling down into Block 103 to turn off at Block 79 and return to its maintenance area. The 747 had proceeded up Block 99 into 98 and the Captain figured it was best to get out of the way of waiting aircraft and manoeuvred himself into the loop of Block 100 where Ted

Thurnblad was looking for the crane. Meanwhile, the Fire Service had roared up the outer taxiway past the queued up aircraft and into Block 99, expecting to find two embarrassed – if not otherwise humiliated – aircraft. By this time the 747 was parked in the loop on the other side of ten right, and the 707 had reached Block 79, ready to turn off the main runway.

Harrison stopped the lead tender and called the Tower. His only question was where the hell were the two airliners?

The Tower didn't know and contacted the Captains of both aircraft. But since the Captains didn't know exactly where *they* were, as Block Numbers meant little to them, they only reported that they were either holding in one area or requesting permission to move into another. Obviously, neither aircraft appeared in any immediate danger, and all the crews had known was that they could not take off without repairs.

Harrison then proceeded to the holding area in Block 98 which was directly opposite the loop where the 747 was sitting, but nearly a thousand feet away. Harrison further directed other Fire Service vehicles to turn off Block 99 and try to find the 707 which had last been seen heading down the main runway with its tail hanging limply across the elevators. By this time, the 707 was ambling back down the taxiway past the queued up aircraft while the Fire Service vehicles were driving around in circles at Block 79.

Harrison was, by this time, convinced that someone was having him on. His information was that a 747 and a 707 had been involved in a collision at the threshold of ten right, or in that general vicinity, and Harrison knew damn well that it was pretty hard to lose sight of a 747 whose tail stuck up higher than a six storey building.

The Tower was adamant that there had been a collision and it had been witnessed by the Captain of the airliner behind the tail-chopping 747. If the Fire Service couldn't locate two aircraft in what was considered a pretty clear area, then they had better get their eyes checked.

Harrison was fuming. Already fifteen minutes had been wasted, and still the whereabouts of the two airplanes was a mystery. He had two vehicles out searching for the tail-less 707 and he himself was looking for the 747. But the line up of other 707's, 747's, 737's, Tridents, Caravelles, a TU 104, and a

Viscount made singling out the aircraft in question impossible. It was only when Harrison noticed the Captain of the plane who had witnessed the incident and who was by this time manoeuvring into Block 98, waving frantically from his window, that he looked across the threshold of ten right and spotted the 747 he was after. Although he had noticed it before, he guessed that since there was nothing wrong with it that he could see the Jumbo was merely holding in the loop for some kind of take off clearance. At last *one* of the aircraft had been found.

Sean Cahill was hot on the trail of the 707. He had spotted a few bits of debris on the turn off point at Block 79 and proceeded up the taxiway along Blocks 89 and 65 until he finally spotted the 707 heading for the 747 docking bays known as White City. Finally, in the middle of 58 Outer, Cahill charged the 707 and blocked his entry into 58 Inner. As far as he was concerned, the 707 was under arrest and had he ones big enough, he would have handcuffed the nose gear to his fire tender.

In retrospect, the entire incident would have made a good old-time comedy – an airport version of the Keystone Cops – but by the time the two aircraft were escorted into their maintenance area, neither the Fire Service nor the Tower were much amused. Among the various flight crews who had witnessed the whole incident, it was hilarious. What made it more so, and what to this day is still talked about with wild fits of laughter, is that both planes involved in the incident belonged to the same airline!

What usually prevented such incidents, however, was the eight-millimetre radar scanner on top of the Tower which gave a concise picture of the airfield. The screen, which scanned at 760 revolutions per minute, could identify any moving object from a roving BAA vehicle to a single wandering person within the airfield manoeuvring area. This screen enabled the lighting director to guide aircraft around the field at night or in near zero zero conditions. It was the same screen that directed the blindfolded driver of the lead fire tender and it was the only radar screen of its type in the world. It made life a lot easier for the gang in the Tower and it took the tension out of ATC work. There were so many divisions and sub-divisions of responsibility in Approach and Aerodrome Control that nobody really tensed up. Occasionally, there would be a flap on when congestion was at its worst, but the jumbo jets had managed to increase passenger movements at Heathrow and decrease the number of aircraft flying in and out. To the ATC Controllers this was a blessing. Bigger planes capable of carrying more passengers was the answer to air congestion, and the jumbos, the Lockheed Tristars and 500's, and the DC 10 would soon make the 707 redundant on long-haul runs, and every jumbo that flew would replace three 707's. Already, TWA, Pan-Am, National, BOAC and other commercial airlines were planning the phase out of the smaller jets like the 707 and VC 10 in favour of wide-body aircraft for long-distance flights. Money was saved – the key to aviation success! – congestion was cut down around the world, and the general public would just have to accustom themselves to becoming one of four hundred on the big jets than one in a hundred on the old 707's.

The advent of the wide-body aircraft did indeed seem a boon to Air Traffic Controllers, commercial airlines and safety in the air, but to airport ground support it created hell. Not only did the arrival of a jumbo herald the onslaught of up to 460 passengers who had to be processed through Immigration and Customs, but the physical touchdown of the 550,000-pound airplane was breaking up runways. At Heathrow, where the main entrance for passengers ran straight under Two Eight Right, the twin tunnel bores were weakening and Engineering knew that one fine day the whole tunnel would collapse. So the East bore had been shored up and reinforced and the West bore was up for strengthening in a year's time. Ground Operations were hardly impressed by the scheduling of this work. Buff Congdon had already seen Block Fifteen sinking and he was fighting for the immediate closure of the over-the-tunnel runway. The impact weight of the jumbos combined with the enormous forward-downward increase in G force when the thrust reversers were engaged was posing a major threat to the now obsolete runways. Hardly a week had gone by when either Congdon himself or Thurnblad or one of the officers from Ops hadn't hauled in a chunk of concrete that had been broken off the runway shoulder, because the taxiing speed of the 747's was still too fast for the taxiways to support the weight. The integrating de-accelerometers on board, which are supposed to retard the speed of a 747 when set to Ground Speed Mode, needed re-calibrating so that the pilot could control his speed, and if these adjustments weren't made soon, the main runways of Heathrow would, in Congdon's words, resemble 'an open pit mine'.

Closure of a runway for any length of time was out of the question. The most Heathrow could hope for was a resurfacing project similar to that undertaken by Prestwick. Though concrete was always considered superior to any other material for runway surfacing, the time involved meant weeks without a serviceable runway. Instead, Prestwick had experimented with asphalt and found it better than concrete. And it meant that runways need only be closed at night when air traffic was at its minimum. But even this idea was months off in Heathrow's mind. With London Transport tearing up the East side of the airport to provide an underground train service direct to London, and the reconstruction of Terminal Three Departures, Heathrow couldn't cope with another major alteration. And the future of Heathrow's lunge into tomorrow's world looked worse still. The underground wasn't going to begin at Hatton Cross on the East side, but at a station that was going to be built right in front of the Control Tower. No one wanted to predict or consider the massive confusion and congestion the project would involve.

So Congdon and his Operations Unit made their three-hourly scours of the runways, continued to haul in broken runway or taxiway shoulders along with the other bits of aircraft debris, and every so often put in a request that something should be done either to the accelerometers or to the runways – preferably to both. Congdon's real worry were the pit covers, slabs of concrete a foot thick and half a yard square, which rested on thin shoulders at various points on the runways. Pit covers acted as access areas to the cables that carried electricity to ground and approach lighting, the radar installations and runway lighting. And they carried the telephone communication lines. They were, in effect, nothing more than glorified manhole covers and, until the arrival of the Jumbos, they had rarely been the source of concern. Now they were being broken up like so many egg shells.

Of particular concern to Congdon was the intersection of Zero Five and One Zero Right. This intersection was saturated with pit covers – dozens of them that crisscrossed and zigzagged in every direction. The intersection was in Block 85 and it was the point at which most aircraft were airborn when departing on One Zero Right from Block 79, and the touchdown point for arriving aircraft using Two Eight Left. Often, during the era of the 707, the pit covers had withstood lift offs and touchdowns and had never presented themselves as a source of trouble, but they simply were not designed to cope with the weight of the 747s. One day, Congdon prophesied frequently, one of those damned monsters is going to go straight through those pit covers and he didn't elaborate on the consequences.

Three thousand miles away, at John F. Kennedy Airport, New York, International Airlines was recovering from one of the worst nights in its fourteen-year operational history. Nearly eleven hours before, their night flight to London – IA 124 – had been delayed due to an engine overheat on a 747B Jumbo jet. Two hundred and sixty passengers had been milling about the departure area for an hour when the nine thirty flight had been delayed until ten thirty. At ten thirty, when International's engineers couldn't promise to remedy the situation in any reasonable time, International's Ground Staff had to figure out what to do with the two hundred and sixty passengers, among whom were an unaccompanied minor flying first class, a grouchy electronic salesman who demanded evidence that his cargo ship of hi-fi equipment for the European market was safely stowed away, three priests and a rabbi, and the usual crowd of tourists. The only answer was to put them up at the International Hotel and the ferrying of passengers had begun at eleven p.m.

Allison Powers had still not solved the problem of twelve-year-old Brodie Washburn, the unaccompanied minor. Once International accepted the responsibility of the boy, it had to be met until Brodie was handed over to his parents in London. She and Brodie were brooding in the International's Crew

Room when the flight crew of 124 appeared, somewhat unconcerned about the bonus stop over.

Captain Huston made for the phone to ring his wife in Chappaqua, New York, while the First Officer, Richard Page, and Peter Sturgess, the Flight Engineer, cancelled their flight plan for the night and thought about preparing an up-date for the morning flight. Lynn Almirall appeared with the other eleven stewardesses and spotted Allison, her room-mate between flights, looking exhausted and undecided.

'Find Paul, could you,' Lynn asked, turning to Toni Rice, the only stewardess on the flight with nursing qualifications. 'I think Allison is having another nervous breakdown.' Toni smiled and made for the confusion in International's departure lounge.

'Phew,' Lynn gasped, pulling up a stool near Allison. 'What do you do with a plane load of unhappy passengers? I'm glad I'm not in your shoes.'

Allison frowned. 'You'll have them all day tomorrow so don't look so smug.'

'And who's this young man – one of your admirers?'

'This,' replied Allison, 'is Master Brodie Washburn, who is at the moment in a bit of a quandary.'

'He is – or you are?'

'We both are. He's unaccompanied. That means someone has to stay with him until tomorrow morning and I don't fancy that your flight crew will be too anxious to share quarters tonight.'

'You mean you don't know what to do with him?' Lynn asked.

'Well, I can't just dump him in the International with all the other passengers. We'd be crucified.'

'What about staying with my young brother?'

Brodie looked up sleepily, hoping that maybe a solution had been found and he could get away from this female gestapo agent.

'With your brother?'

'He's flying with us on 124. Toni's out trying to find him now. I've booked a room at the International for him and your friend could bunk down with Paul. Paul can keep an eye on him.'

Brodie looked insulted.

Allison felt some kind of light relief. She didn't relish the idea of being an all-night watchdog. It had been a hellish day what with disgruntled passengers and an impatient youngster. Besides, she was well into overtime for the third day running. 'You think it would be safe – I mean the two of them together?'

'If I tell Paul to keep an eye on him, he will. This trip means too much to him.'

'How does that sound to you, Brodie?' Allison asked.

Brodie shrugged. He wasn't sure how old Lynn Almirall was and therefore how old her 'younger' brother might be. But his hopes took something of an upward sweep when he noticed an International stewardess dragging a boy about Brodie's age along through the crowded room. The stewardess stopped to speak with one of the ground crew and the boy seemed to be looking for someone. With any luck this would be Lynn's brother, Brodie thought, and he could finally get away to the hotel. The boy spotted who he was looking for and made his way towards them. Lynn turned round in time to see her brother – for once in an ordinary white shirt, blazer and what she called 'conventional' trousers rather than the roll neck sweater and jeans which she was used to seeing him in on the brief lay overs she had at home.

Here in the crowded and somewhat confused crew lounge Lynn thought quickly of the sudden change that had overtaken her family since she had left for training as a stewardess and Paul had left for private school. They saw little of each other, but somehow they seemed closer than they had been when both had lived at home and fought between themselves in the years of growing up as brother and sister. Paul had always struggled to keep up with Lynn in his own way, even though he was several years her junior. Lynn was pretty, and she had been popular. Paul had been a pugnacious waif, fighting to overcome both his size and his stature which made him look a good two or three years younger than he really was. And then at twelve Paul had begun to grow and though he was still barely over five foot at the age of thirteen and he hadn't exactly filled out in any great proportion, he was losing his aggressive attitude towards Lynn after finding his own per-

sonal success at private school. It was Lynn who had urged her
parents to take him away from the highly competitive environment of the junior high school and try him at a small boarding
school thirty miles from the Westchester home. That had been
a year ago. Paul had resolved himself to the fact that he was
being rejected and abandoned by his family – especially by his
turncoat sister who had dreamt up the idea of a boarding
school – but when he had begun to achieve his first measure of
success both in his school work and in athletics, his confidence
returned.

Lynn knew that initially Paul might feel he was being
rejected by being sent away to school, so she had dedicated
herself to convincing him he wasn't. Having been promoted to
flying the international routes which took her to just about
every European city where International flew, she always
found something to send him. He had bull fighting posters
from Madrid, a switch blade from Italy (which had been confiscated by the Headmaster and delivered to Paul's parents),
miniature skis and boots from Austria, chocolate from Switzerland and, on one occasion, a giant Swiss cuckoo clock which
had also been confiscated by the Headmaster after the dormi-
tory had been kept awake for six nights, but which now hung
proudly in the upper school study hall. Slowly, over a period
of weeks and months, Paul took to writing Lynn c/o International Airlines, and a new kind of relationhip began to
develop between them. When the aviation bug caught Paul,
and Lynn was in a position to furnish him with just about
everything except an aircraft, the relationship was sealed and
once again they were brother and sister.

As Lynn considered this while Paul hung back long enough
to talk to the four-stripes-which-meant-captain, she knew she
had done the right thing in urging her parents to find him a
private school. Tonight, out of his jeans and pullover and
wearing instead the somewhat modified uniform of International's ground staff, Paul was a long way from the shy and
aggressive youngster he was fourteen months before. His blond
hair was cropped smartly about the ears and neck but was full
and recovering from the school's barber, and his thin face
gleamed with confidence, his features determined and growing – albeit slowly – into a handsome young man.

'Hi,' Paul grinned. 'Not a very good airline you work for, is it?'

'It's carrying you so it can't be all that bad,' Lynn replied. 'I've got a job for you.'

'Where do you want me to fly to?' he answered quickly. 'Something wrong with the Captain?'

'Paul,' Lynn began, ignoring the offer, 'this is Brodie. He's going back to his parents in England and he hasn't anyone to stay with tonight. I figured you and he could share a room at the International and you could keep an eye on him. You know, make sure he gets settled in. You know the ropes.'

'Sure,' Paul replied, extending his hand across the table. 'Glad to meet you, Brodie.'

Brodie smiled and felt relieved. At least his 'guard' was someone his own age. It could prove an interesting night if anything good was on television.

Allison Powers stood up and yawned. 'Well, if all this is settled, I'd like to get to bed. And I have to go further than the International Hotel to get home. Lynn, be a dear and look after Brodie in the morning. I couldn't face getting up at six and trundling out here if Paul can manage things.'

'No trouble,' Lynn said. 'You can manage, can't you, brother?'

The courtesy car from the International was waiting as Paul and Brodie, last of the stranded passengers, piled in at Kennedy and piled out at the hotel. Paul demanded his key more than asked for it, marched to the lift and found his way to Room 331 without the help of the porter. ('They always expect at least 50 cents just for turning the key in your door,' he explained to his charge.)

'You seem to know all about this kind of thing,' Brodie remarked, flopping on to one of the twin beds.

Paul drew the curtains shut and switched on the television. 'Lynn told me all about it,' he said with a flourish. 'She's been flying for four years. She's been on international flights for eighteen months. That's when you've reached the top.'

Brodie pushed back a wisp of auburn hair from his eyes and stretched. He was tired. He had come in from Los Angeles in the afternoon, spent four hours in the company of Miss

Powers doing generally nothing, and then found himself threatened with a whole evening of this sugary female agent – until Paul had shown up. He relaxed and was nearly asleep. It was the muffled cries that roused him. At first he thought it was the television.

'Paul? You all right?' he asked sleepily. 'Something the matter?'

'Nothing,' Paul groaned, trying hard to fight the sudden stabbing pain. 'Just a stomach ache.'

'Looks like food poisoning to me. Want me to ring downstairs?'

'No!' Paul cried. 'Forget it, Brodie. It's just my stomach.'

Brodie sat on the side of the bed. Paul was sweating and his face was as pale as the sheets. He noticed Paul had clenched his fists and doubled them into his stomach. He began to feel frightened. 'I think you should see a doctor.'

Paul made an effort to rise. He swung his legs over the side of his bed and forced himself to sit up straight. 'There, you see. Almost over. I feel much better. Only if you call a doctor I won't be able to go tomorrow.'

'You mean to London?'

'If Lynn thought there was anything wrong with me, she wouldn't let me fly. And this is the only chance I've got to fly over with her. She's on the Hawaiian run after this.'

'I see,' said Brodie slowly. 'Do you get these pains a lot?'

'Only recently. But I'm sure they're nothing much.'

'I'll get you a glass of water. Maybe that'll help.'

And, as the night progressed, faded and dawn crept from behind the curtains, Brodie had become Paul's guardian and Brodie had a suspicion that Paul was suffering from something more than a stomach ache.

Wilbur Cross was up at five thirty and at the airport by seven. Wilbur Cross was a bad natured person at the best of times, and the delay combined with a rotten night's sleep had made him worse than ever.

'When's our flight taking off?' he demanded at the International Airlines information desk. 'Or do we spend another day in New York?'

'Not goddam likely,' thought the clerk to himself. He had

been trying to estimate the cost of putting up two hundred and sixty passengers – most in single rooms – and giving them a complimentary breakfast as well. He smiled and looked up at Mr. Cross. 'Your flight is scheduled to depart at eight thirty, sir. If you would care to join the rest of the passengers in the departure lounge, we'll advise you when your plane is ready for boarding.'

'What about my hi-fi equipment? You haven't done anything to that while you were fixing whatever was wrong with your plane?'

'No, sir. Your consignment is safely on board. It was a minor technical fault in one of the engines that caused the delay. Your shipment would not have been affected.'

'I hope so. For your sake. That gear is very important to my company. All our European sales depend on that gear.'

'Yes, sir. You can be sure that it will arrive safely.'

Cross didn't seem satisfied, but then he didn't have much choice. His demands the previous night that he see exactly where the equipment was loaded had been ignored – politely, of course, but ignored nonetheless. Reluctantly, he moved away from the information desk and walked slowly into the departure lounge. Some of the passengers had already checked in but he was unwilling to socialise. The bar wasn't even open. He found himself an isolated seat.

Flight 124 was finally ready for boarding. Lynn Almirall had singled out Paul and Brodie and checked them on board before the rest of the passengers. Brodie was in first class and Paul was flying economy, but she knew that Paul could have the seat of his choice if he had an extra few minutes before the remaining passengers scrambled for the best window seats. Although seat assignments had been made, there wasn't time to ensure that two hundred and sixty people were in their correct positions before take-off and frequently, compromises had to be made – with the promise that any misunderstanding would be straightened out after the plane was airborne. By that time no one usually gave a damn. Brodie, however, didn't want to sit in first class. At least, not without Paul. It was a six and a half hour flight and he didn't relish the idea of sitting next to some kind-hearted mother who gave him the third degree, or

44

trapped beside some pompous executive who blocked his way to the aisle.

'Either your brother joins me in first class, or I'll go back and sit in tourist,' Brodie proclaimed to Lynn. 'Paul said this plane can hold three hundred and ninety passengers and it looks to me like there's plenty of room for everyone.'

Lynn sighed. She couldn't bring Paul into the first class compartment because he hadn't paid the extra fare. Paul was a discount traveller because of Lynn's concession as a stewardess, but the concession limited travel to economy. And Brodie was an unaccompanied minor who was booked into first class. The boy's parents could demand a refund if she allowed him to travel in economy.

'I'm sorry, Captain Huston,' Lynn began, as she interrupted the pre-flight check which Huston and his First Officer, Richard Page, were immersed in. 'I just don't know what to do'.

'Let me get this straight,' Huston said impatiently. 'You've got an unaccompanied minor who's made friends with your brother. This rich kid is booked through to London in first class, but he wants to make the flight in economy with Paul. And you don't know what to do?'

'That's it, in a nutshell, Captain. Can we let Brodie sit in economy?'

'Or bring Paul into first class,' Huston thought. 'What do you think, Dick?'

Page looked up from his checklist. 'Is first class full?'

Lynn knew it wasn't.

'Well, if the Captain here won't tell anyone, and I'm damn sure none of the others will, then let Paul have the de luxe treatment. He *is* your brother, and we're all agreed that crew should get preferential treatment.'

'If it's all right with you, Captain,' Lynn replied, hopefully.

'Yeh, sure. Go ahead and stick the pair of them up front. And tell them to goddam well behave and let us get on with it.'

She smiled and returned to the cabin where Brodie had already decided Paul's fate. 'He's flying with me, Stewardess,' Brodie announced. 'You can bill my parents for the extra fare. I am an unaccompanied minor, you know.'

'It's all been cleared with the Captain. But let's just keep

45

it amongst ourselves, O.K.? There won't be any question of padding the bill.'

Brodie smiled as if it were *his* victory. Paul was equally content. Travelling first class, he thought. This meant he could sit in the Sky Lounge upstairs. If things carried on this way, he and Brodie might even be able to visit the cockpit in flight.

Wilbur Cross hunched himself up against the window and gave a cursory glance at his neighbour. The neighbour was reading some electronic magazine and that interested him. Maybe his neighbour was foreign and maybe he, Wilbur Cross, could begin his sales campaign right now.

'You interested in electronics?' he asked somewhat awkwardly.

The neighbour looked up from his reading. 'I work in electronics if that's what you mean. Name's Roger Staunton. I'm with Amplivox.'

The accent gave him away. Staunton was British. Cross had found a customer. 'I deal in electronics. Hi-fi stereo stuff mostly. What's your pigeon?'

'We make hearing aids,' Staunton replied with a smile. 'For people who can't hear hi-fi stereo. I'm responsible for our aviation division. We manufacture special headsets for pilots. We combine the micro circuitry of our hearing devices with a boom microphone. The whole unit weighs just a few ounces and the pilot doesn't even know he's wearing it.'

Wilbur Cross, interested in anything new, relaxed a little. 'Do you have one handy?'

'I think so,' Staunton said, pulling his briefcase down from the overhead storage rack. 'I packed most of my samples in my suitcase, but I think I might have one or two on board'.

Cross hoped he had. Maybe, just maybe, Cross could combine Amplivox Minilite headsets with his hi-fi equipment. A stereo hearing aid. It might sell.

Bruce Ames looked ahead two seats and grinned at the carryings on of the two boys. He thought it must be their first flight – at least in a jumbo. They beamed with excitement and fiddled with the battery of controls on their armrests. The boys reminded him of his own two sons. And of his wife – separated nearly a year now. He had seen Kirk and Lance only twice that year. He desperately wanted them back. But he didn't dare take the case to court. He knew his wife would win if it came to divorce. She had always won at everything. And with him flying around the world every other week on some trouble-shooting job for Pan Am, he wouldn't make much of a father. Not in the eyes of the courts, anyway. At least, under the terms of a separation he could see the kids whenever he wanted to – whenever he had the time. If it came to a divorce, well, it didn't bear thinking about. Because there wasn't going to be a divorce. Ames closed his eyes and tried to rest.

'Tired?' inquired Bruce Ames' fellow passenger. 'It's been a long night for all of us.'

Ames opened his eyes and resolved himself to the fact that he would have to make conversation with this first class passenger. He was getting a grace flight on International as it was the earliest available flight out and Pan Am wanted him in London quick. There was trouble in the maintenance department at Heathrow – something about one of the new 747B Pratt and Witney JT9D engines that the maintenance boys couldn't figure out. It was holding up one of their jumbos – and it was costing Pan Am money. 'I heard you had some trouble last night,' Ames offered.

'Weren't you on board – I mean –'

'No, I've just joined the flight. I'm with Pan Am – the Technical Control Centre here in New York. Had to catch the first flight to Heathrow, so here I am.'

'Alex Trent-Jones,' said the passenger, extending a friendly hand. 'I'm with Decca in London.'

'Bruce Ames,' Ames replied. 'The same Decca that's been developing the navigational system?'

'The same. Omnitrack and all that. I've been trying to get your FAA boys to replace your VOR system with our latest navigational aids. But they don't really seem too eager. '

Ames felt some relief. At least he could spend the next six and a half hours in the company of someone who spoke the same language. It might not be a bad flight after all.

International Flight 124 for London – now twelve hours late in departing – began to roll away from its stand at Kennedy. The two hundred and sixty one passengers made last minute adjustments to seat belts, the nervous read what to do in an emergency, and within another fifteen minutes, Captain Huston announced that they were, indeed, on their way to London and apologised for any inconvenience due to the delay. For the most part, no one cared.

At about the same time that International Flight 124 left Kennedy Area Control and was picked up on radar by Gander Newfoundland Transoceanic Control where Captain Huston was cleared to maintain flight level three five zero on the Great Circle Course, the first of a series of events was taking place at Heathrow – a series of events which would affect not only the combined ground sections of Heathrow Airport, but also every inbound flight scheduled to land at London: including International 124.

Runway One Zero Right was still being used for take offs although the time was 1.45 pm and Met. Section had forecast a westerly wind which would mean switching to the Two Eights. EI-ASH, an Aer Lingus 737 bound for Dublin and the same aircraft that Blake had seen when he was working on the AGNIS system, was holding in Block 79 waiting for permission to roll.

'Shamrock Alpha Sierra Hotel, you are clear for take off,' London Tower announced.

Captain O'Shea acknowledged and checked with his First Officer. He began his run, adjusted critical attitudes of his control surfaces, and made a normal lift off at the intersection of zero five and one zero.

'Shamrock Alpha Sierra Hotel, airborne at three five. Contact radar on one two five decimal eight,' London Tower advised.

'Alpha Sierra Hotel. One two five decimal eight. Good day,' Captain O'Shea repeated.

'We're in trouble,' the First Officer announced coldly. 'Can't raise the starboard undercarriage. Better inform Area Control we'll want a low level priority holding until we know what's causing the difficulty.'

O'Shea trusted his First Officer. He had to. 'Area Control this is Shamrock Alpha Sierra Hotel. We seem to be having some trouble with our landing gear. We'd like permission to hold at Epsom until we can have a think about this. Can you give us a pretty low flight level?'

'Roger, Alpha Sierra Hotel. You're clear to hold at Epsom at two eight thousand feet. Call us when you decide.'

'Thank you. Two eight thousand at Epsom.'

Clipper One Hundred, a Pan Am jumbo, had turned from Block 98 into Block 100 – the extreme end of runway one zero right – and was requesting permission to roll. Captain Rollins was still worrying over the fuel he had burnt up waiting for this roll and was swearing at the delay the French, Germans and Belgians were causing. With the usual go slow strikes which were for ever plaguing French aviation, aircraft had been limited or restricted in using European airspace. So new flight plans had been filed over Belgian airspace. This led to saturation and the Belgians couldn't handle the volume of air traffic now headed their way. So they had issued restrictions. The same thing was happening over Germany. And it all bounced back to Heathrow where the Departure Controller was holding aircraft until the number of jets flying over France had been re-routed and shared out between the three complaining countries. This led to delays of up to forty minutes, and, although Departure Control were now witholding permission to start engines, aircraft were sometimes burning up too much fuel on the ground waiting for their clearance to taxi. Once in the taxiing queue, more fuel had been wasted as aircraft were held for permission to roll off Ten Right. This made the Flight Engineer's job difficult, it annoyed Captains, and it put everyone in the flight crew in a foul humour.

'Clipper One Hundred, you are clear to take off at three nine. Squawk standby Alpha three zero zero five.'

'Roger. Roll at three nine. Alpha three zero zero five.'

Captain Rollins sighed heavily and glanced at Hennigs, his First Officer. 'Let's go.'

The 747B, fully loaded and rolling down the runway with a weight of 698,000 pounds, took up six thousand feet of tarmac before she reached V1, the point at which a take off can be aborted and beyond which the pilot is committed to flight. At this speed the control surfaces would begin to respond and Captain Rollins was able to get the 747's nose off the ground. With the nose up attitude of the jumbo, the four main bogies were taking all the weight and it was in this attitude that Clipper One Hundred lifted off at the intersection in Block 85. The tremendous thrust from its four engines was blasting away at dozens of pit covers.

'You're going to have to hold those departing aircraft,' Mark Meyer announced.

Jim Ramaley, ready to clear a BranAir Charter 707 to take up his position behind the departed Clipper One Hundred, looked up gloomily. 'How long?'

'Five minutes, if we're lucky. The Belgians just sent in another restriction.'

Ramaley squeezed the transmit button. 'BranAir Two Four, you are to proceed to holding position and wait for clearance to roll. There will be a slight delay.'

Captain Hite wasn't particularly bothered. 'Roger London Tower. Any idea how long?'

'About fifteen minutes Two Four. Will clear you for your roll as soon as possible.'

Captain Hite picked up the horn. 'Ah, Ladies and gentlemen, this is Captain Hite speaking. I'd like to welcome you aboard Charter Two Four and I'd just like to tell you that we've been told to hold our position here for a few minutes due to some delays up in the skies. We should be getting our clearance for take-off shortly so please ensure your seat belts are fastened and I'd just like to apologise for this brief delay.'

Meanwhile, Captain O'Shea had decided to cancel his flight to Dublin.

'London Control, Shamrock Alpha Sierra Hotel at Epsom. Permission requested to run back to Chepstow and dump some of our fuel as we're going to have to return. The starboard undercarriage will not retract. Can you give us clearance for a low flight level?'

'Roger, Alpha Sierra Hotel. You are cleared for Chepstow at flight level eight zero.'

Captain O'Shea apologised to his passengers, explained that due to a minor technical fault in the landing gear they were dumping fuel and would be returning to Heathrow, and not to be in any way alarmed. The undercarriage was in the locked down position and there would be no danger in landing. What Captain O'Shea didn't explain was that a local standby would be declared at Heathrow when his plane was on finals, and that the Fire Service would automatically be standing by, waiting for him.

Clipper One Hundred, the last plane to leave Heathrow, was also encountering difficulties.

'Damn it, if it isn't our day for Gremlins,' Captain Rollins swore. 'What's up with that gear?'

'I don't know, Sir,' Hennigs replied. 'I've got two bogies that won't come up.'

Captain Hite squeezed the stick with sweating hands. 'Shall we request a visual check or just get clearance to Frankfurt?'

'You'll be lucky if you can get clearance to Frankfurt. That's what's been holding us up. The high level routes are packed at the moment.'

Hite pressed his transmit button with vehemence. 'Area Control, this is Clipper One Hundred out at three nine. We seem to have some undercarriage difficulties and I would like a visual check unless I can be cleared to Frankfurt.'

'Roger, Clipper One Hundred. Stand by.' Ted Lomax figured it was going to be a good day for lousy undercarriages. This was the second in succession. He picked up the direct line to London Tower and spoke to Meyer.

'Yea,' Meyer answered. 'You can clear him for visual check. We've got enough delays building up here so there won't be much traffic. Bring him in from Biggin and we'll sort things out.'

Meyer reckoned things were getting tricky. He rang down to Bill Auer and asked him to get on to Pan Am's engineer. By the time he arrived from the Pan Am maintenance area on the East side, Clipper One Hundred should be ready for a visual check from the Tower. It would mean clearing the Control Zone and Meyer rang the Met Section to get a report on the cloud base.

At the same time he picked up the slip of paper sent from Approach Control and contacted Air India Four Two Seven. 'Call when established on the localiser. You're clear to descend to three thousand feet.'

'Four Two Seven. Two thousand feet,' Captain Mahurra acknowledged.

'Three thousand feet, Four Two Seven,' Meyer corrected, wondering how in hell those pilots were forever getting their localiser fix mixed up with the glide path at two thousand. It was as if they didn't understand English.

'Big flap on, eh?' Auer said, hoisting himself up the last two steps of the nearly vertical stairs which led into aerodrome control.

Without turning away from his monitors, Meyer replied, 'Everyone's having trouble at once. Departure delays and undercarriage problems. Two in a row.'

'Both off one zero right?' Auer asked.

Meyer nodded.

Buff Congdon was heading out for a runway sweep in Checker. He was still trying to figure out how an airplane could lose a wheel rim without noticing any trouble. Things like that never ceased to puzzle him. How, for instance, could a jet continue its climb when one of the fuel caps was left behind on the runway? And what of the poor blighter who was bringing his 707 in on a perfect attitude approach landing when his nose gear hit that fuel cap? Already the 'bits and pieces' table had been filled and cleared off three times, and Gerry Vimr, one of his junior officers, had rightly suggested they open a used spares store since none of the airlines seemed interested in claiming any of the missing parts.

The threat that runway debris posed to any aircraft – jets in particular – was obvious, and it was little wonder why airlines complained if they discovered a hat pin or broken wheel rim or shattered runway lighting before Ground Ops did. The aggravating situation arose when the airlines denied responsibility – even if it could be proven. The airlines carried their denials to ridiculous lengths, Congdon thought, even when the name of the airline was engraved on the aircraft parts so often found.

Congdon was passing Block 97 where Air India had its maintenance area and he stopped at Block 91. 'Checker. Clearance to turn right into Block 85 to cross onto Outer 72.'

'Report clear,' replied Ramaley, still waiting to clear Bran-Air Two Four for his roll.

Congdon stalled the landrover. The clutch had jammed. Same thing as yesterday and he swore, because he hadn't got the bloody thing seen to. He jumped from his seat and was was about to lift the bonnet when he saw the crane flying overhead making for the Central Area. 'London Tower, this is Checker. Cancel my request. I've got some engine trouble. You've got that crane heading in your direction. See if you can get Seagull near the stands.'

'Roger Checker.' Ramaley was now able to clear BranAir Two Four. The crane could entertain the spectators on the Queen's Building for a while longer. 'BranAir Two Four, you are clear to start your roll. Squawk standby Alpha Two One Zero Four.'

'Roger London Tower,' snapped Captain Hite. 'Rolling, Squawk standby Alpha Two One Zero Four.'

Congdon heard the 707 build up thrust at the end of ten right. He turned from the bonnet of the rover and peered through a slight mist up the runway. He figured this baby was on a long trip. The Skipper was holding her back to give his engines time to build up power – it meant she was fully loaded with passengers and fuel. Unconsciously he looked down along the runway as if his visual check from this remote point would guarantee a clean surface. When his eyes caught sight of the intersection, he froze. What he saw he refused to believe because he knew it was impossible. It was an hallucination – a trick the overcast was playing. He screwed up his eyes, squinted at the intersection, then dived into the rover for his binoculars.

Captain Hite felt the 707 lurch slightly as he released the wheel brakes and his aircraft lunged down Block 100. In a flash he had passed the turn off point in 102, cleared the main turn off at 79, and was approaching eighty knots by the time he crossed the stop bar at Block 80. He knew his First Officer would be calling out V_1 in another few seconds and his eyes skipped over a score of instruments that told him he could pass V_1 and continue his take off normally. The intersection at Block 83 was ahead, and he knew he would be airborne before he reached 84 and 85. He was almost waiting for the call of V1 now, feeling his steering lighten on the nose gear. Soon he could get some response from his control surfaces – a bit of lift from the elevators and flaps – he'd ease back on the stick and . . . His nose gear thudded and he felt a bump that jolted the entire cockpit. Instantly his mind diverted from a take off configuration to diagnosing what the hell had happened. Jesus, if he lost a tyre now – but his First Officer was shouting something, and it wasn't V1.

'Engine Number Four's blasted to hell,' called the Flight Engineer. 'I've got fire in Number Four.'

'Number One, Skipper,' Hite's First Officer shouted. 'Total loss of power.'

'Abort!' Hite returned. 'Hit the extinguishers on One and Four and give me all the reverse thrust we've got!'

At the same moment Hite took a chance and dropped his flaps to their maximum down position. His spoilers went up at the same time as his feet shoved the pedals into the floor. 'The brakes,' he shouted above the ear splitting roar. 'Stand up on the brakes!'

The effect of bringing the 707 from its rolling attitude and speed to a complete emergency stop had shot the force of gravity spinning upwards. Passengers and in-flight luggage were flung forward, the former held into their seats only by their seat belts. The Flight Engineer, facing his console on the starboard wall of the cockpit, gripped his desk after he had hit the extinguishers and was fighting the forward thrust which threatened to send him ploughing into the back of the First Officer. He risked his balance and brought his right hand up to the fuel cut off switches for engines one and four, the knuckles of his left hand white and his fingers digging into the metal frame of his desk. The noise was agonising, the lurching and shuddering of the fuselage terrifying as the 707 struggled to stay in one piece, hurtling across Block 83 and into 84. Smoke was already pouring from the undercarriages as the two main bogies fought for a grip on the concrete while the nose gear burst its hydraulic suspension from the G force that soared over its operating capacity.

As the 707 left Block 84 for 85 and the intersection, Congdon stood alongside his landrover only long enough to see the nose gear plunge into the gaping hole where minutes before a pit cover had been. He heard the sickening bang as the gear snapped off and then the scream of rending metal as the 707 nosed down and ploughed on seconds before he dived for cover behind Checker.

Captain Hite hadn't seen the hole, nor the bits of shattered concrete that had somehow scattered themselves four hundred feet along the runway. His only sensation – and that of his crew – was the sudden downward plunge of the aircraft and splintering sensation in the belly of his cockpit as the runway leapt towards them. He guessed his nose gear had sheared straight off – probably from the deacceleration forces – and, despite his frantic efforts to keep his plane on the runway, he was thankful the gear hadn't buckled and shot straight up into the cockpit.

First Officer Rice was convinced they were going to stand the 707 on her nose as he and his Skipper arched their backs and strained against their harnesses, pouring every ounce of strength into their legs which were pushing the brakes down as far as they'd go. When the rubber on the port bogie ruptured from the intense heat from the runway and the brake drums, Hite gave up on his left pedal and fought to keep the plane from winging over. Without looking, he knew that with the port gear down on its rims, the engine pods were just about on top of the runway and already the plane was swinging to the left from the drag on the useless bogie. His hand shot to the throttles and he opened up number two, cutting out the thrust reverser. If his wing scraped the runway at the speed they were travelling, the tanks filled with fuel would blow them over half the airport. And now, with his number two open and his number three still giving him full reverse thrust, the plane veered starboard, but the right hand undercarriage was still holding. His port wing was up, but unless he corrected his attitude he'd be winging over on his other side with the same catastrophic consequences.

Block 87 loomed up ahead of him, and Captain Hite was staring at the threshold markings of two eight left. He reckoned the threshold to be about a thousand feet away. Even if he was down to sixty miles an hour, he was still grinding along at eighty feet a second. He looked beyond the threshold and saw the grass verge, the approach lighting bars and the localiser. If he crashed into them . . .

But the plane *was* slowing down. Hite was now skidding along the shoulder to the right of the centreline. He closed down number one and cut the thrust reverser on number three. Dropping the spoilers on his port wing in a last minute effort to give the wing whatever lift was left to keep her off the tarmac, he let the 707 veer diagonally across the runway, figuring the extra few yards a diagonal skid would add to his stopping distance was all he needed.

The threshold markings were below him. He could see the wide black and white strips. The grass verge was now only feet away. The approach lights for two eight left looked like ghoulish spectres through the sweat-stung eyes of Captain Hite and his First Officer as the plane ground to a halt at the upper left hand corner of Block 87. From the moment he had been cleared to roll to this second, Captain Hite had used up every inch of nearly two and a half miles of runway.

'Turn to the fire service frequency, one three zero decimal five,' Hite said in a long drawn out sigh. 'Tell them we are deploying escape chutes and using standard emergency evacuation procedures.'

'Yes, Sir,' replied Rice.

The Flight Engineer was rubbing his sides where his harness had bitten into him. 'That was quite a ride, Skipper.'

Hite raised his eyebrows and let his head loll about slightly. 'Cut all fuel switches. Internal power off. Standard emergency procedure.' He paused. 'Quite a ride.'

Auer, Ramaley and Anderson had watched every second of Captain Hite's attempt to abort his take-off. Even before the 707 had ploughed into the broken pit covers and nosed down onto the runway, Auer had pressed the crash button and picked up the telephone. Immediately, the Fire Service, Motor Transport Section, Medical Centre, Management Duty Room and BranAir were informed through the telephone exchange. He gave the pertinent details and nothing more. 'Aircraft accident. Rendevous Point South East. BranAir Delta Two Four. Boeing 707. Nose down on Block 85 and crossing Blocks 86 and 87. Passenger load unknown.'

Harrison was already in the lead tender when the Aircraft

Accident information was broadcast throughout the fire station. All he heard was 'Ground Incident. Boeing 707. Block 87,' but that was enough to spur his men into immediate action. The four doors to the fire station swung open with incredible speed and the first engines were already turning out.

'London Tower. Permission to cross one zero left,' Harrison asked, not as a formality but as a strict requirement.

'You're clear to cross. Will abort landing aircraft.'

Harrison didn't bother to look up at Air India 747 which was heading straight for him.

'Air India Four Two Seven, this is London Tower. You are to abort your landing immediately. Repeat. Fire service vehicles crossing one zero left. Overshoot.' Auer instructed coolly and decisively.

The 747 reacted. Captain Mahurra pulled back on his throttles, retracted his undercarriage, and prayed he had enough lift to make an overshoot safely. When his plane passed over the last of the Fire Service vehicles his main bogies were twenty feet above the foam tender.

'This is Captain Hite,' Hite repeated slowly on the fire service frequency. 'I am deploying chutes. No fire on board. No internal damage.'

Harrison acknowledged and in the few seconds he had time to think, he admired the coolness in Hite's voice. 'They're deploying chutes,' he shouted.

The fire crew took up their positions. The Cardox tender lined up in front of the downed 707 in case the engines ignited. There were thousands of pounds of aviation fuel still sitting in the tanks and, although only the burnt rubber of the undercarriage was smoking, the chance of fire was great. The high pressure Nubian Major stood ready to hit the plane with everything it had if a fire broke out in the fuselage area, while the stewardesses pushed open the emergency exits and rolled out the escape chutes. Firemen grabbed the bottom of the chutes and held them high off the ground so that the passengers didn't come sailing down the chutes to break their legs on the concrete.

Motor transport had rolled up and the local Staines fire brigade was now standing by at the rendevous point, waiting to be called in if needed. BOAC had sent out three coaches as soon as they saw what was happening, to get the passengers away from the plane and into one of the VIP lounges. Though BranAir could have turned out their coaches in time, BOAC figured they had enough to worry about. It was common for one airline to assist another in any emergency.

The Medical Wagon arrived last. If the plane were to blow – or just catch fire – there would be passengers running from the disaster in need of help. There was no point in bringing the Medical Wagon too near if there was a chance of an explosion. But a tentative all clear had been given and frightened passengers were being hustled clear either into the BOAC coaches or into the Wagon. Ground support staff knew that the first priority in any aircraft incident was to get the passengers away before they had time to realise what was happening. Shock set in all too quickly if given the chance.

Last out was the flight crew. Captain Hite and First Officer Rice stood just beyond the nose of their airplane staring at the torn up belly. The Flight Engineer, Chris Dennis, was still in the cockpit, checking and double checking that the fuel valves were shut and all the systems were closed down. Instinctively, he knew that if the darned thing hadn't blown up by now he was safe enough making sure everything was done to prevent a secondary explosion. As he heard the foam tender spraying the red hot belly of the forward section he knew that if a fire did start, it would be in the region away from his centre tank.

Gavin Bartlett had appeared with Ray Milross from Press and Public Relations who had driven him over. Milross knew what his job was. The Press would be hot onto this one and he wanted to see just what had happened. When he returned to his office in the Queen's Building he'd report the on site inspection to his boss, William Bell, and together they would have to make arrangements to ferry the Press and television boys out to the incident when the all clear was given. In the meantime they'd have to make an immediate statement.

Mechanical Transport was already setting up a salvage centre. For the moment all they knew was that runway one zero right was US – out of action – and it was their job to get the runway open again. And quick. Coburn was discussing the problem with Doug Parent, his Salvage Officer, while the

Director of Operations, Ian Turin, was getting information from Bartlett. Turin knew that if it were a BOAC or BEA plane lying there, then Mechanical Transport and Engineering Section wouldn't be needed: BOAC and BEA had their own salvage teams. But BranAir didn't, and this meant calling in the full resources of everything Heathrow had to offer to get that plane off the runway.

Harrison was now satisfied that no fire danger existed. He informed the watchman back at the station who in turn sent out a stop message. 'Stop for GI Block 87, 707. Nose wheel collapsed. No fire. Stand down local authority fire service. Services not required.'

The Marshalling section who had been holding the local fire brigade at the rendevous point dismissed the fire trucks and returned to their section with the airport police.

As far as the emergency vehicles were concerned, the incident was over. For BranAir, Mechanical Transport, Engineering and Ground Operations, the headaches were ready to turn to migraines.

Gerry Vimr had been finishing his sandwich lunch in the Ground Ops building when a violent roar had shaken the flimsy windows – a roar that Vimr knew was some jet throwing his engines into full reverse. Seconds later he saw the BranAir 707 skid across Block 86 and disappear behind the Pan Am maintenance hangar. Immediately, his hand shot to the direct line phone to the tower.

'Emergency's been declared,' was all Vimr heard.

'Let's go,' shouted Cary Rowe, bursting through the door and tearing his jacket from the hook. 'It looks pretty bad.'

'I hope that thing doesn't go up on us. Jesus, which vehicle is in?' Vimr scrambled through the row of keys in front of him.

'Use Ops One. It's free.'

Rowe snatched the keys from Vimr and made for the land-rover. As he crashed the rover into first gear, halted only to allow Vimr to leap into the front seat, he saw Checker belting down the runway towards Block 87.

Congdon had kept his position behind Checker only long enough to ensure the 707 wasn't going to explode all over him.

The moment it passed, he had jumped into the rover and ignored the usual request for clearance to enter the runway. In his mind flashed the Emergency Proceedure rules. *Section A. Paragraph One. Subsection One Three. Sweep Search. Organised as soon as possible to safeguard uninjured and shocked persons who may have wandered away from the scene; locating injured or dead flung from wreckage on impact; also property.* From the way that pilot was handling the nose down 707, Congdon hoped to Christ he wouldn't be staring into a lot of 'dead flung from wreckage on impact'. He had seen that before. He didn't want to see it again.

The chutes gave him confidence. When he saw the long white self-inflating slides being deployed from the emergency exits he knew that the crew had everything under control, and with the Fire Service cooling off the belly of the plane, the chance of a fire now was pretty slim. He whispered thanks to whoever it was who pre-destined aircraft incidents and then noticed Ops One barreling down the runway behind him.

'It's a mess,' Vimr reported when the two Operations vehicles had come to a stop two hundred feet from the 707's tail. 'The centreline lighting is ripped up from the intersection clear down to here. Some of the side lighting is gone as well. And there's bits and pieces of undercarriage everywhere.'

'What about the passenger sweep?' Rowe asked. 'Any idea of injuries?'

Congdon was watching the passengers being hustled into the BOAC coaches while a few were being led into the Medical Wagon. 'I don't think anyone's got it. No fire and no aircraft damage – structure damage anyway. We'd better get to work on clearing up the runway and get a lighting assessment written up. Engineering's going to have their hands full with this mess.'

Vimr looked back up Blocks 87 and 86. The path the 707 had taken was clearly visible. Runway light housings were shattered. Bits of concrete were lying about the intersection, and chunks of pit covers had been dragged several hundred feet. The metal scar from the crushed nose gear traced the pattern the 707 had taken from the instant she went down, and the whole area looked like the British Army had been on tank manoeuvres. He shook his head and trembled slightly. He was just beginning to feel the full weight of what he had seen. It wasn't only the passengers who suffered from aircraft incidents.

The telephone exchange had just finished notifying the various Sections that an Aircraft Ground Incident had been declared, and immediately upgraded to an Aircraft Accident. The entire emergency services of Heathrow were now in full effect. Management Duty Room had notified the necessary personnel to prepare the Alcock and Brown suite for the passengers from BranAir Flight Two Four. This VIP lounge could accomodate up to two hundred passengers and this was the first priority once the aircraft had been cleared. Already the BOAC coaches had arrived and were helping shaken passengers into the suite. Meanwhile, in Building 221 on the North side, the airport Chaplain had been summoned, and Reverend Joseph Baxter was on his way to offer what comfort and encouragement he could to the distraught passengers. The Medical Centre was receiving those slightly injured from the sudden forward lurch of the aircraft when the thrust reversers had been engaged, and a mobile unit was on its way to the VIP suite to administer tranquillisers and minor first-aid to those who were merely bruised or shocked.

The police were having their usual problems with the scores of visitors who had witnessed the incident. Hundreds of spectators had seen the 707 go down from their vantage point on top of the Queen's Building, while plane spotters near the end of One Zero Right had emerged from their rapidly sought shelters and were scrambling over the fence – some to offer help and others to grab some quick photographs. Traffic had built up on the perimeter road which ran within fifty yards of the localiser. Not only had spectators made it their duty to come zipping over to the incident area, but rescue vehicles, heavy duty lorries working on the underground extension area at Hatton Cross and airport employees were jamming the road in both directions. Motorcycle police were trying to sort out official vehicles from the scores of spectators, while other BAA police removed the dozens of unauthorised persons who only managed to creep back from another direction.

Around the BranAir 707 assessment operations had already

begun. The thousands of gallons of fuel stored in the wings would have to be drained before any salvage work could commence. Two Shell tankers had arrived and were fitting the hose couplings to the fuel valves, but with the nose gear down, it was difficult to get under the wings between the engine pods. It would take at least an hour to drain the fuel, and then no one knew how much longer it would require to actually remove the 707 from the runway. David Coburn estimated five hours at the minimum and Kevin Blake who had just arrived from the stands was guessing somewhere in the region of eight to ten hours. And he had seen the runway damage on his way down. Even if they did get the 707 cleared off in five hours – which he doubted – there was a hell of a lot of emergency repair work to be done to the intersection and the centreline lighting in Blocks 86 and 87.

By now the orange and white Incident Post Vehicle had arrived from MT Section, along with two cranes, a fork lift and several radio cars. Coburn knew that he would have to use the air bags to get the plane's nose up before a tug could be hooked up under the nose and he snapped an order to Malcolm Hewitt to have the compressor unit and air bag trailer hauled out. He'd need some winches, too, and some steel plates to lay over the grass areas at the end of the runway. With all the vehicles surrounding the aircraft, the grass verges would turn into a soggy battlefield if some kind of covering wasn't laid down quick.

'It's been a good day,' sighed Blake. 'It's been one of those days that I'll remember when I want a good night's sleep.'

Coburn looked across the bonnet of his land rover. 'We're just goddam lucky that pilot stopped here and didn't go ploughing through the localiser. It'll be easy getting that thing jacked up on concrete. If she was on the grass . . .'

'Yes, easy for you maybe. Have you seen what the runway looks like?'

Coburn shook his head.

'A battle zone. Every damned lighting fixture is gone. Sheared right off their housings. The pit covers are scattered from here to eternity. There's concrete all over the place and Christ knows what kind of damage to the cables running under the intersection.'

'If we get this plane out of here in about five hours, how soon can you get that runway open?' Coburn asked thoughtfully.

'Offhand, I couldn't tell you. It'll mean pulling all our men onto this job and calling some of the boys in from home. With luck – maybe seven or eight hours. We'll have to re-fit the centreline lighting, run a check on all the cables under the pit covers, shore up the pit covers that aren't damaged and replace the broken ones, re-surface the areas where that 707 skidded and then make a final clean. So, between the problems you've got getting this thing out of here and the problems I've got repairing the damage, I'd say that Heathrow's going to be out of two runways for the next twelve hours.'

'Yea, you'd better sound a bit more hopeful. Here comes King Kong,' Coburn replied softly.

Brian Barker, the Incident Officer and a senior BAA police officer with a reputation for knowing just how much power he swung, and Ian Turin were approaching fast. Aerodrome Control was screaming for some answers while the four stacks were building up with waiting aircraft and departures were virtually at a standstill even though runway One Zero Left/Two Eight Right was still open.

'Oh, happy days.' Blake squeezed between clenched teeth.

'Well?' Barker began, 'What's the assessment?'

'Lousy,' Coburn replied, pushing himself away from the landrover. 'We're going to have to air-bag her and that's going to take three hours. They're draining the tanks and that'll take another forty minutes. Once she's bagged we can begin to haul her out, but we don't know what kind of damage the undercarriage's suffered. We could begin to inflate the bags and find ourselves with just two broken wings. Even if we're lucky and the wings take the weight, it'll be a damn slow haul out of here. We've got to winch her around first.'

Barker sighed and frowned. 'I don't suppose your report is anything more promising?'

Blake looked up at the sky. The clouds were heavier. It would rain soon. 'Suppose I told you that we could have the runways open in two hours. It still wouldn't help you until that plane is shifted, would it?'

'It would give us Two Three,' Turin said hopefully.

'Yeah, well, it isn't going to take two hours. My guess is we'll be lucky to have both runways operational inside twelve hours.'

Barker paused to think. He turned to Coburn. 'Do you agree with that?'

'Yes, I'd go along with that. At the outside. Too much depends on how bad that plane is underneath. We ought to have a better idea once we can move around her a bit more. It's just getting the fuel out that's delaying us at the moment.'

Barker and Turin looked up at the sky. Blake was right. A slight drizzle had begun to fall.

Barker wiped his forehead. 'O.K., Kevin. Get all your men on. Call them in from home if you have to. You, too, David. Christ knows what this is going to do up there,' he finished, looking towards the green windows of Aerodrome Control.

Captain O'Shea's Shamrock Alpha Sierra Hotel had finished its fuel dumping run to Chepstow and was cleared to descend to three thousand feet to establish itself on the localiser for one zero left. Meyer was watching the Aer Lingus 737 closing on finals from his console in Tower Control and praying that the undercarriage wasn't going to give way and dig up their one and only runway. Ramaley was cancelling departures, advising aircraft on the stands not to start up, re-routing taxiing aircraft to roll off one zero left instead of one zero right, and, generally, finding himself in one of the worst muddles of his career.

Meyer declared a Local Standby. Any aircraft coming into Heathrow with suspected trouble required a Local Standby. The Fire Service, just having returned from the BranAir incident, took up their positions outside the fire station. If the 737 did run into any trouble on touch-down, four vehicles would attend, and the whole bloody emergency procedures would be initiated all over again.

Alpha Sierra Hotel flared out over the threshold and touched down perfectly. Vimr had been ordered to follow the plane in, just in case she left any rubber or undercarriage parts on the only serviceable runway. But she hadn't. And now that the Gulfstream Two had been finally cleared away from the entrance to Charlie, the 737 taxied in and lined up with the operative AGNIS system. One minor crisis was over.

Now the Pan Am 747 had returned and was slowly ambling about the airspace over aerodrome control. Brent Tenny peered through the ultra high power binoculars fitted to the floor of the control room and tried to distinguish some bits of grey from the rest of the complexities in the two port bogies. He turned to Bill Auer, his eyes still squinting. 'I can't seem to see what they are. You have a look.'

Auer exchanged places with the Pan Am engineer and adjusted the focus. When he had locked onto the bogies, he studied the grey chippings clinging between the tyres. Auer then swung the binoculars around to the intersection where Clipper One Hundred had lifted off. 'There's your answer,' he said. 'The same trouble as that Aer Lingus jet had. Your plane's blown up the pit covers and got some of the concrete wedged in her undercarriage.'

Tenny studied the bogies again. It seemed the only answer. 'If she tries to land with that concrete between her wheels, she'll split everything to bits.'

'And you aren't landing her here, either. That I can promise you,' Auer said. 'We've only got one runway and that plane of yours could do a hell of a lot of damage.'

'What do you suggest?' Tenny asked.

'Well, she's going to have to dump fuel. That's a dead cert. I reckon we get her an emergency clearance to Frankfurt, let her dump fuel on the way, and advise Frankfurt what the trouble is. Maybe they'll bring her down on one of the military bases where the runway can be foamed.'

'Why can't they foam Frankfurt?'

Auer walked over to a cluttered desk where Jim Ramaley was sorting out the departures. 'Foaming a runway is the same as closing it down. The whole thing has to be cleaned off before it can be opened to traffic again. No civil airport does that anymore.' He turned to Ramaley. 'What's Germany like?'

'Not bad now that all our departures are hung up. If you want to route Clipper One Hundred over there, I can't see how they'd object.'

'Well, put her down Green One and get her out of here,'

Auer said. 'It's getting bad enough without having to keep an eye on that jumbo.'

'I'll see if I can get clearance,' Ramaley said. 'We're trying to get some kind of pattern going for arrivals and departures on the one runway and it's putting us way behind. You'd better get a NOTAM out to the airlines and get them to cancel as many of their flights as you can. Either that or prepare the passengers for some pretty long delays.'

Auer nodded. He led Tenny down the steps into radar control. He wondered how Germany was going to feel with that 747 coming in. At least Heathrow wasn't the only airport that was going to have troubles.

A full ground emergency had been declared by MT Section, involving a complete turn out of the hundred odd men employed in Mechanical Transport, and there was a similar flap on in Engineering. The Prime Directive at the moment was to clear the runway and get it back in service. But however hard the pressure was laid on, there was no quick and easy way to remove the offending aircraft, nor clear the mess off Blocks 86 and 87, repair the lighting and shore up and replace the pit covers. Shell was still draining the last of the fuel while every necessary Mechanical Transport vehicle was being assembled around the 707. Coburn and Parent, the Salvage Officer, were assessing the situation as best they could. The only immediate action open to them was the installation of the air bags, and this had to be done within the critical stress limits of the aircraft. At the same time, steel plates were being laid around the grass verges, and the sweepers were out clearing off the debris immediately surrounding the plane.

Blake had retreated to the pit covers two thousand feet away. Fifteen of them had been broken, four totally crushed, and another eight weakened, but serviceable if shorn up from below. There was no way to replace or reinforce the thin concrete lip on which the covers rested without waiting two or three days for new concrete to dry, so wooden supports were called in. And there was still no way of knowing how much damage was done to the electrical and communication circuits below the pit covers.

Blake, satisfied that his men were doing the best they could, called the Tower on his RT. 'Lighting Director,' he asked.

Reed Boyd took the call from his watch over the map of the airfield. 'Lighting Director,' he said simply.

'Blake in Engineering here. Look can you switch on all your ground lights in this area and tell me if you're missing any?'

Boyd studied the map for a few moments before he began switching on the hundreds of runway lights: centreline lighting, shoulder lights, taxiway and apron lighting, approach lighting, threshold lights and touchdown zone lights. The map in front of him indicated which lights were on, whether each junction along the taxiways and aprons indicated red for stop, or green for go, and he found that most of the lighting network along Blocks 83, 84, 86 and 87 were out, and so were many of the lights on runway zero five/two three. Even if MT and Engineering could clear the inoperative runways by nightfall, it would mean bringing in all the mobile emergency lighting available until the broken circuits could be repaired. Boyd knew that the runways would take priority over the ground lighting, but he also knew that his job would be made a nightmare without the use of the map and guidance lighting.

'It doesn't look good,' Boyd sighed. 'Most of the lights in your area are out.'

'That's what I was afraid of,' Blake replied. 'You'd better get Marshalling to organise emergency lighting for tonight. I doubt we'll get this mess sorted out much before morning.'

'Will do,' said Boyd. He picked up his phone and dialled the Marshalling Section, wondering what kind of problems they were having.

Gavin Bartlett was talking to Coburn, trying to decide the best way to haul the 707 off the airfield. Coburn would have liked to chop the bloody beast up and be done with it, but Bartlett was out to keep whatever was left of the 707 intact. He eyed the reporters and photographers and television crews crowding against the fence the police had hastily erected fifty yards from the plane, and he knew that he would be called upon to make a statement. Neither Air Traffic Control nor the Airport Authority could say much since it was up to the individual airlines to release their own statements, but this time Bartlett wished he could let someone else do the talking. He was still waiting for a report on the condition of the passengers, but Sean Cahill had told him that no one seemed seriously injured. Harrison had also reassured Bartlett that the only serious casualty was a sprained ankle or twisted arm which a few of the passengers had sustained when they slid down the chutes. Mostly, it was general shock ranging from the mild to the serious – but no fatalities.

'Smile,' Coburn said. 'You're on camera.'

'I hope this rain fogs up their lenses,' he replied coldly.

'Stop worrying. We should have this baby out of here soon enough. We're placing the air bags now and, with any luck, we can begin lining up the tugs in a couple of hours. Once that's done, we'll winch her around and haul her away.'

'If the wings'll take it,' Bartlett began, pushing back his rain soaked hair. 'How much damage do you reckon that skid did?'

'No way of telling until she's raised. That's what's going to be tricky. Each bag has to inflate at exactly the same pressure. That's what takes time. If the fuselage begins to raise, too, then we're in the clear. If it doesn't, it means that there's structural damage to the spars and we'll have to haul her out in pieces.'

Bartlett shuddered. BranAir was running at a loss as it was. It didn't need the loss of an airplane.

'How's it look?' Coburn asked when Doug Parent appeared from behind the wings.

'I think she'll take it. The belly's pretty badly done in, but if the wing spars haven't been damaged, we'll be able to lift her. If we can raise the nose just a couple of feet off the ground, we'll shove a jack under her and push her up that way. After we get her nose up we'll fit the tug and then wait until the wings are high enough to hook up the trollies. It's the winching about that's going to be dodgy. If we don't get her out soon enough, I bet we get an order to haul her onto the grass.'

Coburn thought. 'Blake's having his headaches over the pit covers and re-surfacing. That'll take him a lot longer than I think he wants to admit. It's just a question of who gets done first. If we can winch her around and get her clear of the runway before Blake gets done, then we're safe. If Blake finishes first, we'll probably be told to haul her onto the verge.'

Parent agreed. 'It's causing almighty hell in the central

area. It'll take them at least a few hours to sort out the delays. But once Blake gets this runway clear, they're going to open her up again – and we'd better have this plane out of here.'

Ray Milross approached from the direction of the reporters. Bartlett knew what was coming.

'Can you make a statement, Mr Bartlett?' Milross asked. 'They're beginning to speculate and that could put you in a bit of a mess.'

'Yeah, sure. I'll make a statement. I don't suppose the medical report has come through?'

'I shouldn't worry about that,' Milross replied, hunching himself against what was now no longer a drizzle, but a steady rain. 'No one was seriously hurt. I can promise you that.'

'Can I quote you on that?' Bartlett shouted over the roar of a jet departing on one zero left.

'I don't like it,' Auer was saying as he leant back in the armchair. 'I'd bet you anything that 707's offset the localiser.'

Alan Manley, Chief Officer of the National Air Traffic Control Services and the second of the two airport Directors, read through the brief incident report. 'You think it's going to need calibrating?'

'I wouldn't want to open ten right until we can check her out. The plane didn't actually hit the localiser, but it came damn close. There's no telling what aberrations we could be getting. I just wouldn't like to rely on it, Sir.'

'Neither would I,' Manley agreed. 'How soon before the runways will be in service?'

Auer whistled softly. 'Hours. This rain's making it impossible for both MT and Engineering. And Blake's called in to say that if the rain gets any worse, it'll flood the open pits. There's a hell of a lot of wiring down there.'

Manley knew only too well. Under the hundreds of pit covers scattered across the three runways lay the lifelines of the airport. Without communications there wasn't a hope of keeping Heathrow operating. There were certain danger levels. Reach any of the prescribed danger levels and it meant an airport shut down. Just like weather conditions. 'I haven't been out there, Bill,' Manley began slowly. 'Just how bad is it?'

Auer thought. He hadn't been out there either, but he had

made a careful inspection from the Tower. He had also talked to Coburn and Blake. 'If I said we might have the runways open by late this afternoon I'd be optimistic. I'd guess that we could have things moving on those runways by late tonight. And there's the question of lighting.'

Manley was thinking of his lads upstairs. 'How's it going in the Tower?'

'We're managing. Plenty of delays. We've got all four stacks filling up and Christ knows how many aircraft waiting on the stands. The airlines have been notified, but we're trying to knit the planes in from the stacks as priority.'

Manley wrinkled his brow and flipped through some papers. He pushed himself away from his desk and walked to the window. A solitary plane – a Trident – shot upwards from one zero left and disappeared from sight in the cloud. A moment later a BOAC VC 10 swooped in and touched down on the same runway. Manley had the authority to divert. He had the authority to close down the airport simply by closing down Air Traffic Control. He was the key man in keeping the central services open and operating. Aerodrome Control was his province, and the only other person at Heathrow who could call for a shut down was the Airport General Manager for the British Airports Authority. Manley knew he had little choice. 'What's Shannon and Dublin like?'

'Shannon's socked in with this storm. Heavy cloud cover. Last report was Cat. Three. Dublin's a little better but you know how limited they are. If you start landing foreign aircraft at Dublin . . .'

'I know. I've been up to my ears in it. O.K., see how many planes you can divert to Gatwick and Luton. Then continue to divert to Prestwick and Turnhouse. Spread the load out as best you can. Notify the airlines to delay all departures for Heathrow. No, better still, tell the airlines that Heathrow is closed to all but essential traffic until 1800 at the earliest. Let the long-haul stuff in, but keep the jumbos away. We've only got one runway for the moment, and I want to make damn sure we protect it.'

'You want me to get onto the General Manager?'

'No,' Manley sighed, returning to his desk. 'I'll do that. You're going to have your hands full for the time being.'

International Airline's London General Manager, Malcolm Wilmet, had heard about the aircraft incident that was blocking two main runways. He felt the same sympathy for Bran-Air that every other airline was feeling: thank God it hadn't happened to *him*. Not that International wouldn't have coming running to help if BOAC hadn't beat everyone else to it. But all the airlines were having more trouble this year – if it wasn't the odd hi-jacking, it was a bomb threat. If an airline escaped either of these, the pilots were on strike – or threatening one. And once a pay dispute was settled among the pilots, the cabin staff figured they warranted a pay rise. Wilmet was now facing a walk-out by his flight crews. As were all the airlines. The one-day world-wide strike of not too long ago had failed to bring any agreement on hi-jackings, and the pilots were planning another. A bigger one. The United States government might make the strike illegal, but Wilmet realised the pilots *knew* that no airline was going to sack their flight crews or let some government imprison them. Besides, from the reports he was getting, public sympathy was behind the pilots. For the first time that Wilmet could remember, the flying public didn't mind an air strike which fouled up their holiday plans or business trips, or kept them waiting for hours in airport lounges.

Wilmet was looking at a cartoon someone had sent him – one of the Managers from the International Air Terminal in London. It was a picture of the front window of a bank and a large notice had been put up which read, 'Do you need to pay ransom money urgently? Large stocks of used notes of small denomination always in stock.' There was no note attached to the cartoon and Wilmet wondered whether he was supposed to laugh or take umbrage. So far, International Airlines had been lucky inasmuch as no one had cared to hi-jack their planes. Jokes had already been tossed at Wilmet about this – no one in their right mind would hi-jack an International plane: they'd be lucky if they could get it off the ground. But, behind the joke, was a tinge of jealousy from those whose airlines had been singled out for hi-jacking. TWA had been given a hard time over the Captain who strangled a hi-jacker, and a moral question had been raised about how much right an airline Captain had in protecting his plane to the extent of murder. And with the Delta Airlines hi-jacking, in which

71

two families had been involved, it seemed now that stealing planes was becoming a family affair. Maybe it was because Wilmet had been out of the United States for too long that he couldn't help wondering why the hi-jackings seemed confined to America. Security at American airports must be about the same as it was at Heathrow, yet England had been completely free of air piracy. Heathrow had taken pretty extreme measures to ensure that aircraft were protected and that passengers were closely scrutinised – even some bright lad in Air Traffic Control had dreamt up an early warning device for pilots whose planes were being pirated. The circular had been sent to all the flight crews which advised them to fly an 'S' pattern on their approach to Heathrow or to leave their transponder switched on, which had the effect of leaving a bright trail of continuous 'blips' on the Approach Controller's radar screen. So far, only one Captain had used either technique and it turned out to be a false alarm anyway. But, regardless of the apparent safety – or sanctity – of Heathrow, the pilots were calling for another massive strike and with present hi-jackings still confined to the United States, Wilmet wondered if non-American pilots would stage the sympathy walk-out that had been called.

The order to strike was lying on Wilmet's desk. Without reading the wherefores and etceteras, he knew what the order suggested. And it was the same order that was circulating among all airlines, at Heathrow, at Kennedy, at Orly – at every major airport in the world. The date hadn't been set, but preparations were being laid. And, on top of this, there was the latest pay claim by senior flight crews. Word had got round that the acceptance of 747's by International meant the phasing out of the 707's on long haul routes. Pan Am had accepted the jumbo, BOAC, TWA, National, Air India, JAL, Air Canada – just about every airline was now satisfied with the performance of the jumbo jet and Boeing's orders were on the increase. BEA had placed a fifty million pound order for Lockheed Tristars equipped with Rolls Royce engines, and Pan American were studying the maintenance manuals on Lockheed's Ten Eleven. The Douglas Corporation were competing with Boeing's 747 by bringing out a DC 10, and, if aircraft carrying over four hundred passengers weren't large enough, there was always the Lockheed 500, a military transport jet capable of being refitted and accommodating one thousand passengers. If the Lockheed 500 ever entered commercial service, the jumbo jets would face the same redundancies that 'smaller' aircraft like the 707, VC 10, and DC 8 faced today. Wilmet didn't smile at such a prediction, either, for he remembered when the 707's entered commercial service in 1958. Airlines balked at the idea of such a monstrous plane as this new jet – there would never be enough passengers to fill a 707, they had said. And, in 1965 it was discovered that the 707 had become too small and Boeing were developing the 747 jumbo. In another five to ten years Wilmet could see the giant jets of today being sold off for scrap while jets like the Lockheed 500 entered service. It made him cringe to think of one plane holding one thousand passengers. Heathrow was only just learning to cope with four hundred passengers per plane. He knew that planes weren't built at the whims of big aircraft companies but developed from the experience of millions of pilots and billions of flight hours under every condition, yet he wondered just how far these wide body transports could be taken. Airports of the seventies if compared to those of the thirties was like comparing man to an amoeba, yet today's airports were still fighting on two fronts: the management of air traffic congestion, and the management of giant sized aircraft pouring out thousands of passengers an hour, who had – on the average – three people per passenger to meet them. Where did one put all those passengers and their friends? But the cold hard facts were facing Wilmet as they faced all the major airlines. By 1976 nearly every air traffic movement would require a 350-seat aircraft if the airlines were to meet the number of people who wanted to fly.

So long to the world's first commercial jets. And so long to the flight crews needed to fly them. If one jumbo could replace three 707's, that meant two flight crews would be made redundant. The cabin staff would be absorbed easily enough because more stewardesses were required on a 747, but it took only three men to *fly* one. The pilots had read the cards, not only in International's hand, but in the other airlines'. The old numbers game was back again: who was staying and who would have to find a job of flying for some back-woods banana republic airline in beat up DC 3's?

Wilmet knew that it was inevitable. The wide body aircraft made flying safer because it reduced air congestion. It made flying more economical for the airlines because it cut down on multiple landing fees, maintenance and crew salaries by axeing flight crews. So, what was he to do? It hadn't been his decision, but the headaches were, sure as hell, his. And he had some pretty loyal friends in the flight crews. Friends who had suddenly decided that he was no longer a friend. He, Malcolm Wilmet, was an administrator. *He* didn't know how the pilots felt. How could he? So there was the anti-hi-jack walk-out coming up soon, and then there was the pay claim dispute among the pilots which would be followed up by a cabin staff pay claim dispute, and when International made the official announcement of the phasing out of the 707, all the disputes and anti-hi-jack walk-outs would be nothing compared to the stink and flap and Lord knew what else that would spring up.

Wilmet nodded curtly to his secretary who dropped a memo into his tray. 'Notice to all Airlines,' he read. 'Time: 1300 Hours. From: Chief Officer, NATCS and AGM, British Airports Authority. Restrictions on all incoming aircraft due to closure of runways One Zero Left/Two Eight Right and Two Three/Zero Five. Essential inbound traffic only. Advise home bases to delay departures for Heathrow until further notice. Cancel departures outbound Heathrow wherever possible. Diversions of incoming aircraft now in effect.' *Poor BranAir*, Wilmet thought. *Thank God it isn't us.* He checked what International Flights were due in during the afternoon. No doubt they were being re-routed already. Then there was Astral One Two Four due in at 1830. It was their jumbo flight from New York – already delayed by half a day. He'd have to get special clearance for that one. He knew it would be easy. Heathrow was still the only 'local' airport that could handle 747's comfortably, and he knew that Shannon was – at the moment – socked in.

Wilmet risked an annoyed controller and phoned the Tower. 'International here,' he said quickly. 'Any chance of bringing Astral One Two Four in this evening? She's an important flight.'

Clive Amery repeated the question to Meyer. Luckily for Wilmet, Amery had just reported for duty and his nerves hadn't been frazzled yet. But Meyer, hard pressed as he was, had sympathy for the airlines. It wasn't their fault that Heathrow was having trouble. And it was the airlines that kept Heathrow an airport.

'Tell him we'll do all we can,' Meyer said slowly. 'We'll try to bring him in on One Zero Left if all the other runways are still closed.'

Wilmet appreciated the effort. He knew that the Tower was having it as rough as he was – in their own way. They were a good bunch. It seemed everyone at Heathrow was a good bunch. It would be a nice place to work if it weren't for the airplanes.

Gander Transoceanic Control had received a navigational report from International (code name 'Astral') Flight 124 at 14.30 British Summer Time, 13.30 GMT or Zulu time, on the Great Circle Course which took the flight directly across the Atlantic. With favourable winds aloft and a bit of a jet stream to push the jumbo along, Captain Huston was quite satisfied with his progress. The auto pilot was guiding his plane through turbulent free air, the passengers seemed relaxed and not too put out by the delay, and the weather report for the next several hundred miles was excellent. Below, the Atlantic waters were an unruffled blue and, above, the sun shone down at their cruising altitude of thirty-five thousand feet. Captain Huston's only concern was the foul weather he and his crew would have to face once they approached the Irish coast, and he reminded himself to get a concise report on how bad that cloud front was.

The Great Circle Course was a lucky break for Huston. The night before when he had to advise International's engineers that something was up with his number three engine, his Minimum Time Path Calculation which took advantage of the winds aloft reckoned he might have to take Flight 124 as far north as sixty-one degrees, or over five hundred miles from the course they were presently flying. Because jets depend on favourable winds at high altitudes and must avoid head winds whenever possible, the Minimum Time Path Calculation took into account the winds aloft and spelt out the course which would get aircraft from one point to another in the shortest possible time even if it meant flying hundreds of miles off the old geometric straight line that connected two points. One Two Four's Great Circle Course was the straight line from New York to London, however, where the Point of No Return was imortalised in *The High and The Mighty*. It reduced Huston's navigation work, gave him one of the favoured flight levels and promised him a pretty trouble free flight.

In the two-thirds filled economy section Julie Stark, Valerie Lewison and Peggy Dawson were cleaning up while Susan O'Burns and Sandra Gesner saw to the after dinner requests of the passengers. There was Mrs. Brannigan in 23 B who was disposing of her lunch in an air sickness bag. Peter Armstradt, a Danish passenger who found the English language impossible, was trying desperately to get it across to Sandra that he wanted two aspirins.

Brodie Washburn and Paul Almirall were relaxing in the comfort of the Sky Lounge, sipping Coca Cola served with two slices of orange, a cherry, a sprig of mint, crushed ice and a dash of vanilla flavouring. They had just finished a combination breakfast and luncheon and were, at this time, considering the first class dinner menu, presented to them for their approval. The simple problem that faced them was one of language:

Déjeuner
Medaillons d'homard parisienne
Sauce mayonnaise
Huitres au naturel

Consommé en gelée Madrilène
Crême Princesse

Contrefilet de boeuf rôti
Sauce raifort

Poulet de grain grille a l'anglaise
Sauce diable

Escalopine de veau Marsala

76

Printaniere de legumes
Pommes Lyonnaise

Salade panachee
Sauce piquante ou sauce Roquefort

Gateau Pavlova
Parfait glace a l'italienne

Choix de fromages

Panier de fruits

Cafe. Cafe sans cafeine

Mignardises

'Do you understand it, Brodie?' Paul asked hopefully.

Brodie shook his head. 'It's French – I know that. And I know some of this stuff like Krem Princess and something of the booeef rotee. Maybe your sister knows what they're giving us.'

'Yea – I'll ask her when she comes up again.' Paul took a leaflet from one of the wall pockets and looked at the goods International offered to sell at International Terminals The World Over. There were mugs, cigarette cases, beach balls, jewellery, neck ties, scarves, luggage and pen and pencil sets – all with the distinctive International Airlines monogram. 'You know,' Paul began when he had studied what International had to sell, 'I bet they make a packet off all this junk.'

Brodie was studying International's World Wide Route Maps. 'You know where we are?'

Paul looked at the map. 'You're looking at the small one. Here, pull out the big one. It unfolds. That's it. Now all we need is a position report from the Captain.'

'How do we get that?'

'I asked Lynn to see if the Captain will let us into the cockpit. I know there are two extra seats up there, and it's just a question of when he has time to let us in. I guess he's got a lot to do.'

77

'You really think we can see the cockpit?' Brodie asked eagerly.

'Of course, it's completely against regulations since all this hi-jacking stuff began. But Captain Huston's a friend of mine. At least, that's what I intend to tell anyone who asks.'

Paul was about to continue when the pains came back. He closed his eyes and dropped his Coke on the table. He wanted to double up, but he fought the knives that sliced through him and tried to smile at Brodie.

'Indigestion,' he cried softly. 'I told you I got these things often.'

Brodie took the drink from Paul's hand which still clung to the glass. 'Lie down a minute,' he said, moving out of the chair and lifting the armrest. 'Please – just for a minute.'

Paul opened his eyes and a tear squeezed out and rolled down his cheek. 'Yea, O.K.,' he managed.

Brodie looked over at one of the passengers sitting across the narrow lounge. It was Wilbur Cross. He returned the stare. 'Too many damned Coca Colas,' he sniggered and went back to his reading.

Alex Trent-Jones appeared from the stairs. He saw the boy, and he noticed Brodie's pleading look. 'The boy air sick?' he asked, pulling out a bag from a wall panel.

'I don't think so,' Brodie replied. 'He had these pains last night. At the hotel. He said he got them often.'

Trent-Jones knelt down beside Paul and put his hand to his forehead. 'You all right, lad?'

Paul turned his head. He nodded stiffly.

'You go get one of the stewardesses,' Trent-Jones said to Brodie. 'I think the lad's pretty sick.'

The rain was heavy. When the wind blew, it blew the rain in heavy sheets. Already, mud was oozing between the steel plates that had been laid on the grass verges around Block 87. Coburn was watching the dials on the control console of the air bag trailer as Simson and Andrews controlled the flow of compressed air into the five bags under each wing. All it would take was one bag out of the ten to inflate one pound faster than the others and the wing could buckle like cardboard. It was a slow agonising job, and the pouring rain made life hell for everyone. Two mobile canteens had been brought in as rest centres and many of the Mechanical Transport staff had sought shelter until they were needed. At the moment the bags were just touching the underside of the wings, edging them up a fraction of an inch every few minutes. Bartlett squatted under the starboard wing between the burnt out landing gear and the belly of the aircraft. He was praying silently. He was praying that the spars supporting the wing internally would hold. Just enough, so that the trollies could be moved into place. If they could do that, then they could save the plane.

Coburn was urging Simson and Andrews to take it easy — nice and slow. The slower, the better. Keep an eye on each gauge. Keep the control levers steady. Each bag must fill at precisely the speed of the others. Gently, and in all this god-dam rain.

Doug Parent was standing at the rear of the plane, watching the bags inflate. They were inflating much too slow for him to see, but he judged the height of the wings against the localiser. So far, the starboard wing had lifted one inch in thirty minutes. There was no way he could estimate how high the port wing had risen, but he was hoping it was an identical inch. The rain was sloshing around the bags and a tiny stream ran along the belly of the aircraft where it had nosed down. He noticed Bartlett was getting the worst of it as puddles collected around his shoes. Why the hell Bartlett didn't take a breather was beyond him. Then, without warning, the last bag on the end of the starboard wing popped out.

Parent raced beneath the tail section and squeezed between the port landing gear, shouting at Bartlett to get the hell out.

'Hold it!' Coburn shouted at the same instant. 'Boost the pressure in number nine! Jesus, she's slipping, too!' He saw Bartlett trying to squeeze past the inside air bag and the starboard gear. Why the hell didn't he go the other way? 'Parent — get Bartlett out of there!' Coburn cried, leaping off the trailer.

Parent turned in time to see the ten feet high starboard bags flatten under the increased pressure. Bartlett was still trying to squeeze past the innermost bag without realising that it was pushing him against the landing gear, for the rain had made the concrete so slippery that the bags couldn't hold their grip on the tarmac. Parent grabbed Bartlett's arms and tried pulling, but the bag had surrounded his waist and was pinning him to the metal. Coburn leapt back onto the console where Simson and Andrews were adding pressure to the bag that was pinning Bartlett.

'It's no good,' Andrews snapped. 'If we increase the pressure, she only rolls toward the gear. The bags can't take the weight with number ten gone.'

'The jack!' Coburn yelled. 'Get a jack under that wing.'

Turin had emerged from one of the mobile canteens in time to see what was happening. He called out his men and leapt into the landrover to back what was to be the nose jack under the wing.

'Easy, Bartlett,' Parent was saying. 'Don't try to move.'

'Fat chance of that,' Bartlett wheezed. 'I feel like a bleeding python's got me.'

'It's O.K. We're going to jack the wing up,' Parent said.

'The hell you are,' Bartlett coughed. 'You jack this wing up and it'll rip the whole damned plane apart.'

'You want to get crushed to death instead?' Parent argued. 'Jesus, man, the plane's insured.'

'Keep that jack away from here, understand? It's my plane. I'm the engineer for BranAir. You just keep that goddam jack away from here and get that air bag back in place.'

'You won't have a chance,' Coburn shouted as the landrover backed the jack into position. 'By the time we get these bags in alignment you'll be squashed like a tomato. And you'll bloody look like one too.'

'I don't care,' Bartlett cried desperately, his breath short. He closed his eyes. 'Don't ruin this plane, do you hear? If I'm going to get it, then I get it. I've been through worse.'

'Met could have warned us of this,' Blake swore, peering into one of the trenches where the pit covers had fallen through. 'We're going to need the pumps.'

'So's radar,' Swithers replied, reaching for a handful of cables. 'You remember what happened last time we had flooding?'

'Yea, I remember. But we're going to need wet suits in here if this rain keeps up.' Blake stood up and faced his deputy.

'Tell me, Mr. Swithers, why in God's name does everything happen at once? I knew this was going to be a rotten day the moment I rolled out of bed. Just something told me – that's all.'

Swithers smiled. 'You know what they say, don't you?'

Blake frowned and waited.

Swithers looked up at the sky. 'It never rains – it pours.'

'You're bloody right,' Hardy agreed. 'I've just had a close look at the lighting again. We'll never have it operable by to-night. You'd better get all the emergency ground lighting you can. And we'll probably need some overhead mobile lighting as well.'

'I have a feeling we're not the only ones who'll need it,' said Blake, looking down towards the 707. 'Just look at that right wing. They're having a right party blowing up those balloons.'

'I heard there's trouble,' Hardy said. 'One of the lads is trapped between the inside bag and the undercarriage.'

'Jesus Christ,' Swithers mumbled. 'Poor blighter.'

'Yea, there's trouble all right. Here comes the ambulance. Well, if they need us, they'll call. We've still got to get these covers shored up. Have those replacements arrived yet?'

'No, Sir,' Hardy said. 'They're still loading them. You think we can shore up such a big area?'

'I'm not sure of anything,' Blake replied. 'But we better figure something out. You'd better get some tarpaulins over from MT to cover up these trenches. I want to keep out all the rain I can. If the trenches begin to fill, it'll take weeks to sort the mess out.'

Hardy nodded and headed for the land rover. He heard a soft peal of thunder in the distance. Maybe it was a good sign. Just a summer squall.

Congdon pulled up in Checker and climbed out of the seat, pulling a mobile spotlight with him. 'Thought you might need this if you're going to inspect those cables.'

Blake wiped the rain from his face. 'Thanks. Any news on what's going on down there?'

'It's Bartlett – BranAir's engineer. The air bags collapsed and squeezed him against the starboard gear.'

'Why the hell don't they jack the wing up?' Blake asked hastily.

'Because Bartlett won't allow it. He said it would knacker the wing. Then he passed out.'

'Sure it would kill the wing,' Blake continued. 'But it's better than being squashed. If you ask me, that's taking dedication a little too far.'

'Well, they're trying to get him out now. The Doc doesn't think anything's broken – the bag seems to have gone around him. But no one seems to know just how to free him without using the jack.'

'If he's unconscious, then there's nothing stopping Coburn from using the jack, is there?'

'It's Bartlett's decision. He could sue us for everything we're worth if we went against his orders. Unless the Incident Officer over-rides Bartlett's decision.'

Swithers thought about a similar accident he had seen at Turnhouse Airport near Edinburgh. 'How bad's the undercarriage damaged?'

'Wheel rims gone, tyres gone – don't know about the hydraulics. Why?' asked Congdon.

'Because there might be another way of getting him out. Look, I saw something like this happen before. It was on ice when the air bags slipped. Instead of jacking up the wing they refitted just one tyre onto the gear and inflated it. As the tyre inflated, they decreased the pressure in the inside air bag.'

Congdon thought. He didn't know much about the technical side of all this, but he reckoned it might be worth a try. 'I'll tell Coburn. He might go for it.'

'It's impossible,' Coburn announced angrily. 'How in the name of hell are you going to refit a tyre onto that gear and just pump it up? Those tyres are tubeless. I tell you it won't work. The only way is to jack up the wing and reduce the air bag pressure.'

'Can't you get a jack under the gear and push her up that way?' asked Congdon. 'Sort of take the place of a tyre like in a car?'

'We haven't got a jack small enough. You just can't stick an automobile jack under a 707 and expect to lift her up.'

Congdon was about to give up when he saw Blake speeding towards them in a land rover.

'Forget the jack,' Blake began, shouting from the rover.

'Look, I haven't got much time to spare with you fellows, but I just remembered something I saw earlier today.'

Congdon looked up angrily at the sky and the rain that was muffling Blake's words. He glanced at Coburn and they left the cover of the wing and walked toward the rover.

'Your idea stinks,' Coburn declared. 'Have you seen that bogie? You couldn't get a tyre . . .'

'I was trying to tell you to forget my rotten idea,' Blake interrupted hastily. 'And it wasn't my idea – it was Swithers'.'

Congdon and Coburn leant on the window ledge, hunched against the rain.

'Listen. There was this kid who got his head stuck between the railings on Queen's Building this morning. It was when I was working on the AGNIS lights. The Fire Service had this sort of jack – a hydraulic ram they called it – and one of the men said it could hoist up something like eight tons. Only they were using it to pry apart the rails – you know, horizontally. If you can get that ram and push up your bogie just enough to take some of the pressure . . .'

'It sounds good,' snapped Coburn. 'I apologise. You're a genius. I might even ask you to work for me. I know that ram – we used it once before when we had that spate of overshoots.' He turned and looked at the starboard bogie as if weighing the possibilities.

Blake started his engine. 'Like I said, it's an idea. And I got my own problems. I just don't like the idea of that fellow being squashed to death.'

'Thanks, Kevin,' Coburn said, pushing away from the rover. 'Good luck with your pit covers.'

'Same to you,' Blake shouted back. 'Let me know if it works.'

Coburn walked slowly back to the plane with Congdon.

'You going to try it?' Congdon asked.

'We have to. It's his only chance.'

Congdon looked down at Bartlett. The rain had soaked him through. If he didn't die from the pressure, he'd die of pneumonia when they got him free. 'I better get back to work, too. There's still an awful lot of junk on that runway. Let me know what happens.'

'Will do,' Coburn said. He watched Congdon drive off and

83

stop fifty yards further on. Just how many pieces of airplane and concrete was Ops supposed to pick up, he wondered.

It is said of Heathrow that the three terminals and the Queen's Building are as individual as if they were separate airports. The departments which run the terminals and the airport as a whole are as individual in power and prestige as the organs of the body. Yet – like the body – if one malfunctions, if there is the slightest infection in any single organism of this vast system – the result is catastrophic. The closure of the two runways combined with the deluge outside had created a catastrophe, but one which Heathrow was facing up to. Having been through pilot strikes, bomb threats, overshoots, undershoots and even air crashes in the middle of the airfield, the staff of Heathrow could be expected to handle almost anything. And during the afternoon the staff of every Department and Section, as well as the airlines, were faced with an airport nightmare.

All three terminals were packed with passengers whose flights were now cancelled or delayed. Relatives and friends of arriving passengers were told that planes were being diverted to other airports throughout England and Scotland. Airline information booths were being machine gunned with impatient questions and complaints. Airline offices and briefing rooms were trying to sort out where their aircraft were and exactly when flights could depart. Flight plans were filed, cancelled and drawn up again. Crew schedules were ruined – lay overs would mean hours of re-scheduling of carefully worked out duty sheets.

Despite the rain the viewing area on the Queen's Building was packed. Spectators had jammed the balconies to have a look at the crippled 707 and those with strong enough binoculars or telescopes could see the mess that was holding up operations down at the intersection. The police were anxious to close the viewing area, but then the spectators would merely march along the peri track until they got within eyeshot of the 707. As it was, the peri track alongside the Pan Am maintenance area and the Ground Ops building was packed, and because there was easy access to the runways from both Pan Am and Ground Ops, people were found wandering near the threshold of

Two Eight in hopes to get a better look at 'all the excitement'.

Today, however, there was little to see. The intersection was messed up, but only staff involved in air traffic movements could appreciate the mess it really was. As for the 707, it just sat on its belly and was for the most part obscured from view by the score of MT vehicles surrounding it.

But Heathrow was approaching a critical standstill. The terminals were jammed, the approach roads were filling up with traffic, and the Tower's handling capacity was more than halved. At the moment London Tower was releasing one aircraft for every two that arrived. The runway visual range was down to an uncomfortable eleven hundred metres, and this further restricted incoming traffic.

The time was three p.m. An hour and a half had passed since BranAir Two Four had aborted its take-off.

With the runway visual range down, the RVR caravans had to be manned. It was Operations' responsibility to monitor the visual range of the runways through a system of spaced lighting along the edge of the runways. If a light placed a thousand feet down the runway could be seen from the caravan assigned to that runway, then there was a thousand feet clear visibility on the ground. But Congdon's men were also responsible for picking up the still plentiful debris from One Zero Right and Two Three. Ops was also responsible for handing in a report on the damaged runway lights so that the works section from Engineering could get on with replacing them. Congdon now wished that the experimental transmitometers had been successful. Rather than pulling in men from his unit to man RVR caravans, the automatic transmitometers measured the visibility at specific spots along the runways by bouncing a light off an opposing mirror twenty feet away. Any low level atmospheric interference was registered and signalled to the Tower. But so far the transmitometer readings and those of the time proven RVR caravans were in disagreement. And until the transmitometers fell in line with the RVR readings, they were kept out of service.

'Checker to Seagull,' Congdon said on his RT.

'Seagull,' Thurnblad replied from somewhere on the airfield.

'We're manning the RVR caravans, Ted. But I need everyone I got here. Round up some lads from somewhere and see what you can do, will you?'

Thurnblad knew the pressure his boss was working under. On the one hand he was glad to be away from the chaos near the intersection, but he never liked avoiding his responsibilities. He was relieved he had an easier job to contend with, and manning the RVR caravans was every bit as vital as the work going on at the incident area. 'I'll have the caravans operating in ten minutes,' Ted said firmly.

Congdon now gathered Vimr and Peter Kaupe together and compared notes on the damaged runway lighting. Vimr and Kaupe had pooled their findings and marked off the damage on an Inspection Form.

'Sixteen centreline lights,' Vimr read slowly. 'Five contact lights, three stop bar lights at 86 and the whole on 87. Seven touch down zone lights – but I think they're some more we haven't found yet, and we've counted twelve threshold lights. We can't find out how many more threshold lights are gone until they shift that 707. Most of the green taxi lights are gone off 85 – but what isn't gone near that Block?'

'Right,' Congdon sighed, handing the inspection sheet back to Vimr. 'You better get this over to Engineering. Were any of the RVR lights damaged?'

'No,' Kaupe replied. 'The Skipper kept his wings clear of the shoulders. Most of the damage is on the runway proper. I don't know how he did it.'

'I hear they've called Elliot in,' Vimr began, glancing over at the localiser. 'I wonder just what's happened there.'

'Probably a check and calibration,' Congdon suggested. 'With all this messing about down here, I guess they reckon the beam could be out of line. Once they get this runway open again, they're going to want everything working perfectly.' He remembered the lights. 'Including the runway lighting.'

Vimr and Kaupe nodded. 'We'll get this over to Works straight away. But they're going to have fun replacing lights in this rain.'

Kaupe looked back towards the intersection. 'And I hear that half the electrical circuits are gone under the pit covers. There's no guarantee that if the lights *are* replaced, there'll

86

be any power to operate them. The lighting director's having kittens in the Tower.'

'His precious board not responding, eh?' Congdon said grimly. 'I don't blame him. If this cloud base drops any more, he's going to need every bit of runway lighting. I don't suppose the approach lighting is working.'

Vimr had made a check earlier on. 'No physical damage to the approach lights, but there's no power. Unless Engineering can sort out the electrical side of things, any incoming traffic is going to be on precision radar or autoland all the way.'

'Well, we've got our problems. File that report and get back here as quick as you can. I want to start a complete runway check on One Zero/Two Three. We'll want to sweep these runways every half hour until we're sure they're clean. Lord knows what bits and pieces are still out there.'

'That's if the rain hasn't washed them away,' said Kaupe.

'Fat chance,' Congdon retorted, and slammed the land rover's door.

Jim Harrison was shaking his aching head. The turn out for BranAir Two Four, then the local standby for the Aer Lingus 737 and an ambulance call for some fellow injured at the incident area had begun to put the pressure on. The Fire Service had a lot of cleaning up to do and it was time he made an inspection. Now another call came in.

'Jim, this is Dennis,' the watchroom attendant began. 'You know that injury in 87? We've been asked for the hydraulic ram. It seems that the BranAir engineer got himself wedged between one of the air bags and the starboard bogie. Engineering suggested we try jacking up the bogie just enough to take the wing pressure off the inside bag. Can we do it?'

Harrison didn't know whether they could or not. But he knew they'd try. 'Yeah, send down a vehicle. Better put Michelson on it. He knows that ram better than anyone. But I don't want any arguments down there. Get a full report before we start jacking up that airplane.'

'Yes, Sir,' Keefe replied. He pressed the siren button and called out on the public address system. 'Michelson and Jeffreys. Number Two Vehicle to Block 87.'

The announcement boomed through the station. Keefe

waited until – forty seconds later – he heard Number Two Vehicle start its motor. He flipped the traffic light stop switch and two red lights halted cars on either side of the fire station as Number Two screeched out of the bay and stopped at the runway shoulder. After receiving permission to cross the only serviceable runway, Michelson turned off Block 17, entered Two Three and crossed onto the taxiway at Block 48 which led him straight into Block 87.

Coburn had consulted the Medical Section. Bartlett was alive and still unhurt, but the pressure from the air bag was slowly suffocating him. Bartlett could die and Coburn would be powerless to interfere with his orders. But if the idea of using the hydraulic ram wasn't another false hope, then Bartlett could be freed and operations could resume. He wondered how far along Engineering had gotten with the pit covers and mangled wiring when he saw the flashing blue light of Number Two.

'He's down there,' Coburn explained. 'Blake said your jack might be able to hoist up the undercarriage just enough to take the pressure off that inside bag. Then we could pull the fellow out.'

Michelson and Jeffreys hauled the ram unit from the side of the tender. When they had squeezed beneath the aircraft and assessed the situation, Michelson wasn't happy. He turned to Coburn. 'How long's that fellow been there?'

'About twenty minutes. It's holding up the whole damn operation. Unless we get him out, we'll have to use the jack – and that means ruining his airplane.'

'So what's he want?' Jeffreys shouted above a clap of thunder. 'His life or his plane? From the looks of it this crate isn't going to be worth much anyway.'

'Look,' said Coburn heatedly, 'Bartlett's got the right to decide what happens to that plane – not me. Can you get him out or not?'

Michelson had already opened the metal box and was removing the vertical shafts of the ram. 'We'll get him out. At least we'll try to raise the gear. But this ram can only take eight tons. How much do you reckon this plane weighs?'

'A damn sight more than eight tons,' Jeffreys replied, fitting the base plate between the ruptured tyres.

'Not with these air bags, it doesn't,' Coburn said. 'All I want is just a few inches. Just enough to get this wing up without straining the spars.'

'I'll stay here and get ready to pull him out,' Parent said. 'You can go back and keep an eye on the pressure gauges. Once we've got him free, we'll hold the ram in place and refit the number ten bag. If we can get some kind of balance back, we'll drop the ram and start lifting her again.'

Coburn nodded. 'Good luck.'

Parent smiled. 'Just have the medical boys ready.'

Jeffreys disappeared into the tender and returned with breathing equipment. 'You know how to fit this on?' he asked of Parent.

'Sure.'

'Then strap the mask on this fellow and set the control to resuscitate. It'll help him breathe. If he comes round, cut out the resuscitator and just give him straight oxygen. There're too many fumes down here for my liking.'

Parent opened the box and pulled out the rubber mask. He took the key and twisted the knob on the oxygen cylinder. With the mask in place, the oxygen would be forced into Bartlett's lungs, released and exhaled, and repeated. If the pressure from the air bag was inhibiting Bartlett's breathing, the resuscitator would act as a sort of iron lung until he could be freed.

'How quick do you want this gear raised?' Michelson asked when he had fitted the vertical shaft into position.

'Slow,' Parent replied. 'Dead slow.' He looked back at Coburn and nodded.

Coburn slapped the pressure controllers on the back to warn them that every square inch of pressure was now critical. One slip and Bartlett would never make it.

Despite the restricted operations of the airport, aircraft were still using runway ten left for landings and take offs. But the rain was threatening to build up on the runway surface as the concrete reached saturation point and the slight camber of the surface became insufficient to keep the water rolling off to the shoulders. Ted Thurnblad had been called away from his crane search when landing aircraft requested a report on the condition of Ten Left. If the surface water, or standing water as it was called, reached a level of three millimetres or more, the water was sufficient to increase the drag from the wheels on a take off, and pose a major hazard to a landing aircraft which could aquaplane, or skid along the runway surface with the same effect as if it had touched down on ice. Thurnblad was out making standing water checks at various points on Ten Left, but unlike Amsterdam Airport which had scientific devices to detect the surface water, the only reference Thurnblad had was two two pence coins whose combined thickness was three millimetres.

The difficulty which faced Thurnblad was getting onto the the runway to lay the two coins down and make his check between the non-stop arrivals and departures of aircraft. He had parked his vehicle off Block 17 and was forced to make his inspections on foot since there was no time to drive along the runway between aircraft movements. Meyer, watching Thurnblad from the Tower, was growing both impatient and frustrated. He didn't like the idea of this fellow darting on and off the runway while jet aircraft were swooping in and out. Yet he had no way of contacting Thurnblad since he was getting pretty far away from the radio telephone in Seagull. Meyer had to satisfy himself with advising pilots that there was a runway inspection going on and to look out for this man who might suddenly sprint onto the tarmac. It hardly seemed the kind of advice an international airport should have to give — and what were the pilots supposed to do, Meyer asked himself. Toot their horns? It was like flying into Kennedy Airport in New York. Meyer had heard stories from Flight Captains of the 707's and 747's who had been calmly warned by Kennedy Tower to watch out for small aircraft crossing left to right at two thousand, or being advised to reduce airspeed because a single engine Piper was just ahead. To Meyer it was ridiculous to combine Instrument Flight Rules with Visual Flight Rules. The big aircraft were thundering in on IFR, relying only on what their landing instruments told them while all around these small planes were peering ahead on VFR, coming into a large international airport with only the pilot's eyes to locate the right runway and keep clear of commercial airliners. How they didn't have more collisions between jet aircraft and the private planes was beyond Meyer, and he knew that Heathrow would never allow such freedom of the skies. Once a flight entered the London Control Zone whether it was a 747 or a small private plane, the pilot had to proceed under IFR conditions or get special clearance from the Tower. But with Thurnblad racing about the only serviceable runway, it bore a close resemblance to Kennedy's situation and Meyer was none too pleased.

Thurnblad wasn't exactly enjoying the between-aircraftsprints he was forced to make and it was equally ridiculous to him to have to head for the centreline, drop his two coins and carefully check the height of the water against this miserable reference. He had carried out this procedure far enough along the runway so as to turn back and head for Seagull where he would drive to the other end of Ten Left. The easterly wind had suddenly picked up to a brisk twenty-two knots, driving the rain hard against him as he trudged along the shoulder towards Block 17. He decided to make one final check before reporting to the Tower and quickly glanced around to see if any aircraft were heading his way. Visibility up Ten Left was pretty poor – maybe a few thousand feet at best – and the pouring rain didn't make hearing aircraft any easier. Satisfied that it was safe to proceed onto the runway, he crossed quickly to the centreline and pulled the two coins from his pocket. His hands were wet and the coins slippery – the wind had numbed his hands just enough to loose his grip and both coins dropped onto the centreline. Thurnblad cursed. He had found the first coin with no trouble, but the second one had vanished. He looked around him, thinking it might have rolled some distance away. But it had disappeared. He swore again for it meant that a foreign object was now somewhere on the runway and it had to be found before any planes landed. He knew it didn't take much more than an object like a two pence coin to damage jet engines or whip from aircraft exhaust and imbed itself in the fuselage or tail section. Smaller things had caused fatal crashes. He debated whether to inform the Tower, but since he still neither saw nor heard any signs of aircraft activity from the end of Ten Left, he continued his search.

Jim Ramaley, the Departure Controller, had just released Air Canada's 747 to begin his roll. He was immediately informed by the Captain that he wanted to hold his roll for a few moments until he had checked out a faulty circuit the Flight Engineer had discovered. Ramaley permitted him to hold and advised him not to roll until he had received further clearance from the Tower since other aircraft might be landing in front of him.

Meyer had a Trident on finals. 'Bealine Three Eight One clear to land One Zero Left. We have a 747 holding so please make your touchdown slightly high.'

'Would you like us to overshoot and come round?' asked the Captain.

Normally Meyer wouldn't have thought twice about saying yes. 'I'd like you to continue your landing as we're pretty tight at the moment, Three Eight One.'

'Roger. Will continue our landing.'

It had been hard enough fitting in the landings and departures and the overshoot of one aircraft would result in more delays. He'd have to be handed back to Approach Control and either re-routed into the stack or squeezed into an already tight approach pattern. Meyer consoled himself with the fact that the BEA Trident didn't need much runway and the few feet he'd lose by touching down beyond the 747 wouldn't pose any hazard.

Thurnblad was ready to give up when he saw the coin. It was wedged between the glass and steel of one of the centreline lights. He bent down and fumbled with the slippery coin. He couldn't seem to get a fingernail behind the coin and his fingers kept slipping on the wet glass. Angered and cold, he stood up and kicked at the light, sending the two pence popping into the air and splashing onto the runway. He picked it up and placed the two coins together in his final effort to measure the standing water. It was a bit above the rim. The three milimetres had been exceeded. The danger of aquaplaning was now pretty great.

As Thurnblad stood up, he saw the landing lights of the Trident. The plane was coming straight for him at a hundred and twenty knots. He scrambled off the centreline and made for the shoulder, but slipped on a light housing and crashed down on one knee. He hoisted himself up and scrambled towards the edge of the runway. His knee throbbed and he limped painfully. In another second the Trident would be zipping past him and the jet exhaust could sear the clothes off his back. Thurnblad made one last plunge for safety, expecting at any moment to feel the heat from the three rear engines. When he reached the shoulder, he toppled down on his bad leg and peered out through the rain. The Trident was just passing him, its engines quiet and ambling along at taxiing speed. Thurnblad blinked at the plane as if to make sure it was the same one he had seen coming towards him. It was, and he suddenly realised why he had been lucky. The standing water. On take off it added immense drag to an aircraft, holding it to the runway with the same grip as Captains of sea planes felt. And often it had the same effect on landing aircraft. Rather than aquaplaning, the wheels of the aircraft made immediate contact with the runway before the Captain had made any attempt to use his wheel brakes and the water gripped the landing gear like glue, enabling the plane to come to rest hundreds of feet before it normally would even on dry concrete. Thurnblad blessed the standing water and limped towards the shelter of Seagull.

'What do you think?' Lynn asked nervously.

Toni Rice counted out Paul's pulse. Brodie was wiping his sweating forehead with one of the Wash'N Dry towels. Alex Trent-Jones looked on.

'You say he had these pains last night?' Toni asked.

Brodie looked up. 'Yes, ma'am. He said he often got them.'

'Has he ever told you about them?' she asked Lynn.

She shook her head. 'He never had any trouble before.'

'I think you better check the passenger list and see if there's a doctor on board. I think I noticed one or two M.D.'s on the manifest,' Toni began. 'I hope I'm wrong, but it looks like his appendix.'

Captain Huston pressed the transmit button. 'Astral One Two Four.'

'Gander Control, One Two Four. Switch to Shanwick Control.'

'Roger, Gander. Good day.'

They had passed the point of no return. Prestwick Control was now in charge of International One Two Four to London at 30° West Longitude.

Dr. Perry Osterton didn't take long to examine Paul. He stood up and drew both Toni Rice and Lynn Almirall aside. 'It's the boy's appendix all right. I understand you're his sister.'

Lynn nodded. Unconsciously her fingernails bit into her palms.

'Did you know he had these pains before?'

She shook her head. 'How bad is it?'

Osterton – who had only just retired from forty years of paediatric surgery – knew just how bad it was. If Brodie had said the boy had had a severe attack the previous night, it meant that Paul's present pain was a final attack. Without surgery, this attack could rupture. Paul would bleed to death in a matter of minutes. 'In any case like this it's impossible to say just how bad it is,' he explained quietly. 'But I wouldn't be optimistic. How much longer before we reach London?'

Toni looked at her watch. 'Three more hours, maybe less. If we're on schedule.'

Osterton frowned, revealing his concern. 'Why didn't your brother tell you he wasn't feeling well?'

Lynn was no longer nervous. She was feeling terrified. She bit her lip and wanted to cry. 'I don't know,' she whispered shaking her head, 'He had been looking forward to this trip, I guess. He just didn't want anything to ruin it. He knew he wouldn't be allowed to fly if he was ill.'

Osterton ran his fingers through strands of grey hair. 'Three hours is a big gamble in a case like this.'

Toni Rice knew it was a big gamble, too. 'Could you operate?'

Osterton seemed surprised. 'What? Here? With no proper facilities?'

'We've got an emergency equipment box,' she began hastily. 'It contains pain killing drugs and sedatives. We can use the emergency oxygen cylinders for anaesthesia.'

Osterton was thinking, but not favourably. Then he heard Paul crying. Brodie looked up and Trent-Jones stood up from the boy's side and faced Osterton. 'That kid's had it, hasn't

94

he?' said Trent-Jones sharply. 'Unless you do something. At least give him something for the pain.'

'All right,' Osterton conceded. 'Let me see this box.'

'I have to get the Captain's permission. He's got the key.'

Toni Rice knocked on the cockpit door. Flight Engineer Sturgess peered through the security hole and turned the knob. 'Trouble,' she announced quickly.

'Ladies and Gentlemen, this is your hi-jacker speaking,' Page began. 'Where to now?'

'Nothing like that,' Toni said hurriedly. 'It's Lynn Almirall's brother – the kid who's travelling in first class. He's had an attack of appendicitis and the doctor thinks it's serious.'

Captain Huston pulled off his headset and turned in his seat. 'What doctor?'

'One of the passengers. He's flying to London for some kind of award from the Royal Society of Surgeons or something. He's retired – but he knows what he's doing.'

'What does he think *we* should do?' asked Huston seriously. 'We've just gone onto Shanwick Control. There's no turning back now.'

'He might want to operate. But he wants to open the emergency box.'

Without hesitating, Captain Huston removed the key from its hook below his side window. 'Give him all the help you can. And keep me informed. We've got clear weather for another two hours, but once we hit the Irish Coast it's going to be rough. If he has to open the kid up, tell him to do it now – otherwise I can't guarantee to hold the plane steady.'

Toni nodded. 'Dr. Osterton doesn't know whether he wants to operate yet, but I know what he will ask,' she paused. 'Can we land anywhere before London?'

'Not a chance,' Huston replied. 'Shannon's socked in and we're on the Circle Course. It would take us as long to reach Iceland as it would to make straight for London. I'll notify Shanwick Control and see if we can't get the best course and speed.'

'Thanks,' Toni said.

Flight Engineer Peter Sturgess was beginning to have his own troubles. He had just completed a fuel transfer from the outside wing tanks to maintain balance when he noticed number three's engine warning indicator blinking faintly. He tapped the indicator. Quickly he scanned the engine monitors for numbers one, two and four. No warnings. 'I think something's up with number three,' he said coldly. 'Either it's instrument error or she's overheating.'

Captain Huston and First Officer Page glanced at the bank of engine indicators on the panel above the throttles. 'Nothing here,' Huston replied. 'Want me to cut back on number three?'

'Give me another minute. This indicator's faulty. It must be. I'm only getting an on and off warning.'

'Can't make up its mind, eh?' Page grinned.

'It's an overheat,' Huston announced sharply. 'I'm picking it up here.'

'Christ,' Sturgess shouted. 'It's a goddam fire.'

'Fuel cut off,' Huston cried. 'Use the extinguishers.'

Sturgess cut the fuel flow and hit the red flashing knob above the number three indicators.

'That's just what we need,' Huston said, cutting out the auto pilot. 'Shanwick, this is International Astral One Two Four at three five zero.'

'Shanwick Control, Astral One Two Four.'

Captain Huston was about to report when the explosion cut off his signal.

'Easy,' Michelson whispered. 'Another inch. Nice and slow.'

'I don't think the ram's going to take it,' Jeffreys replied. 'There's a hell of a lot more than eight tons on this thing.'

'Just keep raising her. If Coburn's right, she'll take it.'

Jeffreys wiped the sweat and rain from his face. 'How much more?'

'Until the Doc says he's got Bartlett out.'

'If this ram pops on us, you're going to get a belly full of steel,' Jeffreys said coldly. 'And Bartlett's going to look like a pancake.'

Michelson looked across the bogie to the Doctor. He shook his head.

'Jesus,' Jeffreys swore angrily. 'The gear's lifting.'

Michelson noticed it as well. If the ram was lifting the bogie, there *was* more than eight tons pushing down. The hydraulic pressure inside the ram could explode like a hand grenade. Coburn noticed it, too. The air bag was rising. Another few inches and the pressure would be off Bartlett.

'You better stand back, Doc,' Michelson warned. 'I'll call you when she's up enough.'

The Doctor looked across. 'I'm fine here, Mr. Michelson.'

'You bloody won't be if this ram goes,' Jeffreys shouted. 'Right now we're lifting half a 707 with an eight ton ram. We'll be lucky if she doesn't collapse and blow all of us to pieces.'

'Occupational hazard,' the Doctor shouted back. 'I think you've nearly done it. I'm beginning to pull him clear.'

Coburn was sweating. He was wet on the outside and sweat was soaking him on the inside. His teeth were clenched nervously. Simson and Andrews gripped the pressure control levers and fought off the rain that was dribbling between their fingers. Coburn took a rag and wiped the glass panes on the gauges.

'She won't take any more,' Jeffreys said. 'Not another bloody inch.'

'Another bloody inch is all we need,' Michelson replied. 'Keep her going.'

Jeffreys' frown bit through Michelson's concern. The ram wasn't built to jack up aircraft. Not 707's anyway. Even if the airbags were absorbing some of the weight, he knew too well that the eight ton limit had been exceeded long ago. The recollection of his brother didn't help, either. Another ram in another place at another airfield. His brother had been careless – or brave – or just plain stupid. Whichever, the ram had exploded. It had ripped his brother to pieces. His chest and stomach had taken the full impact and the only thing that kept him in one piece was his spinal column. The rest of his abdomen was blown to bits. And for what, Michelson had asked himself. For some damned pilot who overshot the airfield and parked his DC 4 halfway through the localiser. Bits of propeller had spun off in every direction. One bit had sliced open a fourteen year old plane spotter. Another bit had soared seven hundred feet across an adjacent field and landed in someone's living room. The number one engine cowling had wrapped itself around a party of youngsters four hundred feet to the left of the localiser. It was rough enough clearing up the human

97

debris – worse holding back the parents who had witnessed the disaster. But then the ram blew. All because runway priority demanded the removal of the aircraft. With the least amount of damage to the plane. Just like now. Just like this bloody minded engineer who would rather suffocate than lose his starboard wing.

And if the hydraulic ram couldn't take the weight now? It was his order that kept Jeffreys hoisting the ram up, inch by inch, minute by minute, while all the downward pressure per square inch was multiplying in some crazy geometric progression against the upward force of the hydraulics. And the undercarriage was at least two inches off the runway. He could spin the shredded tyres if he wanted to. He could probably see the steel bulging on the ram shafts if he wanted to. He could visualize the pressure inside those shafts. Pressure that would crush solid rock into dust. He turned to Jeffreys.

'Clear out,' he snapped.

Jeffreys stared hard at him. 'No way, mate.'

'I said move.'

The two men were facing each other. Rain and sweat dribbled down their faces, mixed with oil from the leaking bogie. 'We work as a team,' Jeffreys began. He had been reading Michelson's thoughts. 'Remember, it was me who hauled your brother out of that prop.'

Michelson remembered. He remembered because *he* couldn't do it. Would Jeffreys be hauling him out of this one – or would he be scraping up the flesh from Jeffreys' shattered body?

'She's leaking,' Jeffreys said coldly. 'Look.'

Michelson stared at the ram. Hydraulic fluid was oozing down the shaft in tiny rivulets, different from the rain only in its colour. 'She'll go any second,' he whispered.

Coburn had guessed how bad it was. He leapt down from the trailer and pushed the Doctor nearer Bartlett. 'Right, pull. Both arms.'

'There could be chest injuries,' the Doctor warned.

'Yeah. And there could be five of us wearing slivers of ram shaft.'

As carefully as they could, but as quickly, they hauled on Bartlett's arms. Simson jumped down from the console and wedged himself between the air bag and bogie, pushing back against the bag. In another second, everything popped at once.

The Doctor and Coburn had given one final tug on Bartlett's arms. Simson's added pressure pushed the bag away and Bartlett was freed. Then the ram collapsed and with a dull thud the 707's weight settled back onto the runway. But rather than exploding, the cracked ram shaft blew hydraulic fluid downwards and over the bogie. Simson was flung clear of the gear as the bag popped back against the undercarriage and Michelson and Jeffreys had been long prepared to leap away from the ram the second Bartlett was freed. The five of them were now on the runway, all laid flat out and all staring up at the rain. Michelson began to laugh. He looked over at Coburn, and at Jeffreys, and they were laughing. Even Bartlett was regaining consciousness as Simson pulled the mask away from his face and sat him up.

'It's been quite a party you've missed, Bartlett,' Simson said. 'But we saved your plane.'

Bill Auer, the ATC Training Officer, was back in his office facing another cup of coffee. Meyer and Ramaley were coping, and Clive Amery was one of the quickest trouble shooters in Aerodrome Control when it came to sorting out delays. His mind worked like a computer, systematically, logically and with a fairness to each airline. At the moment the stacks were being cleared by re-routing to other airports across England and Scotland and extra motor coaches were being laid on at every airport to carry the diverted passengers back to London. Local airport hotels were being notified to accept passengers who couldn't face the coach ride, and at Heathrow final departure cancellations had been decided upon and the passengers either returned to their homes or pitched camp in the terminals, resolved to wait out the delays. It was a costly business. The runway damage was extensive and expensive. There was overtime to pay and shift allowance for the extra men called in. There were the hotel bills the airlines faced. There was the simple loss of revenue from the runway closures. At least it wasn't his problem, Auer contemplated, somewhat relaxed. Air Traffic Control was on one side of things, and the British Airports Authority on the other. He was thankful the two were distinct in power and relationship. BAA would be faced with the reams of paperwork for this miserable day. BAA would be answerable to the airlines. BAA would have to pressure the boys to get the runways open. ATC just had to sit back and wait until the all clear was given to resume normal operations.

'Maintain speed and heading,' Auer thought again. 'Take every bend just like banking an airplane. Turn and bank indicator, vertical speed, rudder and elevators adjusted perfectly, throttle up to maintain correct altitude. And don't stall.' Auer seemed pleased. It equated nicely with motorcycling. If his son could master the fundamentals of that damned bike as easily as Auer did flying, he just might pass his test someday. Auer pushed the Met reports away and picked up the Owner's Manual for the Honda CD 175. It reminded him of *his* first Owner's Manual. For a single engined Cessna. He had studied that manual until he could recite it. Then he had bought the Jeppersen Private Pilot's Course and memorised that. He had gone through the 'Flight Briefing for Pilots' series and he had studied all there was on instrumentation. Then war came. All his book work was applied in the RAF and he shot ahead of his fellow volunteers. After two years of flying, he had forgotten the number of bomb runs he had spearheaded. He had lost count of the number of half shredded aircraft he had nursed back to base – or at least brought near enough to the English coast to swim home.

Then the war ended. He walked out of the RAF as quickly as he had jumped at the chance to enlist. He had flown commercial and in the early days he had enjoyed it. But flying today was pushing buttons, setting auto pilots, fighting the air congestion like so many cars on the M4, and now pilots didn't even have to land their own aircraft. There was the Autoland system that took care of that. Smith's took care of the flying, Decca took navigation away from the navigators and Plessy and Elliots provided the ground systems to land an aircraft in near zero zero conditions. No wonder commercial pilots spent their days off flying single engine planes. At least they could do some real flying. At least they knew that when they had landed a single engine Piper it was an individual – a human – who landed it, relying on human judgement and not on a complex network of computers, ILS localisers, glide paths, Autolands and radar that could 'talk' a jetliner right down to the ground.

Auer sipped his coffee and stared out at the rain. The airport was strangely quiet.

'It's the Titanium blades, Sir,' Sturgess reported. 'There's no way of stopping the fire.'

Huston could have guessed that. The Titanium would burn until every blade was gone. 'Fuel cut off.'

'Fuel cut, Sir,' Sturgess replied.

'Getting any other warnings?'

'Not yet, Sir,' said Sturgess, checking every instrument on his panel.

'Page, you go back to the cabin and make a visual check. See if there are any passenger injuries. Get everybody calmed down.'

Page pushed himself from his seat. 'You give me all the easy jobs, Skipper.'

Huston had been flying for too long to think about anything but his aircraft. The fact that they might be wallowing in the Atlantic at any moment never crossed his mind. The possibility that decompression was imminent was equally ignored. He knew that an engine had overheated, that the Titanium blades had ignited, that the extinguishing equipment couldn't stop the fire, and all he could do was wait for the Titanium to burn itself out. If they were lucky, the sixty below air outside would cool the engine down, and the lack of oxygen in the atmosphere would starve the fire. His real job was finding out how badly the explosion had damaged the aircraft – especially on his starboard side.

'Shanwick Control, this is International One Two Four. May Day. May Day. I repeat. International One Two Four. May Day. May Day.'

'International One Two Four. What is your position?'

'Heading two six zero. Flight level three five zero. Position twenty degrees west. Fire and explosion in number three. Damage assessment being made. Request priority flight level and escort. Over.'

'Roger, One Two Four. Will notify Rescue Co-ordination. Keep your present frequency open.'

The explosion had had the effect of thrusting the 747 in an upward and sideways arc, throwing Julie Stark into the arms of Ronald Lambert, a passenger on the port side of the aircraft. Mr. and Mrs. Reginald Poinsett had the window seat directly opposite and slightly forward of number three. But they had remained calm even when the engine nacel slammed against the fuselage – probably more from the immediate shock than deliberation. Katheryn Mayhill had pushed mid-way up the economy section several seconds after the blast and was bracing herself between the centre and outside aisle, starboard side. Peggy Dawson had taken a similar position on the port side while Sandra Gesner made for the 'phone in the mid section galley. The immediate presence of the cabin crew had the affect of reassuring passengers that death wasn't exactly imminent, but each of the stewardesses knew that the initial shock would soon wear off and panic would set in. Whatever had caused the explosion, it had been heard and felt throughout every inch of the 747, and the only calming element at the moment was the fact that the plane was still in the air.

First Officer Page had emerged from the cockpit into the first class lounge. He found Trent-Jones and Lynn Almirall lifting Paul off the floor and laying him back onto the port side seats. He spotted another young boy holding his head. Blood was trickling between his fingers. The Doctor and Toni Rice had been thrown across the table in the middle of the lounge, but neither seemed hurt. Wilbur Cross, who at least had the sense to keep his seat belt fastened throughout any flight, was trembling violently and Page knew he was going to throw up. He pulled a sickness bag from the wall rack and held it over Cross's mouth.

'Don't let go,' he said, but Cross just shook his head and gripped the bag.

'What's happened?' Toni cried, as she pulled herself up. 'Bomb?'

'Engine fire,' Page said quickly. 'I'm going downstairs to see how bad it is. Everyone all right up here?'

Toni glanced about the lounge. 'Looks O.K.'

'You'd better tend to the lad over there. He's done something to his head.'

Page made his way down the circular staircase and as he

descended he knew the Skipper was testing the control surfaces. The aircraft was slipping one moment to port, then to starboard. He felt the slight thrust of acceleration, then a retarding of the three operating engines. So far it seemed that the control surfaces were responding. This reassured him and he stepped into the first class section with more confidence than he thought he could manage.

Bruce Ames, the Pan Am engineer, was the first out of his seat. He had easily guessed what had happened, and he knew what the probable corrective action would have to be. 'You've got trouble in number three,' he said casually to Page.

'Nothing serious, Sir. I'm just going to have a look . . .'

Ames had pulled out his identification. 'I know things are pretty rough up there so I just thought I'd let you know. I'll be glad to help any way I can.'

Page stared at the ID. 'Glad to have you on board, Mr. Ames. I'll tell the Skipper.'

'You've got two other fellows on board who might be able to help you as well,' Ames persisted quietly.

Page was impatient. He wanted to see that engine, but he also wanted to know just who might be able to sort things out if it came to a real crisis.

'There's a representative from Amplivox – the fellow there,' said Ames pointing, 'And you've got a senior rep from Decca upstairs. I'm sure they'd be as willing to help . . .'

'Thanks,' Page replied, glancing around the cabin. 'I'd better see how the rest of the passengers are.'

'Mind if I look at the engine?'

Page wanted to say yes he did mind, but he thought again, and he still wanted to know there might be some extra help on board. 'No. But don't make it too obvious.'

Marjorie Osterton grabbed Page's arm as he moved towards the rear of the cabin. 'I know you're very busy,' she began apologetically. 'But my husband's up there with that boy. Are they all right?'

Page looked down at the elderly face. There wasn't a trace of fear in her kindly features, only a look of concern for someone who might be injured. 'Everyone's fine, ma'am,' Page replied. 'There's a young lad who hurt his head a bit, but I'm sure your husband is taking care of him.'

Mrs. Osterton smiled up at the First Officer. 'I know we'll be all right.'

Page mumbled a few words of assurance to the remaining first class passengers who had felt less of the explosion. Ahead of the engine and in the most stable part of the aircraft, the violent shaking that had upset economy hadn't been felt with the same severity in first class. Page had opened the door to economy section on the port side when he heard the Captain address the passengers.

'Ladies and Gentlemen, this is Captain Huston,' he began in his unruffled, pre-take off voice. 'We seem to have had some trouble with our number three engine as most of you have guessed, but I'd just like to assure all of you that no structural damage has been done to the aircraft and we are continuing our flight route quite normally. My First Officer will gladly answer any questions you may have about what happened, and we have a qualified nurse on board for any of you who may have suffered some bruising when we had that pop. I'll keep you informed of our progress, and in the meantime I'd just like to say that there is no danger and that we are able to maintain our height and speed with no difficulty.'

That saved Page some headaches, he thought. But he didn't like the bit about answering questions. Already, passengers were milling about the starboard side trying to get a good view of the ruptured engine. He made for the forward galley and picked up the microphone. 'Ladies and gentlemen, this is First Officer Page. I would like to ask all of you to resume your seats if you would until we can get a better idea of just what that engine is doing. You may continue to smoke, of course, but please fasten your seat belts until we have made an assessment of the damage.' He hung the mike up and flicked on the 'Fasten Seat Belt' switch.

Page noticed that Ames was already looking at the engine from the aft windows, so he crossed over to Mr. and Mrs. Poinsett's seats. 'You had a pretty good view of things, huh?' he asked as casually as he could.

'Suddenly bang,' said Mr. Poinsett shakily. 'I looked out the window as soon as I heard the explosion, but all I could see was what looked like a fire inside the engine – you know – just inside the front.'

'I'm afraid she just overheated and popped,' Page replied.
'I'm wondering if I could ask you and your wife – you are
married? – to change seats. We'd like to be able to have a
clear view of that engine from time to time, and I'd hate to
keep bothering you. Why don't you both go up to the first
class area? There're plenty of seats up there.'

'Oh, that's very kind of you,' Mrs. Poinsett gleamed. 'You
mean we can sit in first class?'

'I don't think the airline will mind. Besides, you're our
chief witnesses so it's the least we can do.'

Page inspected the engine from the front. There wasn't
much to see. The first stage compressor fans were shot to hell,
and he imagined it looked just as bad from the rear. He wished
he could see the skin of the fuselage, but he knew he'd have
to wait until the escort plane arrived. He was certain that
none of the passengers was going to know about it. He saw
Ames signalling to him, and slowly he made his way aft, stopping to talk to the passengers as he went.

Shanwick Transoceanic Control had pushed the panic button to Rescue Co-ordination and had given the brief details
of International One Two Four's trouble. An escort had been
requested from Captain Huston which meant there was the
chance the 747 would ditch somewhere in the Atlantic, but
at the same time the message received had not indicated an
immediate distress. A single RAF Nimrod was dispatched
from the air base at Bally Kelly, Ireland, and the May Day
call was passed on to International's offices at Heathrow.
Astral One Two Four was two hours forty nine minutes from
London when the distress call went out. The Nimrod would
rendezvous in less than an hour and a half. On three engines
the 747 might make Heathrow in three and a half hours, but
the weather from Iceland to London couldn't be worse for a
plane with engine trouble.

Malcolm Wilmet received the message and didn't want to
believe it. Not with Heathrow in the state it was. The details
were insufficient to declare an all out emergency, but Wilmet
knew about overheat problems with the 747's. On the ground
the engines overheated with painful regularity and had to be

shut down. In the air the 747 engines overheated less frequently and an engine's power could be cut to cool her off. But a 747 flying the Atlantic run with three engines, possible aircraft damage, and lousy weather conditions coupled with the troubles at Heathrow made Wilmet sweat. He forced the thought of an engine overheat on any of the good engines on One Two Four from his mind and made for Aerodrome Control.

Bill Auer had left his desk and was peering out through the gloom. His office in the tower building faced due north, and he couldn't see the activity at the incident area which was south east of him. Instead, he counted the number of take-offs and landings on one zero left. He had a message from Met that the wind was slowly veering about and soon ATC would reverse the pattern to two eight right. Auer had known busy days at Heathrow – days when planes took off and landed seconds apart – but he had never seen the number of aircraft zipping in and off the one runway before him. Tower Control was down to the absolute minimum criteria for aircraft separation so that the greatest number of planes could be brought in and sent out, and he was glad he wasn't in Aerodrome Control. When conditions demanded runway operation at minimum criteria, the slightest marginal error on a controller's part meant an undershoot – critical separation could be misjudged either vertically or horizontally, and in the end Auer knew he would be answerable for any incident. But he had faith in his crew. He was the Training Officer, and he knew that he had given his lads every bit of his own experience and the experiences of others. He knew that when he assigned a man to ATC, that man could handle any emergency. He could stay calm and use logic rather than hasty miscalculation. The twenty per cent of applicants who were rejected each year he knew were not suited to work at Heathrow. There were just too many airlines with too many planes. The responsibility was too great for anyone but the best.

Feeling somewhat confident in the situation before him, he returned to his desk. Malcolm Wilmet knocked softly on the door and entered.

'I've got troubles, Bill," Wilmet began.

'You too, eh? Must be a virus going around the airport today,' Auer grinned. 'Since when does International Airlines have troubles. The odd strike, a few walk-outs, maybe a bomb threat or hi-jack – but we're all used to that by now.'

Normally, Wilmet would have taken the ribbing the way it was meant. He and Auer had been neighbours long enough to chide each other without hard feelings. But Wilmet put on his not-to-be-chided face. 'Have a read of this.'

Auer took the memo from Wilmet and read the skimpy details on International Astral One Two Four. He read it a second time. Slowly he let it drop onto his desk. 'The first thing I'll tell you is don't jump to any conclusions. The skipper hasn't declared an imminent distress and he's getting an escort. The next thing I'll tell you is we can't bring him in here.'

'I thought you'd say that. Where do we bring him in then?'

'That I cannot tell you,' Auer said slowly. 'There's one chance in a million they'll open up one zero right by the time your flight is due in. Your skipper is going to need all the runway and approach guidance he can get.'

'You tell me any other airport that could take him – Shannon?'

Auer stood up quickly and walked to the window. 'Normally, I'd say yes. We all would. But Shannon's got it worse than us weather wise. I wouldn't trust Dublin even if they'd accept her. She hasn't got enough runway. But we can't route her into Heathrow, Mal, the skies are just too damn . . .'

The phone rang. Auer picked it up, listened, and handed it to Wilmet. 'More news.'

Wilmet took the phone. He listened expressionlessly, trained long ago not to show fear, hope, elation or grief. Not when he represented an airline. When the call ended, he dropped the phone onto its cradle.

'It's not just the plane, Bill,' he began in a tone Auer had never heard. 'There's a boy on board. He's got to have an emergency operation or he'll die. They want to operate in flight.'

Auer rested his hands on the window ledge and was thankful he didn't have to face Wilmet. 'What's their ETA?'

'Twenty hundred, Heathrow.'

Auer glanced at his watch. It was nearly five thirty-five. If it was a normal day, he'd be home in an hour. 'How about the aircraft? What sort of condition is she in?'

'All we know is that she's still in the air. Captain Huston's last report to Shanwick said he was on three engines, air speed down but fuel O.K., starboard control surfaces heavy and he thinks some of number three may have imbedded itself in the tail. He's trying to assess the damage now. He's waiting for a visual check when the rescue escort arrives.'

Auer had decided. He never liked to waste time – even though quick decisions could cost him his job. 'Let's go up-stairs. We'll see what can be done. Then I think we had better see Manley.'

Wilmet prayed that there was a hope Astral One Two Four would be cleared to maintain her heading for Heathrow.

The three flat tops rolled slowly along Block 73 and ground to a halt on the edge of Block 85. Blake looked up from the pits and made an expression that said it's bloody well about time. Ken Patrick hopped out of the lead cab and hunched himself against the rain.

'All we could get, Kevin,' he began, looking back at the three transporters. 'Eighteen pit covers. Fourteen new and four slightly used. It's the best we can do.'

Blake didn't have time to argue. 'Get a crane from Works and pile those covers alongside the stop bar. We won't sink them until we get some of the wiring sorted out below. See if you can get some boys to rig up a tent over these pits. It's damned impossible to work on these cables under a tarp.'

Patrick made for his transporter. Blake shouted after him. 'Take one of the rovers. You'll make it quicker. We haven't got time.'

Thinking of time, Blake looked through the rain towards the 707. The aircraft was nearly two thousand feet away and it was hard to make out if Coburn was having any success. He had heard about Bartlett's rescue, and of the man's deter-mination not to lose his plane. Blake admired him for it. Bart-lett was as dedicated to his company as Blake liked to think he was to his Section. It was dedication and guts that kept an airport like Heathrow ticking over. It was a calm head when most people would break down. It was loyalty to a job or an airline. Above all – in Blake's book – it was concern for everyone else. Whether it was a passenger or an employee Blake made it his principle that life at Heathrow centred around concern. Everyone pitched in and did his bit without grumbling. And if he grumbled, he grumbled good naturedly. Even with the rain, the shattered concrete and severed cables, pressure from BAA and ATC to open the runways, and a bloody great 707 sitting like a lame duck in 87, Blake resolved himself to his work and he was certain that Coburn felt the same way.

Coburn did. But his concern was being strained. He had been concerned for Bartlett and – like Blake – he admired Bartlett's determination to fight it out, but he also had his job to do. The 707 had to be shifted and Coburn had the responsibility of deciding whether to take the easy way out and remove the plane piece by piece, or spend hours air bagging, trolleying, winching and eventually tugging the beast off Block 87.

Once Bartlett had been freed, he compromised. He had been held up for at least forty minutes by the accident and while on the one hand he respected Bartlett's wishes, it would be his – Coburn's – head which would lie on the chopping block if he didn't shift the plane quickly. Brian Barker, the Incident Officer from the constabulary, was more than willing to rely on Coburn's discretion, but there would come a time when Barker would have to push. He'd have to order the plane out of Block 87 in the quickest way available. Coburn knew that there was no Conga line at Heathrow – no massive trucks with massive plows which could push the 707 onto the grass verge like so much garbage – but he did know that the Fire Service and Engineering could make short work of the plane with cutting saws. It didn't matter who would foot the bill. It was worth paying for a brand new aircraft if they had to. Coburn had seen the tarpaulins being stretched over the pit covers in Block 85, and he guessed that Blake was having about as much trouble as he was. This gave Coburn time, but he didn't know how much. If Blake was lucky, he could repair the main electrical circuits, replace some of the lighting transformers, shore up enough of the pit covers and re-fit new ones and then declare the two runways serviceable in a lot shorter time than Coburn could manhandle the 707 into the clear.

Bartlett was tucked safely away in the Medical Centre. Coburn was now entirely his own boss. So he had made the decision to compromise. He wouldn't let Bartlett down – not after all he'd been through to save his plane – but he wasn't going to play it as safe as Bartlett would have wanted. Within minutes after the ambulance had whisked Bartlett off, Coburn took his first gamble. Ideally, the ten air bags inflated at equal pressure to keep the aircraft balanced, but the starboard bags had slipped and the plane was angled slightly off centre. He ordered Simson and Andrews to hold the pressure in the starboard bags while he jacked up the wing enough to push the bags back into position with two of the land rovers. To prevent them from slipping again, he had dumped sand around the bags and improvised a system of chocks to make doubly certain there would not be any more slips. He then hauled out the jacks and told Simson and Andrews to resume inflation, but more quickly than the limits set to insure minimum stress on the spars should they be weakened by the nose-down skid. Inflating the bags at a quicker rate meant everyone keyed up. Simson and Andrews had to watch each indicator for correct and equal pressure in the bags and for compensation for varying weights in the two wings. The rain made it hard to keep an eye on the gauges and with both hands firmly on the control levers, it was impossible to wipe the rain from either their eyes or the indicators. So Coburn had instructed Ben Kitchley to stand between Simson and Andrews with a towel in each hand. Kitchley felt like he was doing an assist in some operating theatre. He kept the dials wiped, drying each indicator in turn. Whenever Simson or Andrews called out, he mopped their faces with the other towel. Ben Casey Kitchley, he thought, and he wondered who was going to give him dry cloths, when after five minutes both towels were soaked.

The stepped up inflation presented a personnel danger problem. If the spars between the wings were weakened, the wings would snap suddenly and without warning once the stress point had been reached. If they snapped with the belly of the 707 still on the ground, the danger was less and the chances were that the wings would bend upwards and remain fixed to the fuslage rather than break away completely. But the belly was lifting. The nose was easing off the ground, and if the spars gave way now, one or both wings could shear off in any direction. The sensible thing, Coburn knew, was to keep his men clear of the aircraft until he was certain that the spars were firm. But he was compromising. It was unfair to the aircraft to suspend the fuselage between the wings: it put too much weight on already injured spars. He had to get the nose trolley in place at the quickest possible moment in order to take some of the burden from the wings. Doug Parent knew what was in Coburn's mind. When Coburn reversed the nose jack into place, Parent told the men to stand ready with the wing trollies, then slid under the nose with Coburn.

'You know what's going to happen if this gamble fails?' Coburn said to Parent.

'I know," Parent replied, eyeing the runway below the nose. 'You think this concrete will take the jack?'

'I don't know,' Coburn said simply. 'If our luck carries on the way it has, you can bet she'll sink straight through it.'

'How about a steel plate? All we need is one more hold up and you know what the answer will be.'

'If we use a plate it'll mean we'll have to raise her that much more. I'm praying she'll take the stress as it is.'

'It's your baby,' Parent said, watching the port air bags suspiciously. Coburn followed his gaze. He knew Parent was wondering just how long it would be before the port bags began to slip. Already rain had washed much of the sand away from the starboard bags and the only sure thing that was keeping them in place were the chocks. Coburn racked his brains, fighting against his job and Bartlett. 'O.K., stick a plate down. I'll get more sand around the starboard bags and we'll do the same chocking on the port side.' He paused and through the rain dribbling from the nose which hung ten inches off the ground, he looked at Parent. 'If we make it, I'll pay for the drinks. If the spars go, well, I just hope I'm under this nose because my job won't be worth a tuppenny fart.'

Parent suddenly froze. There had been a crack. A groan of

steel and rivets from the midsection. 'I'd say she'll hold, but we don't have much time.'

Coburn looked down at the scorch marks on the belly and at the scars the runway lighting and concrete had cut into the fuselage. 'You just keep holding, my pet,' he whispered. 'We'll have you out in no time.' ·

International One Two Four had been maintaining cruising altitude for exactly twenty two minutes since the number three engine had caught fire and exploded. In those twenty two minutes Captain Huston and Flight Engineer Sturgess had gone through sixty eight checks. In those same minutes Captain Huston had prayed. He prayed because he knew there was no one else. He was skipper of an aircraft carrying two hundred and sixty one passengers, twelve young stewardesses and two flight officers. He was in the right hand seat of God's will and irrespective of his years of flying, the thousands of logged hours, the countless technical faults that had preceded this one, he was shouldering more responsibility than any man ever faced. It was Huston's unlucky honour to be the first captain in charge of a floundering giant carrying more passengers and cargo than could be crammed into two 707's. He had many jobs to do. He had an airplane to fly and damage to assess over and over again. He had to instill confidence and tranquillity in every passenger. He had to prove to his crew that he was capable of making critical decisions every bit as quick as any sudden emergency demanded. And he had a boy in the next room who could die at any moment. These were the headings of his immediate problems. The sub-headings were more intricate. They involved using every trick of flying to keep the 747 in the air: he would rely on every instrument, every navigational aid, every control surface, his fuel tanks – and each of his three good engines. He had added to his prayers that the Boeing Corporation had built this aircraft with the same reliability as the 707. He prayed that somehow this monster of a flying machine had the guts of a Dakota and the aerodynamics of an eagle. His sub-headings regarding the passengers were drawn from his experience and his ground school. He had been told all about hi-jackers and how to handle them, and suicide nuts with bombs – the psychology had been the same. Passengers had to be reassured. Passengers didn't share the same faith in the aircraft that captains had. They didn't know – and couldn't know – just how many things were being done in the air and on the ground to protect them. Besides, if they feared death at thirty odd thousand feet, so did their skipper. The flight crew wanted to live every bit as much as any passenger. Flight crews just didn't give up when a critical situation arose. The difficulty was conveying this to a plane load of nervous passengers who had been brainwashed with Hollywood interpretations of the survival rate in crippled aircraft. Huston hoped that Page was coping: that he wasn't overplaying the nothing-to-worry-about bit, or that the 747 was built like a tank. Tanks sink fast in water and there was plenty of that five miles below.

Another assessment. Paul Lloyd Almirall. The doctor wanted to operate, but only if there was some surety that the plane could be held steady. Half an hour ago Captain Huston could have given Dr. Osterton that guarantee – with a reservation about clear air turbulence. Now there was no telling how steady he could hold three hundred tons of aircraft. If he didn't give the promise of even flight, Osterton had said the only alternative was morphine to kill the pain. Whether the boy lived or not would be in the hands of the gods. But if he administered morphine, an operation was out. The body could not be suppressed with a potent analgesic and be expected to fight the internal shock of surgery: the boy couldn't be anaesthetised for surgery with morphine running about his bloodstream. And every minute that Captain Huston used up assessing a multitude of situations, the chances of survival for both Paul Almirall and the two hundred and sixty other passengers diminished.

First Officer Page had never really given ministers anything but the due respect he estimated they deserved. His beliefs were limited to what he knew was going on in his own life or in his aircraft. He felt guilty as he pulled himself up the staircase to the lounge, now, because if it hadn't been for the three priests in the economy section, he would have been up against odds which didn't leave room for winning. There was the rabbi, too. All it had taken was a quick conference with the four of them, and panic among the passengers had disappeared within the fifteen minutes he spent below. Father Giordino had covered the port side in the forward section, and Father Anthony the starboard. Rabbi Eidel and Father Balliston worked their way down the aft section and together with the cabin crew, they had restored faith in the immediate situation. Page had known passengers respond to the gentle, unflappable attitude of stewardesses, but what he had just witnessed he reckoned was something akin to a miracle. Everyone had returned to their seats and had strapped themselves in, upon his announcement, but there was a lot of nervous chatter going about and Page sensed the tension. When he had told the ministers a few of the details of the damage to the plane, which as far as he knew was minimal, the priests and the rabbi had descended on their congregation, and if Flight One Two Four did end in disaster, Page now felt there wasn't a soul on board who wasn't ready for the pearly gates.

On his return to the lounge, Page rounded up Bruce Ames and Roger Staunton. He pooled an assessment of the aircraft's external injuries with Ames, spoke briefly with Staunton, and figured he could give a pretty concise report to the skipper. Page reckoned that Huston and Sturgess would have estimated the internal damage, and since they were still in the air, maybe the situation wasn't as bad as at first thought.

When he reached the lounge, Dr. Osterton had opened the emergency medical case and was wiping blood away from Brodie's forehead. Lynn Almirall and Trent-Jones were kneeling beside Paul. Toni Rice was about to escort the still quivering Wilbur Cross back into the first class section. Cross's only conviction was the imminent end of his forty-two years of earthly existence, and, more the pity, the total destruction of his equipment for the European market. Page made a mental note to get the priests working on him.

'I'll need sutures,' Dr. Osterton said to Page. 'This boy's cut his head pretty badly.'

'I'm sorry,' Page began, 'but we just don't carry things like that on board.'

'My case,' Osterton replied hastily. 'You've got my case somewhere.'

'Did you have it checked on board?'

'No, no. I'd never do that. I carried it on with me. But

your Security friends took it away. You see I always carry my bag with me. I guess it's from habit. But it contains scissors and forceps and other sharp instruments. The Security Officer said he'd have to have it put on board in a special place and one of your cabin staff would hand it to me when we landed.'

'It's the hi-jacking, Sir,' Page explained, bending over to inspect Brodie's wound. He grimaced at the jagged tear. 'If your bag was handed to one of the cabin staff then we can get it.'

'Well please do,' Osterton said quickly, 'and please tell my wife that everything's all right up here. I know she'll worry.'

Toni Rice had returned. She shook her head. 'Quite a passenger,' she whispered to Page. 'He's certain we're dead.'

'Let him dig his grave, then,' Page replied. 'Look, Toni, the doctor said his bag was handed over to one of the crew just before he came on board. You know, the metal search. See if you can find out who it was given to and get it up here. That kid's going to bleed to death if he doesn't stitch that wound.'

'Nonsense,' Toni retorted as she headed back down the staircase. 'All head wounds look like that. It's the other boy you want to worry about.'

'How's it going,' Page asked, squeezing into his seat.

'I was just about to ask you that,' Huston replied. 'How are the passengers?'

'Thanks to a few preachers down there they're all as happy as a church outing. Beats me how they do it. I don't think you'll have anything to worry about unless we hit more trouble.'

'What about the fuselage?'

'Number Three's gone – that's for certain. She blew off her tail end and it's lodged in the stabiliser. There's no internal damage that I can see, only the outside window in twenty four is cracked. There's a Pan American engineer down there who seems to know what he's talking about and we got two other airline guys on board.'

'Who?' asked Huston.

'One of them is from Amplivox. They make all the headsets for BEA and EuroControl. He's got a pack of them with him. Wish to Christ International would order them. Damn nice. And we've got a senior rep from Decca Navigation who's been helping out in the lounge. It's not too good out there, you know.'

'You mean Lynn's brother . . .'

'I don't know how bad Paul is, but the other kid – the unaccompanied minor – he's got a bad head wound. The doctor's got his case on board but those damn Security guys took it away. Toni's trying to find it. I hope it's in the passenger cabin and not stowed below.'

'What's he doing about the kid with the head?'

'Wants to sew him up. That's what he needs his bag for. Now you tell me what's going on.'

'So far it doesn't look too bad. I figured something messed up our tail because the rudder and elevators are heavy. I can hold her pretty steady but we haven't got any trim so it's going to mean fighting her in all the way. We'll have to do it in shifts.'

'There's something else bothering you. Engine overheat?' Page had noticed Huston's frequent glances at the centre console.

'That's about it. All we need is an overheat and the flight's finished.'

'Cut our speed. We're in no rush.'

'You tell Lynn that. The Doc's been in here giving me the report on her brother. He's got a real bad appendix, Dick. The Doc wants to open the kid up, but only if I can promise to keep the plane straight and level. And *that* ain't going to be easy with no trim. If he doesn't operate, he's pretty sure the boy won't make it to London. If we cut our air speed, then we'll be sure to kill him.'

'Jesus, tell him to operate, Don,' Page said impatiently. 'I know this isn't exactly the ideal place and time, but it's better than letting Lynn's brother just lay there and die.'

Captain Huston checked the clock. 'We're still two and a half hours out of London. Our air speed is down and we'll be losing time all the way in. I reckon we'll make the Irish coast in an hour and forty five minutes if we keep the taps open on all three. The weather front begins about eighty miles from the coast. If we cut back on our speed, we can give the Doc about two hours pretty clear flying. I reckon that's about all that's open to us.'

'How about a touch-down at Shannon?' Page asked.

'I'd rather stick her down in the Channel. Once we begin our approach it's going to take everything we've got to put this thing down. If the starboard surfaces are heavy up here, I'll give you any money we don't have flaps and spoilers. Once we drop the gear, it's anybody's guess which way she's going to swing. I'd like to drop down and try a few things now, but I don't think the passengers would believe we're just testing out our controls.'

Page knew damn well they wouldn't and he didn't want to try for any more miracles. 'What's our rendezvous with escort?'

Huston smiled. Page knew a lot about him. 'I'd say thirty minutes. I've been dropping air speed so it's up to him to pick us up.'

Peter Sturgess had been absorbed in too many calculations to hear the conversation. Fuel was his big worry, and he had gone over his figures until his eyes ached. Before he gave his report to the skipper, he was going to have one more go. Somewhere there had to be a mistake. If there wasn't, then one more critical factor was about to influence their flight.

'We can't do it, Bill, and you know it,' Meyer argued heatedly. 'Take a look at this report. It just came in. Met's giving us the worst weather this summer. There are squalls coming in from the south and that front over Ireland is holding things just where they are. Look, it's not that I'm worried about losing Two Eight Right. That's not *our* problem. But you try to bring in a 747 through this kind of weather and it could tear him to pieces if he's had structural damage. The RVR is down to eight hundred metres, the runway is ready to flood with standing water and we got pumping units at the radar points. Engineering is up to their neck in water in the pits and Clive's expecting a loss of all his lights at any minute. You tell me, do you really think we could bring that flight in?'

Auer didn't bother to think. The decision wasn't his. All he had to do was get the facts from the Tower – including an opinion or two, and then report the situation to Alan Manley. It would be his decision whether or not to bring International

One Two Four into Heathrow. 'All right, Mark. I appreciate what you say. Now suggestions for an alternative.'

'Prestwick's the nearest bet. They're monitoring that flight as it is. The weather isn't exactly ideal up there, but it isn't half as bad as we've got. And they've got all their runways open.'

'Do you think Benson would take her?' Auer persisted.

'That I don't know. What the military do is their worry. If I were in charge there, I'd say hell no. If that jumbo falls apart on his run in, well, it would mean too much damn damage. Everyone's at their wit's end out there,' Meyer continued, pointing towards Block 85. 'The Fire Service are out on pumping jobs, Engineering's got every man on the intersection, Coburn's risking everybody's neck trying to rush that 707 bagging and there isn't a man to spare to plan an approach for a plane that big and with that kind of trouble.'

'If the decision was made to bring her into Heathrow,' Auer said slowly, 'would you be prepared to help?'

Meyer frowned. He stared at the distance-to-touchdown indicator which showed him an approaching aircraft sliding down the ILS beam. 'Yes, I'd do it,' he conceded. 'If you order it. We all would. Christ, you know we'd do anything we can for those poor bastards up there, but I'm just thinking of his chances if the skipper bounces straight into a squall. If number three's blown up, it could have ruptured his outer skin. It could have put a rent in his wing. It could have done a hundred other things including foul up his control surfaces. If it were a clear day with no cloud and a nice headwind to glide him down, then I'd be all for it. I'd even put him on Two Three if I had to.'

'O.K., Mark. That's all I wanted to know. I know how you feel. We're all a bit frayed. Including that poor captain up there.'

Meyer took his eyes from the touchdown indicator only long enough to see Auer pause at the top of the stairs. 'You might want to hear what happened to that Pan Am 747. Clipper One Hundred.'

Auer looked back. He grinned. 'Let's hear it.'

Meyer smiled for the first time that day. 'He shook the concrete loose.'

'He what?'

'He found some turbulence on the way to Frankfurt, told the passengers to hold on tight, and shook the bloody plane until his First Officer could raise the bogies. Made a perfect landing.'

'I'm glad someone's having success,' Auer said. 'I always knew Pan Am could handle anything.'

Meyer knew why. Auer had flown for Clipper in his commercial days. Nothing Pan American could ever go wrong. It looked like he was right.

'Christ Almighty,' Coburn swore. 'Have you got stock in BranAir or something?'

Bartlett looked out from the yellow land rover and made an attempt to smile. 'How's it going, David?' he whispered.

Coburn shook his head. 'It's going beautifully. Now get your ass back to the Medical Centre and I promise I'll let you know everything that happens.'

'I'm fine,' Bartlett wheezed. 'As long as I don't breathe. Nothing's broken. I'm just a bit flatter around the stomach.'

'Does Barker know you're here?' Coburn asked, wiping the rain from his face with gritty hands.

'No, and it doesn't matter. I've got an airside pass, remember? Just like everybody else. I'm going to sit here and watch. I won't bother you.'

Coburn still shook his head. 'Well, we're risking it a bit, but I had no choice. Doug's getting a plate under the nose and we're going to push in the trolley anytime now.'

'Turin told me you and Doug took quite a chance under that nose.'

'We're all taking chances. So far we've been lucky.' Coburn turned to look at the nose high jet. 'She's just about ready. I gotta go.'

Bartlett caught his arm. When Coburn turned, he saw the look of pain in Bartlett's face. 'Thanks Dave. I mean it.'

'Don't thank me yet,' he smiled. 'Wait until your precious aircraft is tucked away in its hangar. There's still a lot to do.'

Bartlett looked up at the grimy face. He nodded. He closed his eyes and wanted to sleep.

'O.K., Bob,' Parent shouted from just beneath the nose. 'Roll her back nice and slow.'

The nose jack was dropped into its lowest position. With luck, the 707's nose was just high enough to manoeuvre the jack in such a position that when it was raised, the jack wouldn't shear through the fuselage. Inch by inch, Bob Hughes eased the tug backwards, keeping his eye on Parent's hand signals every foot of the way. Coburn stood alongside the tug, his hand on the jack unit that had been specially fitted onto the trolley. Once in position and secured to the underside of the nose, the jack and trolley took the place of the battered nose gear and the first of the moving operations would be complete. Coburn wished he could be on the compressor wagon at the same time. He knew that if any of the air bags went now, there wouldn't be a hope of saving the aircraft. But each bag had been sanded and shored up with chocks. A check had been made of the hose connections and the pressure gauges on both the compressor and inflator had been checked a dozen times for accuracy. Simson and Andrews, still being wiped down by Kitchley, held the pressure steady. There was no point in risking extra stress on the spars if they could manoeuvre the jack trolley into position at the plane's present height.

'Cut!' Coburn shouted, and Hughes braked hard. 'I think that's done it. What's she look like, Doug?'

'Perfect. If we get her secured, then problem number one is solved.'

Coburn called down Simson and Andrews and instructed them to secure the jack. He chocked the trolley just to be safe and ordered the caterpillar wing trollies to be rolled into place. When the air bags were deflated, the weight of the wings on the trollies would hold them in place and the winching about could begin. He and Parent backed away and grinned broadly. The worst was over. It had nearly killed the lot of them, but they had done it.

Bartlett opened his eyes in time to see the wing trollies being rolled into position. He knew the nose trolley had been secured. The job was nearly over. But the pain in his chest was killing him. He closed his eyes again and wished he could take a deep sigh of relief.

Nine of the eighteen pit covers had been shored up with timber supports wedged between the covers and the base of the two foot deep trench and Blake called a halt. There was no point in replacing the rest until the electrical circuits had been restored. Works Section of Engineering were scattered along Blocks 85, 86 and 87 replacing runway lights, and Blake wondered just how many men were on duty. He knew that an emergency call had gone out hours before to everyone in Mechanical Transport and Engineering, and there were rumours that men from Gatwick were being driven in by coach, and as he looked down the two thousand feet of runway towards Block 87, he reckoned someone had called in the Army Engineers as well. He had never seen so much activity in one area at one time. He remembered when a 707 – Whiskey Echo – had plopped herself down in the middle of Zero Five and ninety-seven fire vehicles had been called out from the London Fire Brigade. Fortunately the order to stand down was issued before Heathrow had turned into a firemen's convention. Whiskey Echo had been dealt with swiftly and thanks to the quick action of the Fire Service, nearly everyone was saved. Removing the burnt out wreckage had been done with little damage to the runway, and Blake was wishing that BranAir could have hit the grass verge rather than One Zero Right, carrying nearly every light with it. But he knew the pilot had done a hell of a job. Controlling the plane must have been the worst few seconds of his life, and Blake bore no grudge. After all, it was what he was paid for.

'Astral One Two Four, this is Rescue One, over.'

'Rescue One. This is One Two Four.'

'We have you on radar, One Two Four. Rendezvous in zero nine. I'll make one pass over you and come up from behind. Will report visual check when complete.'

'One Two Four, thank you,' Captain Huston looked over at his First Officer. 'Well, if we go down, at least the RAF will be here.'

'The figures are correct, skipper,' Sturgess began, swivelling in his chair to face Huston. 'We lost just about everything in number three's wing tank and the starboard transfer valves are US. The explosion either froze them or destroyed them altogether. The tanks for one and two are fine and I can transfer the fuel as needed, but you do not have much for number four.'

Huston, looking suddenly tired, took the report. Page was holding the stick as steady as he could, and he wished another miracle would happen to restore One Two Four's trim control.

'We'll make the English coast on number four. From there on we'll be on two engines. We'll make Heathrow with not a drop over. That's what your figures say, isn't it?'

Sturgess nodded almost sorrowfully. 'I've checked them over and over. The gauges tell me what's on that report: the starboard valves are seized up and that's all the fuel we have left. There's nothing I can do about it.'

'I know,' Huston replied. 'Just keep an eye on our consumption. Do everything you can to conserve. I'll request a higher flight level and maybe we can save some fuel.'

'Negative,' replied Sturgess. 'I thought of that, but I worked it out and we'd burn up as much fuel in climbing as we would save staying right where we are.'

Huston stared at him for a moment, then nodded. 'There's one thing we can do. Cut back on our air speed. Throttle down on number one.'

Page looked at the skipper. He obeyed, but he also wondered.

'These engines have a habit of over-heating,' Huston began, as if he felt an explanation necessary. 'We saw what an overheat did to number three. When we begin our run in, we'll be on two engines. Number four will be out and there won't be one way in hell of opening her up with no fuel in the tank. So I want security. I'll bring this thing in on one engine if I have to, and I want to be sure we have that one engine. Everybody agree?'

The skipper's word was law. There was no question of disagreement. But when Page and Sturgess nodded, they did so because they knew the skipper was right.

'Well,' Huston began, 'if we're all happy about that, then I had better have a look around myself. Can you handle her for a while, Dick?'

'Without trim it's going to be a damn few hours, but just don't forget I'm up here, will you?'

'If you get tired, our Engineer can take over,' Huston grinned. 'Doesn't look like he's got much to do now there's no more fuel and we're under escort.'

Sturgess glanced up. 'I wouldn't fly this overstuffed 707 if Page dropped dead at the stick. You show me how to lock her onto auto pilot and I'll just keep an eye on where we're going.'

'You're a great comfort,' said the skipper, sliding past his Flight Engineer. 'It's nice to have a crew I can rely on.'

Page winked at Sturgess and turned back to his controls. He knew that within a few minutes the ache in his arms would grow worse, and he wondered just how long a man could fly a jumbo which has lost its trim.

Huston entered the lounge. He wasn't planning on going downstairs – after Page had settled the passengers, a visit by the Captain might frighten a few of the nervous types. So he left his cap and jacket behind and approached Dr. Osterton. 'Did you get your bag?'

Osterton didn't look up. 'Yes, I did. With any luck we might get those two boys home in good shape.'

'You still want to operate on Paul?'

'We don't have much choice,' the doctor replied, cutting strands of matted hair from Brodie's forehead. 'I've given him a mild sedative to help him relax, but his fever's up and it's just a question of time before that appendix ruptures. After that, well, there just isn't a chance.'

Toni Rice was laying out the Doctor's instruments. She was surprised at the number he carried. She guessed he was the type of doctor who had the reputation of always being prepared. He'd be the type of doctor who would risk law suits by helping injured motorists, who would ignore religious and parental taboos by operating without prior consent. He was trained to save lives. He didn't give a damn whether the transfusion of blood was against a particular belief if it meant a child might be saved. Toni Rice knew she'd be working under a no-nonsense, no-compromise surgeon, and she hoped she could remember her surgical training.

Osterton stood up. 'There. I think we can begin to sew him up now,' he said to Toni. 'Prepare me an injection of zylocaine – about four c.c. You'll find some pre-wrapped sutures on the bottom right hand side. I'd like a couple of forceps, too.'

Brodie had been laid out on a hastily improvised operating table. The table in the middle of the lounge had been covered in blankets, and the blankets tied down with string. Lynn had brought up several pillows and these had been tied around the edge. If the aircraft did encounter any rough weather, there would be less chance of either boy sliding out from under the doctor's scalpel, and the height of the table was just about right for Dr. Osterton to operate comfortably. He had joked, however, that the table was suited to the two boys: an adult's legs would have hung over the end. He had operated in strange conditions before, he admitted, but never in an improvised operating theatre at thirty-five thousand feet.

Toni stood at the end of the table and held Brodie's head still. The wound began about two inches above his right ear and extended to the crest of his forehead. When the explosion had hurtled the plane to the port, Brodie had been thrown against the cabin wall where two panel sections joined. A tiny bolt in one of them had caught his head and ripped downwards as he fell. The wound was deep, but it had done no serious damage. The hair would easily cover the scar above his ear but where the wound showed about a half-inch down his forehead, Osterton knew he'd have to do some pretty careful suturing to avoid leaving an ugly souvenir of the flight. He'd use extra fine nylon the whole way, he thought, and use his own special stitch for the forehead. It took longer, but he had never known it to leave a bad scar – if any at all. Brodie looked up at him and at Toni. He was still slightly dazed from the accident which had left him groggy, but he wasn't frightened. The fact that blood had covered half his face when he pulled himself from the floor hadn't really bothered him either. He had felt for the wound, made his own estimation of his personal damage and he had the sense to pull a pillow over his forehead which neither hurt nor let more blood dribble down his face.

'Have you ever had stitches before, Brodie,' Dr. Osterton asked, taking the five c.c. syringe from Toni.

Brodie eyed the syringe skeptically. 'In my ankle,' he replied, determined not to show any fear. 'Playing football.'

'Good,' the doctor replied. 'Now this is an awful big syringe, but it's only because I want to make sure you don't feel anything when I start sewing you up. You'll feel a few slight pricks when I stick the needle in, but head wounds are pretty painless to repair. You just let Miss Rice hold your head still, and it'll all be over in a few minutes.'

Brodie stared up into the wrinkled face. Somewhere in the pit of his stomach he was frightened, but it was one of those situations where he knew he didn't have much of a choice. He looked up at Toni who was looking down at him and smiling. 'Are you enjoying this – or do you have to smile?' he asked.

'He'll be coming down Green One,' Alan Manley began, looking over the upper airways chart for Southern England. 'And he'll want a pretty slow descent to be at eight by Woodley. He can hold his height until he's approaching Woodley and we'll put him on a heading for Ockham. He can use his own navigation when we turn him for Two Eight Right, but again I think he'll request a pretty long run in. Once he's established on radar we'll talk him all the way down and give him every inch of the runway.'

Bill Auer glanced across the table to Malcolm Wilmet. There was no guarantee that Heathrow would commit themselves to bringing in his jumbo, but at least a tentative routing was being prepared. Auer knew that once Manley began figuring a safe approach for a priority landing, he usually saw it through. But this was a new situation. This was a jumbo and it would be making a long slow level approach over some of the largest built up areas in England. It would be flying directly over London in poor weather conditions, a heavy cloud base which was already down to eight thousand feet, strong westerly winds which were gusting, and pouring rain. If Manley committed Heathrow to accepting IA 124, Auer knew that a full emergency situation would be declared – an emergency situation unlike any other Heathrow had experienced. Not only would the airport Fire Service be called out in full, but every one of the London Fire Brigades would be on stand-by. Local services from Hayes, Feltham and Staines would be held at the runway rendezvous points long before IA 124 was on finals, and once the R.A.F. Nimrod Comet escort had made a visual assessment of the damage to the 747, emergency appliances might be told to come to readiness at points all along the Green One approach route. There would be vehicles standing by for a hundred miles out of Heathrow – just in case the jumbo didn't make it.

Local hospitals would have to be notified and with two hundred and sixty one passengers aboard, plus the crew, a fleet of ambulances would have to be called out. The old KLM building would have to be organised. This would be the last priority on Manley's list. The old KLM building was the morgue.

Manley had been planning every detail of the approach and at the same time he had been considering the same emergency preparations that Auer had foreseen. If the decision was made to bring IA 124 into Heathrow, then Manley knew that he'd have to call a conference. The AGM – the Airport General Manager, Mike Wise – would have to approve the plans on behalf of BAA and other Section heads might have to be called in to give their opinion of both the idea and the plans. At the moment the Section heads of Engineering, Mechanical Transport and Ground Operations were being overworked as it was. But Manley knew they would push themselves further still – throughout the night if necessary – because once they had worked at Heathrow, they knew that aviation was their life: at the best of times and in the worst.

Both Manley and Auer faced another problem which was unavoidable however discreet their preparations might be. Once an emergency situation on this scale was declared, the Press had to be informed. It would be Wilmet's task to release details of the actual aircraft situation, but the Press would realise instantly that there were the makings of a jumbo size story in both the engine fire and the plans to bring IA 124 in with two main runways out, the weather 'exceptionally dangerous for aircraft' and the emergency services which would have to be laid on. Reporters at Heathrow made it their job to anticipate the various emergency plans for any declared incident, be it on the ground or in the air, and through their devious sources of information, they somehow always managed to find out just what was going on. A low level approach ('Could this Plane Land on *Your* House?'), with gusting winds and poor visibility ('Crippled Jumbo Fights for Survival over London'), coming in on three engines with possible structural damage ('Peril in the Skies: 747 Limping into Heathrow'), and whose final approach would be so critical that an undershoot was more than possible ('Heathrow Residents May be Warned to Evacuate their Homes'), would give the Press enough panic stories to double at least one day's circulation. For the Press wasn't interested in taking the common sense view that emergency preparations were in effect emergency precautions. In Manley's words, 'The Press want to dress up age old problems in new guises so as to disturb your peace of mind.' The fact that fire services a hundred miles from the touchdown point on Two Eight Right might be told to stand by meant – said the Press – that this aircraft was in bad shape and the odds were that she'd never make Heathrow. The fact that a fleet of ambulances would be called into readiness meant that if the 747 *did* stumble onto the runway, it hadn't a chance of making a safe landing. Then there was the question of morals. Was it Heathrow's prerogative to endanger the lives of hundreds – maybe thousands – by bringing this aircraft in over residential areas? If IA 124 went into an irrecoverable slip over London, who was going to pay for the reconstruction of perhaps several square miles of flattened city?

The situation was not just a meal for the Press: it was a banquet. Manley, Auer, Wilmet, Mike Wise and Heathrow's own Press Office knew that there wasn't a thing they could do to stem the exaggerations the papers would make. The only thing to do would be to keep the details of both the aircraft's own troubles and the provisional approach plans as secret as possible until the very last moment. With any luck, IA 124 would be down and safe on Two Eight Right before any story went to print. The only thing Heathrow would then face were the accusations thrown at them by the aviation geniuses who guessed at what *could* have happened if IA 124 didn't make it. Somewhere in the pit of Manley's stomach was a twinge – what would Heathrow do if IA 124 did fail to reach the runway?

With all these thoughts, Manley rang the AGM's office and requested to see him immediately. If the decision to bring

IA 124 into Heathrow was going to be made there was no time to lose.

Coburn and Parent were facing their second real problem of the day. Having solved their initial difficulty of air bagging the 707 onto the trollies, the plane had to be winched about one hundred and eighty degrees. The captain had done his all to keep his plane on the runway surface – had it overshot the end of one zero right, it would have nosed straight into the ground and buried itself up to its engine pods. The salvage operation would have been far more difficult and damage to the aircraft would have been severe. Captain Hite had therefore accomplished his plan to keep BranAir Two Four on the runway, but with not an inch to spare. Coburn couldn't swing the plane about without either the port or starboard trollies rolling onto the grass verge. With the verge now nothing but a sodden grassy mire, one of the trollies could easily sink and salvage would have to begin all over again. The only thing to do was pull the plane back towards the centre of Block 87, swing her nose starboard and tug her into Block 94 in front of Pan Am maintenance. Although BOAC had offered to handle the aircraft in its own maintenance area, Coburn was worried that the 707 might not make it up Blocks 76, 56 and 50 and the Pan Am maintenance area was a hell of a lot nearer – and relatively more isolated from operational taxiways.

Simson and Andrews had deflated the air bags. Parent had rounded up just enough men to load the bags onto the trailer and order the compressor and trailer returned to the MT Garage. It also gave him an excuse to get Simson and Andrews under cover for they had been in the rain long enough. What he reckoned they needed were hot showers and fresh clothes. With a full ground emergency declared until the runways were opened, neither he nor Coburn could send them home, but they could be sent back to the garage and given a well deserved rest. Meanwhile, the winching unit had been driven into position at the tail of the 707 and Coburn was supervising the task of hooking the cables onto the trollies. The instability of the aircraft meant that reversing her was many times more critical than simply tugging her forward. Tugs could be hooked onto the wing trollies from either side, but there was only one tug for the nose trolley – and each trolley had to pull or push with the same precision and timing that Simson and Andrews had inflated the air bags. If a trolley slipped, then it was back to square one.

'Ready to roll?' Coburn asked when Parent appeared from beneath the port wing. 'I think we're ahead of our friends in Engineering.'

'We're ahead of them, all right,' Parent shouted over the engine of one of the tugs. 'They can't fit the new covers on until they get some of the cables fixed up. Apparently the rain's seeping in and fouling up the transformers. Blake's asked for a power shutdown until his men can seal up the wires. This whole area will be switched off until they're finished. Works are bringing in all the mobile lighting they can find and Gatwick's sending down some additional mobile lights and spare runway lights. I'd say old Blake's up to his ears in it.'

'What's the idea of requesting assistance from Gatwick?' Coburn began suspiciously. 'Surely there's enough gear in Works to keep that area lit up.'

Parent shrugged. 'Maybe there's another flap on. All I heard was that assistance was being called in from Gatwick and Luton's been told to stand by.'

Coburn shook his head. 'I've been here too long not to notice a rat. I'll bet we've got something else coming up.'

'Well it won't bother Gatwick or Luton. They've shut down operations. It's one of the worst air days they've known. The nearest to zero zero everything. Low cloud, minimal RVR, bad cross winds and flooding on the runways. I'd say this one'll go down in history.'

'Well, we better get on with it. Get onto Buff Congdon and tell him we're just about ready to winch this one back. He'll want to start his lighting check and sweep just as soon as we've got her onto the apron. It's going to be fun to see just what this plane's done to the threshold lighting. I expect the whole bloody lot's gone.'

Parent bent down and looked towards the nose. 'It's not as bad as you think. But there's plenty of re-surfacing to do in the touch down zone. It's like a dirt road out there.'

Coburn saw the tug headlights switch on. Everyone was in position and ready to roll. 'I'll take the port and you take the starboard side. I've got Reynolds watching the nose. I've told the drivers to lean on their hooters the second either of you sees something slipping. We'll take this nice and slow, O.K.?'

Parent nodded. He signalled to one of the radio cars and passed along the message to Ground Operations. In another minute the tugs had eased into first gear and were awaiting Coburn's order to roll.

Manley's meeting with Mike Wise was brief and direct. The report from the R.A.F. Nimrod had been radioed in only minutes before Manley, Auer and Wilmet reached the AGM's office in D'Albiac House, the headquarters of the British Airports Authority. International's office had sent the message through and Wilmet read it with growing consternation. He passed it around to the others even before Manley's preparations had been mentioned.

'Reporting time 1539 Zulu. Visual inspection reveals explosion number three engine. Parts imbedded in fuselage beneath wing believed to be nacel fragments. Turbine shrapnel visible along fuselage with damage to tail assembly severe. Starboard rudder sections and forward spars most affected. Outboard starboard elevator US. Inboard Krueger flaps US. Impairment to inboard starboard spoilers, ailerons and flaps unknown. Undercarriage impairment unknown but fragments visible on starboard wing gear cover. Critical structural damage on vertical fin approximately fourteen feet above fuselage. Further critical damage to starboard wing at junction of fuselage. Suggest first stage compressor explosion shattered nacel, exposing forward honeycomb and spars. Actual cause unknown. Captain reports minor internal damage, no loss of pressurisation and is maintaining straight and level flight. Captain further reports total loss of trim control and Flight Engineer reports loss of fuel in starboard tanks with critical impairment of transfer valves. Number four engine isolated and instrument monitoring US. Operational safety of aircraft satisfactory in present conditions, but Captain is uncertain of aircraft stability at lower altitude. Captain is continuing on his reported flight plan and we are escorting. RAF Nimrod – Rescue Co-ordination. Endit'

Mike Wise didn't share the same fear that Malcolm Wilmet had for his passengers, his plane and his company. Wise feared the unavoidable action that must be taken to safeguard nearly three hundred lives up in the air and at the same time the many more lives and homes beneath the approach route IA 124 would follow. He wasn't hesitant about offering the services of Heathrow – and he didn't give a damn about what remarks the scandal happy Press would make. Air travel was part of the times, and whether or not aircraft posed a threat to the lives of private individuals mental or physical, his job was to manage an airport in the best way he knew how. From the start he made it clear that among other things, his first priority was aircraft safety and however sympathetic he was to the communities surrounding Heathrow, he wasn't going to tolerate stringent noise abatement procedures which endangered outbound aircraft. He had been truly upset by the old age pensioner who committed suicide because he couldn't live with all the noise, but he had been far more upset when a Trident stalled in the middle of his critical climbing altitude and crashed with a complete loss of life. For months he had tolerated the telephone calls and petitions, the demonstrations and results of 'scientific enquiries', but he swore that one day he would publicly point out that if he enforced the noise abatement procedures that would in any way effectively reduce aircraft noise, the chances were that between seven and twelve jet airliners would crash on take off every day. Which did the communities want? A drop of a few decibels or a drop of several hundred tons of aircraft?

But emotions had to be kept personal. The public wasn't interested in simple facts, or the single fact that their demands for quieter take offs which required steeper climbs with slower throttle settings endangered not only the lives of the passengers, but of the very complainers themslves. It was when the government stepped in and legally imposed flight procedures for noise abatement that Wise had to succumb to the public's demands, and he knew that the poor blighters on that Trident might soon be joined by others. It was perhaps because of all this that Mike Wise was prepared to go along with Manley's tentative approach plans. He and Manley together ran Heathrow and if Manley was prepared to stick his neck out to bring in this jumbo then Wise was just as willing to back him up. If any single man could guide this injured aircraft down Green One and route her onto the Precision Approach Radar for two eight right through some of the worst meteorological conditions Heathrow had faced, it was Manley.

'If you think it can be done with any reasonable margin of safety to both the aircraft and the people down below,' Wise said confidently, 'then do it without hesitation. I've called in extra help from Gatwick on this Engineering problem in eighty-five, and we can get all the assistance you might need from either Gatwick or Luton. They're both closed down, you know.'

Manley nodded. From his rough calculations, he and Bill Auer would have to narrow the details of 124's approach down to a needle thin line, and even before some kind of ETA for 124 could be estimated they would have to find out from Captain Huston what plans *he* had in mind. It would be a mutual arrangement of agreement and compromise all the way along.

While Manley and Auer had the approach to plan, Wise knew he'd have to organise the emergency services. He'd have to use his discretion in alerting both local and London fire services and the brigades stationed anywhere near 124's low level approach. Although the intricately detailed emergency procedure manual left little room for guesswork, it didn't cover a situation with implications as far reaching as the one Heathrow now faced. Wise would rely on the manual as a guide and from there it would be up to him, the Medical Centre and other emergency co-ordination sections to decide the proper precautionary action to be taken. He would have to consult with the airport Safety Officer.

Manley, Auer and Wise had volunteered to devote their efforts to bringing in 124. Little time was left. Now Wilmet had his job to do. Rescue co-ordination was out of his hands. But in a very short time, his hands would be stomped on by the Press, and he crossed the rain soaked Central Area to his office in Queen's Building to prepare himself for the onslaught. Already, word had begun to circulate that another big flap was on at Heathrow and the Press boys were rallying round.

Captain Huston was sitting in his left hand seat, but he wasn't flying the aircraft. Page still clung to the stick and the effort of the last half hour had put any hopes of idle conversation out of his mind. Likewise, Sturgess was sweating out his own problems at his desk and he knew they were in real trouble. It was Huston's task to co-ordinate their situation and call for remedial action. The combined facts from Sturgess and the latest Nimrod report gave a clear picture that IA 124 might never make Heathrow. It might not even make the Irish coast. Already Huston was considering setting his 747 down in the Atlantic – he was considering every possibility that would guarantee the lives of the greatest number of passengers. A sea dumping was always dodgy, even if he had the time to organise immediate rescue of the survivors and the Atlantic waters below were being tossed about by the storm front several hundred miles ahead. Every mile his jet devoured brought him into rougher seas and brought him nearer the weather situation that had destroyed his hopes of a clear routing to Heathrow.

Normally, Huston would have risked turbulent air fifteen thousand feet below and juggled his plane across Ireland and the Irish Sea, across Wales and down Green One. But the Nimrod had reported possible structural damage to his starboard wing. Even a tiny rent in his leading edge where the wing joined the fuselage was dangerous – rough air and strong headwinds could shear his wing clean away. And according to the Nimrod, this rent wasn't tiny. Then there was the fuel situation. With reduced speed number four would carry them to Strumble – near the Welsh coast – and maybe a bit further. Much depended on his winds aloft. He would then be left with his two port engines, one of which was already throttled back. Once he lost number four and was putting all his hopes onto numbers one and two, the danger of an overheat in either engine was too great. He could reduce this danger and make a high level approach across Ireland and England, which would also keep him above much of the turbulent air, but once he began his descent, he would be juggling two engines far beyond their rated capacities. He would be over-riding company minima, if that mattered, and he'd be waiting for his useless starboard wing to rip away if he plowed into a squall. He knew that a

707 *could* fly with half a wing gone – it had been done before – but he didn't fancy his odds in turbulent weather. He was playing God again and the sweat on his forehead and pallor in his usually ruddy face gave a clear indication that he was beginning to face the inevitable. He'd make his decision, he'd take another few minutes and go over every possibility, he'd weigh every fact and when the decision was made, either to ditch in the Atlantic or make Heathrow, knew his chances were pretty slim.

Brodie was sewn up and sipping tea. He wrinkled his forehead, and as the zylocaine wore away, he felt the tingle of stitched flesh. But he was watching the flight crew intently as his seat faced the door of the cockpit which was now left open. He couldn't sense Captain Huston's tension nor could he see First Officer Page sweating it out on the stick, but the glowing dials, the hundreds of switches and lights, and the banks of circuit breakers fascinated him.

Brodie turned from his view and looked at the table. Dr. Osterton and Toni Rice had lifted Paul onto the blankets and he knew that they wanted to operate. Trent-Jones hadn't left Lynn's side for what seemed to Brodie an awful long time, but he knew that Lynn Almirall couldn't be expected to carry out her duties downstairs when her brother was as sick as he looked. He wished he could talk to Paul, to stand next to him and smile the same way Miss Rice had smiled at him. To do anything but sit in the lounge and wonder what was going on – either in the cockpit or in Dr. Osterton's mind.

'Here,' Toni said to him. 'Take these. Your head's going to start throbbing soon and this will keep the pain away.'

Brodie looked up at her, and at the two tablets in her hand. 'What are they?' he asked softly.

'Codeine. They won't hurt you.' She smiled at him again.

At that moment the realisation of everything suddenly hit Brodie with the force of a jack hammer. The shock of the explosion, the impact and the trickle of blood, the captain's forgotten announcement and the gloom in the cockpit – it all flashed before his young mind and he let his gaze fall away from Toni as shuddering sobs shook his body. Toni put away the pills and sat down next to him, pulling his head gently into her lap and stroking his hair. She knew the only thing she could do was hold him in some kind of quiet reassurance.

'Captain Huston?' called a voice from the cockpit door. 'May I see you for a minute?'

Huston turned from his controls and saw Dr. Osterton. 'Sure, Doc,' he grinned. 'I was hoping someone would take over for me.'

'No, no, no,' tisked Osterton. 'I never could do your job. With all these buttons and levers and dials . . .'

'It's all right, Doc,' Page said. 'He'd let one of the kids fly this thing if it meant he could get away from it all.'

'Well,' Huston began, 'what can I do for you?' He hadn't yet made his decision, but he had long ago learned the secret of hiding his emotions. The Captain Huston before Dr. Osterton was confident, assured and talking to him as if London was just ahead, clear and smooth.

'I think I'd like to begin operating on Paul Almirall if you think it's safe enough. We have everything ready. I admit I'd like a bit more equipment – special instruments and proper anaesthesia – but I think I can manage. It's really a very simple operation.'

Huston had grown suddenly more pensive. Another decision. He ran his fingers through his perspiring hair and glanced at Sturgess. 'How long do you need?'

'If you can let me have forty minutes of pretty smooth flying, then I can operate with no trouble at all.'

'I can give you thirty minutes, Doc,' Huston said firmly. 'And not a minute more. We'll be holding at this altitude for another half an hour. After that, we're going to begin a slow descent and once we leave this altitude, we're going to hit some rough air. Can you do it in the time?'

"I'll do it, Captain.' Osterton said confidently and he left the cockpit.

Captain Huston's decision to lose height in thirty minutes was the opening move in his plan, now firmly and irrevocably set out before him. He had considered every alternative, every possibility and had weighed every bit of information. For IA 124, the next two hours would bring a plane load of people nearer to death than they had ever been before.

'Alan, it's Mike Wise here. How far along are you with 124's approach?'

'We're pinning him down now. He's past fifteen west and Prestwick have given him over to Shannon. We're trying to get him direct on London Airways communications but with that storm front over the East Coast West Drayton's been having some trouble.'

'Can you give me an idea of your approach plans?'

The phone crackled slightly. Manley caught a glimpse of lightning. 'We're advising a gentle descent to be at twenty five thousand feet by Strumble. He'll continue on a further descent of one thousand feet per minute to cross Woodley Beacon at eight. That'll take him about twenty five or thirty minutes. We'll direct him to Ockham and give him a fifteen to twenty mile approach into two eight right. He'll be on a northerly heading of zero eight zero off Ockham onto a heading of three zero zero closing to the centreline. We'll give him an extended centreline heading of two eight zero at eleven miles when we can pick him up on Precision Approach Radar. If he can maintain his altitude and headings as well as his speed, he'll be over Woodley at six thousand feet, Ockham at four or five and a final descent to three. But he's going to need that long approach.'

'I take it that long approach you're talking about means he'll be coming in over London,' Wise said with concern.

'As far as our present plans go, he'll be right over the city. It's the standard approach for the Two Eights. We can't cut his turn short with the damage he's got and with the weather as it is, the Tower wants a good long run in.'

'No chance of using the Tens?'

'The winds are gusting westerly fifteen to twenty knots. It could get worse. Try to drop him on Ten Left and he could fall out of the sky like a rock.'

'Are you asking Area Control for a special clearance?'

'I'm asking you to close outbounds once he's over Strumble.'

Wise paused. It was a big favour to ask. 'How long is this close down to last?'

'Thirty minutes, at the most. That'll give us time to clear every square inch of sky on his approach routes and it'll give you time to deploy your emergency services wherever the hell you want them.'

'Once I send out that information you know the Press will be onto it.' Wise said cautiously.

'The Press be damned,' Manley replied. 'My one answer to them is, would they rather we order that jumbo to ditch in the Irish Sea?'

'They're just cruel enough to suggest that, Alan. I'll get P & PRO on to it straight away. Maybe they can cook up some story that'll put them on the wrong trail.'

'You have a hope!' Manley laughed. 'I'll bet they're monitoring our VHF signals right now. You just get your emergency plans sorted out and I'll send over our final approach routings. From what the Captain said, he's going for broke.'

'So are we, Alan. So are we.'

The receiver clicked dead.

The time at Heathrow was 18.45 GMT. In one hour and fifty eight minutes IA 124 was due to be closing on finals. So far the Press had been picking up bits and pieces of information about an injured airliner staggering in from New York, but despite their efforts to pinpoint which airline and exactly what had happened, there had been no official statement. Press and Public Relations had conferred briefly with Malcolm Wilmet and it was decided the only sensible thing to do was to call a Press Conference and together they would release the information. Brenards, the resident press agency at Heathrow, was informed first of the conference and it would be up to them to organise the rest of the newspaper reporters and television newsmen. It was decided to open the de Haviland VIP Suite for the conference and fifteen minutes before Wilmet and Ray Milross were due to make any announcement, they discussed what details they would release.

Mike Wise had sent down just enough information to make it appear that BAA were co-operating with the Press and not withholding too much 'juicy information'. Normally, the public relations office for BAA had very little to do with disabled aircraft; it was up to the airlines to release pertinent details about whatever difficulties their aircraft might be having, but since the BAA were committing themselves quite heavily to the landing of International's jumbo, they were obliged to reveal what the nature of their involvement was. Wise was reckoning on the time factor. The Press Conference would be over by 19.15 if the reporters didn't push for more information. The evening papers would have gone to press and the most that a reporter could file would be a somewhat dramatic story of this poor crippled airliner. It would be too chancy to go overboard and give the old bit about how this aircraft could be coming down anywhere under Green One. The plane was due in by nine o'clock – just when the BBC broadcast their evening news, and an hour later when Thames Television broadcast 'News at Ten' the full outcome of the incident would be known – be it a happy ending or otherwise. Wise's only worry was that the television boys might make a newsflash over TV and radio which would invariably bring in the sightseers, plane spotters and every second rate reporter and photographer within a fifty mile radius. It had happened when the Trident went down in Staines, but unlike the Trident disaster, there was much more time to re-route traffic, close off the peri track and ensure that only authorised personnel and bona fide passengers were allowed through the entrance tunnel. In anticipating this, Wise had explained the situation to the BAA's Chief Constable and already extra men were being called in to organise the vetting and re-routing of traffic.

Normally, men from the Marshalling Section would handle traffic diversions on the peri track, but with the two runways still out of operation, and the main electrical lines under Block 85 cut off, Marshalling was busy on the aprons and in the stands and all spare Marshallers were helping either Engineering or Ground Operations. Wise decided to co-ordinate control of the perimeter road with the Roads Administration Section whose offices were in Building 221 on the Northside. If any Section knew the peri track well enough to organise some way of keeping spectators away, it would be the men in Roads Administration. Wise thought of asking David McKeon, the Director, to drive over to D'Albiac House to discuss the problem, but he changed his mind. Northside had been the original airport many years before Heathrow grew, and the old buildings which still housed various airport and airlines offices meant a lot to Wise. He had begun his career at Heathrow in

Building 221, working for BEA when they used it for flight briefings along with BOAC. He decided he'd brave the rain and visit his old hunting grounds – and at the same time visit the airport Chaplain who would need to know what was going on.

With the message passed to Air Traffic Control that there was to be a priority descent on Green One from flight level two five zero to Woodley and an airport closure from 2030 until 2115, Approach Control, Departure Control and the London Director had to do some quick re-routing and rearrangements with West Drayton Area Control, who together formed the London Airways network. Since it seemed that air traffic over southern England was already about as restricted and re-routed as it could be due to weather and loss of Heathrow's runways, once the priority message was sent out to the pertinent controllers in arrivals and departures at Heathrow and to West Drayton Area Control, another message had to be sent to all the airlines. Mark Meyer guessed that another bit of bad news for the airlines wasn't going to do much damage since air and ground movements were at a minimum anyway. If the runway now being used began to flood, then all movements would cease long before the priority restrictions were imposed, and Meyer was waiting for the first aircraft to aquaplane along Two Eight Right and give Coburn something else to work on now that that BranAir 707 was on its way to Pan Am maintenance.

Coburn was having pretty much the same thoughts as he stopped the tugging operations long enough to give everyone a breather. Since the 707 was now clear of Block 87 and heading down the apron into Block 94, the threshold of Two Eight Right was clear and his job was pretty much over. At least, the worst of it was. There had been some tense moments when the trollies and tugs fought to grip the slippery runway surface on the turn-about, but so long as the plane held together it looked like BranAir's 707 had gotten off lightly considering the last few hours.

With the rain sloshing about the trollies and tugs while his men sipped tea in the mobile canteens which followed the plane, Coburn sheltered himself beneath the starboard wing and looked out over the airfield. A brisk westerly teased the soggy wind bag down by Air India's maintenance area and Coburn remembered a time when Heathrow had suffered an entire week of this sort of weather. It was in December, 1968, and he had been promoted to a senior officer in Engineering only a few weeks before – he had guessed it was the airport's way of giving him a Christmas bonus. But the promotion turned out to be more a trial by ordeal than anything else as freezing rain, fog and snow made landing conditions impossible. Three jets had overshot Two Eight in as many days and if the captains hadn't blamed ice on the runway, they said their wheels had aquaplaned. It had given Engineering the roughest going over they could remember, and Mechanical Transport had an equally rotten week towing the aircraft out of the cabbage patch that had then formed the overshoot end of Two Eight. Coburn had wondered what the farmer thought as day after day he saw his garden turned into a docking bay for overshooting jets. Harrison remembered that week, too, because he knew that one of the three planes didn't just aquaplane as the captain had said in his official report. The plane had overshot simply because he touched down four thousand feet beyond his threshold – he had touched down right in front of the fire station and all the thrust reversing and gear braking couldn't bring any jet to rest in the remaining few thousand feet of the runway. It was damned convenient for the captain that the weather conditions were so bad that they provided a good excuse, Harrison admitted to Coburn later. But Coburn also knew that the overshoots could have been caused by the protective jet exhaust blast screen which had been stuck up near the thresold of Two Eight Right. It was frightening the pilots who figured they might easily drop their landing gear straight into it if they made too low an approach, and in time the screen was removed.

Coburn liked looking back on how things had gone at Heathrow, and he knew that someday he'd be looking back on this miserable wet shift with the same feelings of involvement – being a part of an efficient and well trained team whose job it was to keep one of the biggest and busiest airports in the world ticking over – no matter what.

He crumpled the plastic cup in his hand and shoved it into

his pocket. Tea break was over and they still had a long way to go.

Captain Huston had relieved Page, and Page was rubbing his arms. 'Of all the controls to lose on this thing,' he was complaining, 'the trim has to go. There are four and a half million parts and over a hundred miles of wiring in every 747 and the odds have to be so lousy that the one in a four and a half million chance that we lose our trim has to come up. I call that just plain unfair.'

Huston grinned. It was hard flying any plane without adjusting the trim control – an automatic device that corrects an aircraft's attitude to even flight – and Page had every right to be bitter. 'How many other parts do you reckon we've lost as well?'

'Well, if you count each of our blades in number three, the pieces that flew off our tail, the fuel tanks and transfer valves, the bits that are sticking out of our undercarriage, a few feet of our wing and Christ knows what else, I'd say we have about four or five parts left.'

'Optimist,' Sturgess said. 'That's what I like about you.'

'Astral One Two Four, this is Escort. Over.'

Huston peered forward and saw the belly of the RAF Comet a thousand feet above him. 'One Two Four,' he replied.

'Can you give us a status report, Captain Huston?'

'If I were an astronaut I suppose I'd say all systems functioning normally under the circumstances. How do we look from up there?'

'Bloody terrible. But your heading's good. I'd say you're having a tougher time down there than you want to admit.'

Page's eyes glanced heavenward. 'What's he want us to say? We're running around hysterical and the skipper's drunk?'

'It's kind of hard without our trim, but we're managing,' Huston replied. 'I'll notify you of any change. One Two Four out.'

'We'll be reaching the Irish coast in about forty minutes,' Sturgess began. 'And number four's still doing fine. I wish to hell I knew how much fuel we had for her.'

'Isn't there any way of guessing – even at the outside?' Page asked, stretching in his seat.

'I could guess – sure. So could you. We know number three's tank just emptied itself as soon as the engine went. What's in the reserve tank and what's still in number four's is anybody's guess. All we can do is wait till she kicks out on us.'

'No luck with the transfer system, huh?' Huston asked.

'None, Skipper. I'm getting readings for the starboard valves but I know for sure they're wrong. Every so often they skip about – probably from the atmosphere if one of the tanks is split – but I wouldn't rely on them. We're just lucky nothing's affected our belly tank or the port valves. If I begin to get any funny readings on those, then I figure I'm just going to strap on my life jacket and make a jump for it.'

'Yea,' said Page. 'It's a pity they don't equip the crew with parachutes. Everything's so goddam automated nowadays all we ought to have to do is get her off the ground, set the controls, and bail out. If it's this automated today, you just think what flying will be like in five years. Automatic pilot, automatic land, automatic take off, automatic stewardesses, auto- . . .'

'And automatic crash if something like this ever happened with no crew aboard.' Huston cut in sharply. 'There's a thin red line that has to be drawn between man and machine, my boy. There's got to come a compromise. You can take aviation and automate it until a commercial jetliner will fly by remote control as easy as those plastic and wooden models do, but just remember those models don't carry human beings. I know what's being said. I've heard as much as you and Peter and I've read a damn sight more about all this autoland and auto take off stuff. It's nice gear. It takes a lot of extra work off us guys and it cuts down the guess work a bit, but you just look at the three of us sitting here in this miserable cockpit and you pick any one of us that a machine could replace.'

Page looked around the cockpit as if he was thinking what Sturgess would be like if he were a machine.

Huston continued. 'The more technical gear they build into these planes, the more monitors and switches and gadgets have to go with them. And then most of those systems have back-up systems. Each of the back-up systems has a set of its own monitors and switches. You get the ordinary passenger in here and he looks at us as if we're geniuses. How many different individual controls are there in this cockpit? How many are added or taken away every time Boeing or Douglas or our friends back there from Decca and Amplivox invent something new? How many hours do all of us spend with the 747 Owner's Manual and Guide to Safe Flying? How often do we read the rubbish they release on The New Approach to Airline Flight Service? All the boys down there in the labs are sweating their guts out trying like hell to replace you and me and Peter with so much metal – fancy as it may be. But they'll never do it, son. They tried to cut down on flight crews with BOAC when the 747 first came out and what happened? BOAC was left with a hangar full of jumbos and not a skipper would touch them unless he knew he had the crew he needed. And who won in the end? Did the boys down there who said this thing could fly with two men in the cockpit? With one even? No. *We* won. We won because *we* fly these planes – whether they're 707s or DC8s or 747s. Boeing could launch the biggest advertising campaign their millions could buy to convince the public to fly in a jumbo with just two crew members, and all it would take was one word from us – the pilots – and it would blow their campaign to pieces.'

Page looked across at Huston. 'That word being strike.'

Huston frowned. 'No, not *strike*. Go back to what I said about what a passenger thinks when he sees all those controls. The average public don't even begin to think about how we master this. They look at us as if we've been programmed or something. But what they *do* know is that we can get an aircraft up off the ground, fly them along at six hundred miles a hour, and put them down safely. That's what Mr. Joe Public cares about and that's what the public respect us for. Why do you think the public was behind us when we had this world-wide hi-jack strike thing going on? Because they respected us for knowing what we're doing and doing it pretty damn well.'

Sturgess swivelled in his chair and faced forward. 'If there was an aircraft that just had one crew member and people did trust it, what do you think would happen if something went wrong on the scale of what we face now?'

'All the machines at his disposal couldn't help him,' replied Huston. 'Sure, I'm Skipper of this ship and in theory I give the orders. But there's hardly a decision I make that isn't influenced by the opinion of my First and Second Officers.

Maybe in an all out emergency when there isn't time to have a discussion over what to do I'll act on my own, but there are three men who fly this aircraft and I figure you can't fly any big airliner with anything less. If anybody ever asks you two whether or not you think one of these babies could be flown with anything under three crew members, you just think back on our situation right now. Once we hit the cloud front, the party's going to be over and we'll all be sweating ourselves silly about getting this thing down.'

'That sweat of yours is coming up in about twenty minutes, Skipper,' Page said.

'Astral One Two Four, this is Shannon Control. Over.'

Huston pressed the transmit button on his stick. 'One Two Four.'

'One Two Four, I have your approach procedures which London Airways would like you to follow. Are you ready to copy?'

Huston looked at Page who nodded. 'Roger, Shannon. We are copying.'

'Continue on Green One to cross Strumble at flight level Two Five Zero. You are cleared for a priority descent to be at eight over Woodley. You may use your own navigation for your descent and contact London one one nine decimal two. This frequency is being kept open for you and all outbound traffic is being held. Should you require any extra emergency facilities on your approach, London Airways will be standing by.'

Captain Huston let Page read back his approach instructions. Shannon confirmed they were correct.

'Thank you, Shannon Control,' Huston replied. 'Good day.'

'Good day. One Two Four. Good luck.'

'One Two Four, this is Escort, over.'

'One Two Four,' said Huston hastily. 'Don't you have a captain on board?'

'One Two Four, this *is* the captain.'

'Well, for God's sake tell me your name. We've been flying together for a thousand miles and all I know you as is Nimrod Escort.'

'I am Captain Pilkerton, Captain Huston. We will be listening in on your frequency and we shall be standing by to relieve you of any communications should you find yourself too engaged to reply. Is that satisfactory?'

'Very satisfactory, Captain Pilkerton,' Huston replied. 'I tend to think we'll be more than engaged once we begin our descent and you might be a big help but don't get too close. There's no way of telling how this plane will behave once we lose altitude. Keep your frequency open and I'll monitor our progress.'

'Roger, One Two Four. Is there anything else we can do for you before you begin your descent?'

'Yes, there is, Captain Pilkerton. As a matter of fact there are two things you can do. The first is to pray. The second is to let me know the minute you spot any deterioration on my starboard wing.'

'The first will be easy, Captain Huston. But once we settle into that cloud base, I'll be lucky to catch a glimpse of you from time to time. We shall have to maintain standard separation if not a bit more.'

'Yeah, well if you do get a glimpse of us, give me a shout. It'll reassure me that we're still airborne.'

'Roger, One Two Four.'

Captain Huston took a firm grip on the stick and thought. He had the well known habit of throwing himself into a trance-like state immediately before he had to make decisions, and there had been many First Officers who had made the error of thinking that Huston had frozen at the stick. Page had flown with him often enough to know otherwise, and he and Sturgess waited for what would be the next stage in bringing International's One Two Four onto her final approach route. Once Huston began his descent, there would be no more idle chatter. But there was a lot to do before Huston wanted to push his stick forward, and right now he was thinking about his passengers.

Brodie Washburn was asleep. After crying out his fears and hurt on Toni Rice's lap, he made a brave effort to sit up and suddenly felt dizzy spells whirling the aircraft about. As soon as he raised his hand to his forehead, Dr. Osterton recognised the probable symptoms of concussion. Brodie's pupils were normal considering the circumstances, but with an operation to perform in the least ideal conditions and unable to make a firm diagnosis of Brodie's dizziness, Osterton gave the boy an injection of pentathol and Toni and Lynn Almirall had set him on the row of seats which formed a couch when the arm rests were raised. Bruce Ames improvised a safety harness for the boy by removing two seat belts and fitting one pair of the ends between the panel spring clips. He used two of the dado panel fasteners located on the floor of the lounge to anchor the other ends of the two straps and in this way he was able to strap Brodie onto the seats at his chest and legs. To prevent any chance of whiplash should the plane encounter sudden turbulence Ames rigged up a third set of seat belts in similar vertical fashion and after cushioning Brodie's head with pillows, he tightened the straps over his forehead. Ames felt confident that whatever might be ahead of them in the way of a rough ride at least the boy would not be affected badly.

Osterton began his operation after a hasty scrub in the Sky Lounge toilet. First, Paul was anaesthesised with Sodium Pentathol and while Osterton scrubbed up, Toni and Lynn prepared Paul for his operation. They removed his shirt and slipped down his trousers before covering him with a sheet one of the passengers had brought as a gift for relatives in London. Toni cut a hole in the sheet where she knew Dr. Osterton would be operating and finished up by checking over the instruments which had been put on a galley trolley.

Bruce Ames had again helped with strapping Paul down. Removing more seat belts from vacant first class seats below, he bolted the loose ends together with the bolts that had originally held them down and looped the belts under the table. Strapped in much the same as Brodie, Paul would be protected from any sudden movement of the aircraft – as long as Dr. Osterton was as quick with his scalpel.

Alex Trent-Jones then took Lynn down to the economy section where Sandra Gesner was waiting. However much she wanted to be by Paul's side, Lynn knew it was best for everyone if she waited it out below. In *this* passenger's case there was nothing she could do. Sandy took her into the galley and made some fresh coffee. 'It'll be all right, Lynn,' she said with all the conviction she could muster. 'Believe me, it will.'

Trent-Jones had picked up Roger Staunton on the way back to the Sky Lounge and together with Bruce Ames, they sat on the starboard side waiting for anything to happen that might require their help.

William Bell, BAA's Senior Press Officer, threw down an evening paper onto Ray Milross's desk. 'We're in for it now, old boy.'

Milross glanced from the updated statement he was preparing on BAA's involvement with the landing of International's One Two Four to the copy of the *Evening Standard* Bell had tossed at him.

'They've guessed the lot,' Bell admitted resignedly. 'There isn't much, but what there is is enough to get everyone excited.'

Milross knew there had been a chance that one of the papers could snatch enough information on International's difficulties to make it first page material. Newspapers always held Page One until all the other pages had gone to press just in case some important news flashed in. In a matter of minutes the pre-set page could be re-edited, the format revised, and news originally billed for Page One shifted to the back page. Today, the *Standard* had made a snatch, and they had managed to squeeze the news just below the lead article on BranAir's head-long plunge down ten right.

'747 DOODLEBUG. Following the runway disaster of a Bran-Air Charter 707 at Heathrow Airport in which one hundred and twenty passengers narrowly escaped with their lives, a spokesman for the airport revealed that a 747 Jumbo Jet carrying three hundred passengers and crew had encountered engine failure over the Atlantic following an explosion on board the aircraft. It is believed that the 747 belongs to International Airlines and though there has been no official comment from International, it is understood that the plane is in no real danger and is expected to land at Heathrow later this evening.

'With two of Heathrow's three runways out of action, airport officials have expressed concern over landing International's 747 at Heathrow rather than diverting it to another airport. If an explosion has occurred on board, it is possible that the Jumbo may have suffered structural damage which would make its approach to Heathrow exceedingly dangerous for those people whose homes are under the landing route.

One airport official likened a possible crash of a Jumbo Jet to a "Titanic disaster of aviation" and he thought that it was "both risky and unfair to the families who live near Heathrow". to allow International's flight in. Other airlines at Heathrow have said they have received a notice from the Airport Authorities advising them of a temporary stop on all outward flights and it is believed that this action has been taken in order to clear the air routes around Heathrow for the stricken Jumbo.'

Milross looked up at Bell and wondered when the phones would start ringing. He knew that the paper had guessed much of the situation, and 'official spokesman' for Heathrow, or 'airport officials' mentioned in the article were probably maintenance men who had caught snippets of rumours going round and had simply elaborated. All the papers did it. Kitchen staff in Terminal Three had been quoted as being 'high ranking airport officials' when the reporters needed some kind of statement from Heathrow.

'Well, I wouldn't get too bothered. That latest statement you gave with Wilmet was obviously too late to catch any of the other papers. What worries me is the nine o'clock news. It'll all be happening then if One Two Four is on schedule and the newsmen are going to be sitting on us until she's down safely or otherwise. We better get the conference room set up again and lay on some flat tops to get the barriers up as soon as that jumbo stops. We'll get a couple of coaches to take the reporters out once the passengers and crew are off.'

'What about interviewing the passengers – or a word with the Captain?'

'Not a chance. I'll make damn sure the reception areas for the passengers are sealed off. You had better get Wilmet back down here and stick with him until all this is over.'

'If I can find the poor blighter,' Milross replied, picking up the phone. 'If I were him, I'd be out having a few drinks. He's going to be on pins and needles while that plane of his is coming down.'

'It's not just him, old boy,' Bell said. 'Just keep in mind what part our bosses are playing in this one. I don't want any lines crossed between what Wilmet might say and what we say.

That's why I want you to stick with him. There're probably reporters all over the airport looking for some news. If they get Wilmet before we do, it's going to sound like the right hand's lost sight of the left.'

'O.K.,' sighed Milross.

'I'll be in my office if you need me.'

Kevin Blake eyed the BranAir 707 jealously. Coburn was way ahead of him. Already Pan American were out in force, guiding the tugs towards their single hangar. When the decision had been made to use Pan Am's hangar rather than risk the longer route to BOAC, Pan Am had done a hasty minor servicing of the only 707 in their dock and had pushed it back to make way for BranAir. It was the kind of gesture that kept all the airlines free from the worry of finding themselves with a damaged aircraft in an airport far removed from their home base. Pan Am would do all they could to strengthen the weakened spars on BranAir's 707 and probably carry out any repairs necessary to insure the plane could be moved to another location without risk of further damage. Beyond that it would be up to BranAir to decide what to do with the plane, whether or not their small ground support unit at Heathrow could manage the repair work on their own. An initial assessment would have to wait until Pan Am had completed their work and it was possible that BranAir could request Pan Am to repair the aircraft in total if Pan Am were agreeable. Otherwise, the task might be handed over to BOAC. Either way, BranAir would still have to foot the bill. In that case, it wasn't going to be cheap.

Blake's problems were by no means near the completion stage. He didn't think he could finish the job until the rain let up and with night coming on he knew that even with arc lamps and all the mobile lighting Heathrow could throw in there was no way of sorting out the ruptured cables from telecommunications and the electrical sub stations. If the worst came to the worst, he would temporarily shore up the pit covers and finish off the re-surfacing so that the two runways could be opened by morning and then he'd have to wait until better weather set in before opening up the covers again. With luck, and if the Met boys were right, the storm front would be gone by mid-day tomorrow with reasonably clear skies forecasted for the afternoon. The runways could be closed around seven p.m. if ATC did some extra homework and he could plan to repair most of the cables by the morning of the following day.

But until the priority order went out to open up the runways regardless of the damaged cables, he and his men had to defy the rain and cold and oncoming night. He'd work on the cables for another hour – that would bring the time up to a quarter to nine – and then he'd hand in his work sheets and find out what the orders for the evening were.

Buff Congdon, Gerry Vimr and Cary Rowe were working in Block 87, cleaning up the last bit of debris from both Bran-Air's 707 and the runway lighting. So far they had made three trips and had dumped every scrap of twisted steel, shattered glass and broken concrete just inside the Ground Ops Building. Both BranAir and the Airport Authority would want to sift through the mess because there would no doubt follow an inquiry into the incident. Normally, Congdon knew that the 707 should never have been touched until one of the Civil Aviation Inspectors from London had had the chance to examine the incident area, but since it was a priority to clear the runway and get the intersection repaired, the Inspector was relying on eye witness accounts, taking into consideration the undercarriage problems that both Aer Lingus and Pan Am had immediately before the BranAir captain aborted his take off. Congdon had been surprised, however, that the order had gone out to move the 707 even before the Inspector had a chance to at least see the incident area and he guessed that the order was issued by some over-zealous civil servant in D'Albiac House who wasn't too familiar with Aircraft Ground Incidents. Luckily, the time taken to drain the fuel from the 707's tanks and the initial difficulty Shell's men had in coupling their hoses to the drain valves, was long enough for the Inspector to arrive from London before any real salvage work had commenced. It was a pretty straightforward incident, the cause, result and effect were obvious. No time had been lost through the Inspector's presence: he seemed a bit eager to get out of the rain.

Mechanical Transport vehicles were rumbling back to their garages when Congdon and his crew completed their collection. As though Coburn guessed that Ground Ops had finished, three runway sweepers appeared through the gloom, coming down Block 75 with Coburn leading in a land rover. Congdon figured that MT would sweep up 87 and work their way down towards Blake, then swing back to clean up any bits that might have fallen off the 707 when it was being towed along the apron. He also figured that he and his men would have to comb that apron in a few more minutes before the sweepers got there. It was important to find any additional aircraft parts which might have fallen off and a check had to be made of the lights along the apron in case any of the tugs or caterpillar trollies mashed them up. It was twelve hours since he, Vimr, Rowe and Thurnblad had come on duty, and he smiled to himself when he thought of the TWA engineer working on the Gulfstream that morning – he should have been home three hours ago, the engineer had said. Congdon wondered if he ever did get home with all the flap on. Thurnblad was still out running standing water checks on all three runways. If the rain kept up much longer, they could open the runways to sea planes.

'Ever felt like a sponge?' Coburn asked when his land rover ground to a halt alongside Checker.

'You just mind that that banger of yours doesn't drop any pieces on this runway,' Congdon replied. 'All we need is a lug nut in with our airplane collection and the Inspectors will do *their* nuts.'

'You all finished, then?'

'Looks that way, doesn't it?' said Congdon, as he nodded for his crew to take a break in the rover. 'Any more news?'

'On which topic? Blake, Bartlett or our latest flap?'

'What latest flap?' Congdon asked suspiciously.

'Haven't you heard anything?' Coburn said. 'I mean where have you been all afternoon?'

'Out bloody here,' Congdon retorted. 'Where the hell have we all been? Unless you've been taking a cushy break in Pan Am's hangar.'

Coburn saw the sweepers were ready to roll off the threshold of Two Eight and the two land rovers were blocking the way. 'Let's go over to your place and I'll fill you in. I figure you're due for a bit of rest, anyway.'

Congdon peered across at him. 'Bloody right we are.' And he rammed the motor into first gear and led the way to Ground Ops.

With nearly an hour to go before International One Two Four would begin its descent down Green One for Woodley, Wise had finalised his emergency procedures. Bill Auer had brought over a detailed estimate of the exact headings One Two Four would be on, the minute by minute position, altitude and air speed calculations and a TWA Flight Captain with two years experience in the jumbos had given Manley his idea of what IA 124 was in for. This was included in Auer's report. It helped to forecast what to expect every inch of the way and though TWA's Captain Douglas hadn't been overly optimistic about 124's chances, he reckoned there was a good chance the 747 could hold up structurally as long as the skipper of that jumbo knew exactly what he was doing. Wise had integrated Auer's estimates with the emergency procedures and because he wanted to be in Aerodrome Control when the 747 came within radar contact, he called in his Deputy, Roland Cohen, who would be responsible for initiating each stage of the procedures.

'To begin with,' Wise explained across his desk, 'we want as little indication slipping out of what's up as possible. I know the Press have cottoned on to this thing, but at the moment they don't know how serious it is. Even we don't. But if word gets out about these plans, it'll make more news than the first moon landing.'

Cohen nodded his head in firm understanding. He knew that certain sections of the Official Secrets Act were theoretically designed to protect them from the Press – that tuning in to the air bands on a VHF receiver was illegal, and, to quote, in any way anything said over the air bands was a punishable offence. To take action on the basis of anything overheard was equally illegal, but anyone could purchase VHF receivers which could pick up aircraft communications and police bands. These transmissions were what often gave the Press their leads to a hot story, and although the United States equipped their civil aircraft with Selcal – selective calling – which guaranteed some kind of protection from being overheard, no such frequency was used in England. The Official Secrets Act was supposed to be enough.

The emergency procedures that Cohen waited patiently to be outlined for him to initiate would be handled whenever possible by telephone. Once the 747 was maintaining constant radio contact with London Airport, there would be no way to keep things secret and the balance of the emergency plans could be sent out by RT whenever necessary, as the Press would be keeping their ears on the jumbo's situation anyway. Cohen realised that the use of VHF receivers by the general public was widespread.

'It is now seven forty-nine,' Wise began, leaning back in his chair. 'ATC estimate that One Two Four will be approaching Woodley at eight fifty. We are stopping outbound traffic at eight thirty until the plane has safely landed. At eight o'clock I want the Constabulary to begin sealing off all access roads to the airport. The tunnel will be kept open, but officers will be checking all vehicles and only ticket carrying passengers or airport service vehicles will be allowed through. I want all the roads giving access to the perimeter road closed and the traffic must be kept moving. I imagine the radio has already released news of this jumbo and we should be getting some kind of spectator turn out. You can call in assistance from the Metropolitan Police to keep the main roads outside the airport clear of people who want to stop their cars – as well as the local police, of course. At the same time I want you to put out a general call to the London Fire Brigade Stations and notify them that this plane will be over London in about sixty minutes – around nine o'clock. I don't want any turn outs – don't give them that idea – but they better be ready to roll if One Two Four can't make it.'

Cohen grew pensive as the gravity of what Wise was admitting began to sink in. Until now the entire picture Cohen had formed of the approaching airliner would have necessitated nothing more than the standard procedure for a full emergency.

'Green One covers a wide area. This plane is going to be cleared for a slow descent from twenty five thousand feet at the coast down to six thousand feet at Woodley. According to ATC this is the first critical stage. We don't know just how bad that starboard wing is damaged and whether or not it'll hold up to a descent through gusting winds, squalls and all this bloody rain. We don't know how much control the skipper of that aircraft will have once he gets into heavier air, and at the moment we don't even know if he'll be able to drop his starboard undercarriage. The escort plane's said there's some kind of shrapnel sticking out of his bay doors. So I want you to contact the fire brigades along the route that I've marked on this map. And I also want you to notify the hospitals in those areas – particularly in the areas I've marked. The only information you are to give is that there is a jumbo jet which has suffered some structural damage in flight and will be passing over their area at some point during the next hour. Don't give them any suggestion that the plane might come down on top of them – just advise them that their assistance may be required in the event of anything going wrong.'

Cohen stared down at the map on Wise's desk. He again felt some kind of relief in that he had an identical map on his office wall and he knew the approach route of Green One well.

'Next comes the procedures for Heathrow. I'm drawing much of the plans from standard procedure for two reasons. The first is that everybody knows what they should do. The second is that it's the only guide we've got that'll be of any use in effecting immediate rescue if it becomes necessary. At eight forty-five ATC will declare a full emergency, but the following procedures will be taken in addition to those specified in the manual. It'll be your job between now and eight forty-five to get these supplementary instructions sent out to those concerned. The Fire Service will turn out on Two Eight Right with all of its appliances from the main station and the sub-station. Harrison will decide where to deploy his vehicles, but I want him to use four positions on the runway rather than the usual three. Feltham, Hayes, Staines and Hillingdon Fire Brigades will stand by at Rendezvous Points West, North and East where Marshalling Section will hold them until they're needed. Because we will be turning out with all our appliances, I'm more interested in having plenty of firemen around that jumbo, so let the local brigades use their discretion as to how many vehicles they want to send. Just make sure they get as many men out there as they can spare. Those policemen from our

Constabulary who aren't otherwise involved in sealing off the airport will stand by at the positions they would normally take in a full emergency. It is important that the Incident Post vehicle be ready to roll the moment a call comes through. Since there may be a shortage of officers to carry out the normal procedures involved in a full emergency, I want Engineering, Mechanical Transport and Ground Operations Units standing by in their radio cars in Block 115, 116, 117, 35, 36, 37 and the outer taxiway on the north side. MT Section are to be on full alert with the emergency vehicles, Medical Wagon and First Aid Post, and I want them to take up their position at Rendezvous Point North rather than waiting for the call out in their garage.

'Marshalling Section will be at their posts at the Rendezvous Points, but I want every extra man to help Engineering load up every available mobile light we've got on the airfield, including the ones we've called in from Gatwick. They can get a transporter from MT for handlighting and emergency runway lighting – but I want to have as much light available as we can gather and I don't care what kind it is. Once you've got them organised, advise them to stand by on the outer taxiway along with the radio cars. There'll be extra men laid on from Roads Administration and some of the other departments who don't normally attend this sort of thing, but I've already arranged that. Most of them will be keeping spectators away around the perimeter area of the airport, but we can call them in as needed through the police.

'The Management Duty Room is notifying the restaurant staff in the Tower to prepare it as a reception centre, and we may open the Alcock and Brown Suite. MDR will be one of the first to know if it become necessary to use the VIP Suite and they'll be in radio contact with the incident area to divert the coaches as necessary. Needless to say, International are standing by with passenger steps and coaches and they will be given priority to turn out onto the runway once the plane comes to a rest. I understand that they have requested permission to stand by in Block 36. With two hundred and sixty odd people to shuttle around, I think they'll be asking some of the other airlines for assistance so it might not be just International's coaches sitting out in 36.

'Now, the final step. At eight thirty I want you to advise the Duty Medical Officer to leave for Block 35. The Medical Centre has been informed of what we might be faced with and they are planning rescue operations with the local hospitals now. If the plane doesn't make a successful landing, it'll be the job of the fire services to get the passengers out as quickly as they can, and the ambulances that are being called in will be holding at the three Rendezvous Points. I have decided to use the DeHaviland Suite as an emergency reception area for minor injuries and shock which will offset the load on the Medical Centre. Should there be an excessive number of serious casualties, Hillingdon, West Middlesex and Ashford are still standing by and if necessary they will contact other local hospitals as the situation dictates.

'A few final items. The old KLM building will be opened as the temporary morgue, but this time I've asked for additional police after our last experience with the Trident. You'll have to remind the Incident Officer to detach more police to the building area if its use becomes necessary. Also, there will be one ambulance from Hillingdon Hospital waiting in Block 115 as the skipper of One Two Four says he has two injuries on board requiring hospital treatment when they land.' Wise stopped and glanced up at Cohen. 'I hope and pray that's the only ambulance we're going to need.'

'It's a big operation, Sir,' Cohen said. 'You aren't taking any chances, are you?'

Wise stood up and stretched slowly, the twinge in his stomach growing. 'No, Roland, I am not. Any questions?'

'What about all the relatives and friends – where are they going to stay?'

'I thought about leaving them in Terminal Three where they'd usually wait. But that might prove dangerous if something goes wrong. You'll be faced with a few hundred hysterical people. So I got onto our friends at BOAC and wondered if they could suggest anything. Naturally, they were willing to do all they could so they've opened their main staff canteen and the friends and relatives of the passengers on One Two Four are being taken to the BOAC maintenance area now. They're shuttling them over in coaches. Which reminds me. I want you to get on to the Padre and ask him if he can go over to the canteen now. Tell him to take the airport counsellor as well. I know that Traveller's Help are going to be in the Tower restaurant, but I think some professional counselling among the passenger's friends might reduce the tension.'

'If all goes well,' Cohen began, 'what are the plans for dealing with the passengers once they're in the restaurant or VIP Suite?'

'Once we know that everyone's safe, the International coaches will drive them over to the BOAC area where Immigration will process the passengers as quickly as they can. As far as the passenger's luggage goes, I believe International is bringing that over to one of the BOAC hangars where passengers can claim their things whenever they feel up to it. I've also asked Customs to go as easy as they can on them.'

'Then I better get on with things,' said Cohen rising. 'I take it you'll be leaving for the Tower soon.'

'In about ten minutes, Roland.'

Cohen stood at the door. 'A prayer or two might help. That's about the only thing you left out.'

The door clicked silently into place as he walked down the corridor to his office.

The Precision Approach Radar caravans – the mobile radar scanners which monitored the critical attitude of an aircraft's approach to the runway – had to be shifted to their concrete platform off Block 13 before Bill Auer could work with Approach Control in talking One Two Four out of the torrential skies. The PAR caravans had been left for approach landings on the Tens, but with the winds blowing westerly and International's 747 coming in on the Two-Eights, the PAR gear had to be shifted. Auer had sent the order to move the caravans when One Two Four was ready to begin descent to Strumble. This was the responsibility of the Board of Trade vehicles rather than BAA's Mechanical Transport Section as the delicate equipment came under Air Traffic Control's jurisdiction. Normally, Auer's request to have the radar scanners moved was met with indifference and the equipment was quickly shifted. But the lead caravan which towed the secondary radar systems was sloshing around in a pond of water on its concrete base and Derek Wilks, in charge of the shifting operation, was reluctant to rely on the lead caravan. The highly sensitive electronics could be set out of calibration if there was a bad skid or a lot of spinning wheels, and there was no guarantee that the new site off Block 13 would be any less water-logged than this one.

'You're going to have to ask for help from MT Section,' Wilks radioed. 'We can't shift the caravans in all this water without risking damage to the scanners. And that new location off Block Thirteen might have to be pumped dry.'

'I'll see what I can do,' Auer said wearily from the glass confines of Aerodrome Control. 'But keep at it. There isn't much time left. That jumbo's got enough problems without asking him to circle around the airport while we haul the caravans into position.'

'We'll stick with it, Bill,' Wilks began. 'But you haven't got a hope if MT don't get here quick.'

'Where's MT now?' Auer asked the Tower. 'PAR's rained in and Wilks won't shift the caravans. Christ, what the hell is going to happen next?'

Meyer rubbed his eyes and looked up. 'Listen, Bill, you're cutting the odds too thin. The both of you are. I know you and Manley've got more hours behind you than I've had hot dinners, but I still say risk her on Ten Left. The caravans are ready to bring her down on Ten, it would save her making the circuit over London and it would make all our lives a hell of a lot easier.'

'Sure it would,' Auer snapped. 'And with the winds shooting westerly the way they are, all it would take was one strong gust and that 747 would have about as much chance staying airborne as a concrete block. Besides, we're committed to Two Eight Right. If we go for landing on Ten, it'll mean cancelling the emergency plans and re-routing every vehicle that's been asked to assist. If we did that, it would mean holding that jumbo on her approach. It's the Two Eights or nothing. Now where is MT?'

Meyer clenched his teeth and the muscles around his cheeks rippled. He looked away from Auer and out into the mist that obscured the end of the runways in both directions.

'I've got Coburn on the phone,' Jim Ramaley called out. 'He's with Congdon in Ops.'

Auer walked over to Ramaley's console and snatched the phone. 'David – it's Bill Auer here. Look, we've got a priority shift on the PAR Caravans and our boys can't handle it. The caravans are swamped in the approach for the Tens and we've got to get them moved to Block Thirteen damn quick. Can your men take some heavy moving gear out to Wilks and give him a hand?'

Coburn looked over to Congdon and frowned. 'Here we go again,' he snickered, holding the phone away. 'O.K., Bill. I'll get out there myself. I gather this is for that 747 you're talking down.'

'You gathered right. And there isn't much time. Let me know as soon as you've begun moving the Caravans.'

'Will do,' Coburn sighed.

'Need any help?' asked Congdon, tossing a pack of cigarettes across the desk to Coburn.

'I need some bloody rest, that's what I need. And a good meal. Christ Almighty, you'd think we're bloody machines the way they push us around.' Coburn stood up and took a cigarette. 'All bloody day in the rain hauling out that damned 707, then out sweeping the runways so we don't have a reservoir on our hands and now they want us to shift the PAR's 'cause their boys can't handle the job. And I'll give you any money you want that in an hour's time the whole bloody lot of us will be out picking up pieces of that 747. They're bleedcrackers up there in that Tower. It's not bad enough that Blake's out there drowning himself in those pits all afternoon and we're operating on one runway, but now those clots in the Tower are bringing in a jumbo that might not even make it over the threshold. I don't know,' he finished, pulling open the door. 'It just never bloody ends, does it?'

Congdon watched the door slam shut and saw Coburn hunch himself against the rain as he left the garage area and jumped into his land rover. He heard the rover start up and roar off in an angry grinding of gears and black smoke. If Coburn had to haul the PAR gear across runway Two Eight, it meant that Ops would be cleaning up after him. He pulled off his boots and rested his wet socks on the desk. He'd have a few more minutes to rest anyway.

'One Two Four, this is Shannon. You are clear to begin your descent to flight level two five zero. Contact London Airways on one two eight decimal five, over.'

'Descend to two five zero. One two eight decimal five. One Two Four,' Captain Huston repeated. 'Got that, Captain Pilkerton?'

'Roger, One Two Four. I'll be following you in and maintaining one thousand feet vertical separation. I'd estimate you'll hit the clouds at twenty.'

'If we're lucky. One Two Four out.' Huston turned his head slightly and looked back at Sturgess. 'Any chance of juggling Number Four Reserve?'

'I'm trying now, Skipper, but these gauges are useless. If she's transferring, it isn't showing on my board.'

'Well, let's just hope she is. I don't fancy our chances on two.'

Page glanced across at him. 'You think we'll make it, Skipper?'

For what seemed a long few seconds, Huston didn't answer. He was in another one of his trances, assessing every possibility. At length he looked out and ahead as if searching the mountains of cloud for an answer. 'If we don't, it won't be for want of trying.' Huston willed himself alert. His face began to colour and the hours of strain seemed forgotten. Richard Page studied his Captain and felt confident. Huston was preparing himself to face whatever challenges lay ahead. 'Fuel transfer to centre tank,' he ordered briskly.

'Done, Skipper,' Sturgess replied.

'You just keep your eyes on Number Four's gauges and let me know the second anything happens. If she's going to cut out, see if you can guess her first.'

'Right, Skipper. But you'll probably pick it up on your gauges before I do.'

'Dick, I want you to go back and find Mary Stewart. Bring her up here. And tell the Doc that he'd better be finished and get strapped in. Make sure those boys are strapped in as well. Christ knows how they'll do it. Then you can get that Pan Am engineer in here along with the Decca fellow. Bring the other one, too. The headset guy. We're going to have to do some quick planning before I begin pushing her nose through those clouds.'

Page rose stiffly. 'Want me to tell the passengers anything?'

'Wait until I see Mary. Then we'll make an announcement.'

Page felt the stiffness in his arms and legs as he left the cockpit. When he entered the Sky Lounge, Dr. Osterton was standing over Paul, but he was out of his operating gear and the boy was covered up to his neck in blankets.

Osterton turned to see the First Officer. 'I think he'll make it,' said Osterton, smiling. The wrinkles in his face seemed to offer some reassurance to Toni Rice who had never seen such skill in the hands of any surgeon. 'I hope we don't get shaken up too much on the way down, though.'

'You think it might hurt the boy?' Page asked.

'No, no. The boy is fine. I mean, for all that we could do. I just get very nervous when these big planes start shaking. I know they're very well built, but I can't help feeling nervous about being so high up with nothing below. I guess it's just that I'm an old man who should keep his feet on the ground.'

Page faced him. 'I'm glad you didn't. Not this flight, anyway.'

The Doctor chuckled. 'Yes, you're right there, my friend.'

Page looked at the others who had assembled in the Lounge. 'The Skipper wants to see all of you in a few minutes. I'm going to get one of the stewardesses now but I won't be long.'

Bruce Ames looked up sleepily. 'We aren't going anywhere.'

The cockpit was crowded. Page had taken command of the three hundred ton airplane and was feeling all the more insignificant with the loss of his precious trim. For the first time in his career he wondered if man was really supposed to be up here, guiding this monster of an aircraft with nothing more than his control stick, two pedals and he had forgotten how many instruments, gauges and buttons.

Captain Huston was standing. So was Mary Stewart, the senior stewardess who had been managing first class. Alex Trent-Jones and Bruce Ames sat in the two observer's seats behind the Captain's seat, and behind them stood Roger Staunton and Father Giordino. It was cramped, and Huston had to stoop slightly as he spoke.

'I've called you up here because I'm faced with one of those problems which needs a few extra people who know what they're doing to sort out. The problems I speak of involve first – and most importantly – the passengers.' Huston paused for a moment while the aircraft shook from the rough air already buffeting the fuselage. 'The other principal problem we have to contend with is a technical one, and that is the function of this aircraft in its present condition. In taking into account the deeper complexities of both of these problems, I do not hesitate to say that I and Mr. Page – our First Officer, whom you met downstairs – and my Flight Engineer, Peter Sturgess, need your help. I am under the impression that you are all experts in your respective fields and though I know that Mary here and the rest of the cabin staff are more than capable, she and the others will need the help of you, Father, and of your friends down below.

'We know roughly what our damage is and because I need all your help I must tell you that the aircraft is in pretty bad shape for the descent and landing that we're forced to make. But I *am* sure we will make it safely. However, there may be some periods when it isn't going to look like we'll get her down in one piece, and this is where you, Mary, and Father Giordino can help most. I'm going to ask the passengers to put on their life jackets and the stewardesses will instruct passengers in the procedure for a crash landing. This is merely a precaution – I swear this to you, but with the uncertainties that face us, I am sure you can see where the old ounce of prevention comes in handy. Now I know that when I inform the passengers that full emergency precautions will be taken, they're going to get scared. I imagine there isn't one of ahem who has some doubts about whether or not we'll get this plane down safely, and these emergency procedures will only add to their fears. So between what you and the other cabin staff can do, Mary, is going to be vital. My First Officer has told me about the effect you and your fellow ministers had on the passengers after our difficulty over the Atlantic, Father. I am hoping that you will help the cabin staff in doing whatever is necessary to calm them. I don't care whether you lead them in prayers or hymns or even the last rites. Just do what the hell – whatever the heck you can to keep things as relaxed as possible under the circumstances. Can you do it?'

Father Giordino smiled. 'There are three priests and a rabbi, Captain. If between the four of us we cannot convince the Lord to give us all another chance, then at least we will prepare everyone for what must come – one way or the other. So far, the Lord has kept us on a straight and level course – as I think you say – and He wouldn't have brought us this far only to ditch us in the Irish Sea. But Captain, we are putting all our faith in you to bring us to safety, so I hope you are putting the same faith in Him whose decision it will be at the end.'

Captain Huston looked deep into the eyes of Father Giordino. 'I read somewhere recently that if the good Lord wanted jet planes to fly, He would have given them propellers. Let's see who's right.'

Father Giordino smiled again. 'I would appreciate it if you would keep this up here. Captain,' he began, pulling his crucifix from his collar. 'Put it somewhere where it'll remind you of who is flying this plane.'

Huston took it respectfully. 'Thank you, Father. Now if you return downstairs with Miss Stewart, I can give you five minutes to get together with your respective parties and prepare yourselves to help the passengers after I make the announcement.'

Father Giordino nodded and smiled. 'I shall say a prayer for those two boys first if you don't mind. And I shall pray for you. All of you whose skill shall be guiding us down.'

'In that case, make it six minutes,' Huston replied. His hand wrapped itself around the crucifix as he watched Mary Stewart squeeze her way out of the cockpit.

'You may need these,' Roger Staunton said when the door had shut. 'I know the company regulations about using equipment that hasn't been approved, but if Bruce and Alex here are going to be of any help to you, they'll probably want to be plugged into your RT.'

Huston took the three Minilite headsets from Staunton. They looked incredibly small compared to the bulky double head sets and boom mikes that were International's standard equipment. 'Are they wired for this sort of aircraft?'

'I've already rigged them up for this plane. I guessed some

time ago that you would be asking for extra help when I knew who Mr. Ames and Mr. Trent-Jones were. Besides, I'm a representative of Amplivox, Captain, and I never pass up an opportunity to make a sale. Especially to an airline like International.'

'Eight minutes until we begin our descent, Skipper,' Page called out. Huston handed two of the headsets back to Staunton. He turned to his seat and unplugged his own headset. The crucifix was still in his hand. He glanced around for somewhere to put it.

'How about letting me hold it for you, Skipper,' said Sturgess. 'I've got a nice little corner for it right here next to these gauges.'

Huston hesitated, then handed it to him. 'You take good care of that Peter. That's our link with the Big Man.'

Sturgess grinned and turned to his console.

Captain Huston had little time in which to assess the ability of the three men who now occupied his cockpit and who – minutes before – were merely passengers expecting an uneventful trip to London. Unlike his First Officer and Flight Engineer whom he knew inside and out and whose behaviour he knew he could predict under any given situation, Huston hoped that because these three men were involved in aviation, they appreciated the dangers inherent in taking a few hundred tons of metal into thin air. His present assessment of Ames and Staunton was reassuring, but he might have expected Ames' presence of mind in fashioning special harnesses for the sick boys in the Sky Lounge. Ames *was* a trouble shooter and most trouble shooters have been through some pretty trying incidents both on the ground and in the air. Stanton seemed relaxed in the atmosphere of the cockpit – no more nervous than if he were at a sales meeting in New York or at a private demonstration of his mini-micro headsets – whatever he called them. But Staunton's experience pretty much ended with headset communications. Though the extra communications link might prove useful, there wasn't much else Staunton could do up front. So Alex Trent-Jones was left. Huston guessed him to be at least fifty with approaching middle age bulge, greying hair and rather efficient manner. He knew that Trent-Jones had acted swiftly when Paul had succumbed to his appendix, and when Brodie had smashed his head against one of the dado clamps. So far the explosion and condition of the aircraft as he described it moments before hadn't seemed to upset Trent-Jones who was observing the instruments around him with the curiosity of one who has designed them but never really seen them in use under real-life situations. Of the three, Trent-Jones was the quietest, but his actions in the Sky Lounge gave Huston a clue to just how far he could be relied upon to act in an emergency. None of them seemed anywhere near the stage where nerves and tension and fears, both real and projected, took away all sense of judgement. As he listened to Staunton explain the simplicity of his headsets, Huston creased his forehead and decided that these three men could be depended on. Just how far was yet to be determined.

'The two clips swivel out,' Staunton explained, twisting the clips which held the ear piece and tiny boom microphone forward. 'You can adjust the head band by pulling down on the clips. There. Now swivel the ear piece until it fits comfortably and move the mike just forward of your cheek. There's an attenuator on this model which cuts out any excess noise.'

Huston fiddled with the headset until he thought he had it correctly in place. He felt insecure without the bulky earphones and heavy head band, and he couldn't even see the tiny four-inch long tube which was his only vocal link with the outside. Hesitant, he plugged the jack into the socket and pressed his transmit button. Staunton leant over him and clipped the clasp on the automatic gain control onto his shirt. 'One Two Four to Nimrod Escort, over.'

'Nimrod Escort,' came the immediate reply, crisply and clearly into the single ear piece which was no larger than a small hearing aid.

'How do you read, over?'

'You are loud and clear, One Two Four. Five by five. Any trouble?'

'Just testing some new headset that one of the passengers has given us. I've brought in some extra help.'

'With all your problems it's good to know you've still got time to play around with someone else's toys, Captain. I am estimating six minutes to descent.'

'Roger, Escort. Will advise. One Two Four out.' Captain

Huston was beaming when he unplugged the headset and turned to Staunton. 'They have my approval. They're incredible little things.'

'You're more than welcome to use it, Captain. No obligation.'

'I would like to, Mr. Staunton,' Huston replied honestly. 'I really would. But if anything went wrong and I wasn't wearing standard equipment . . .'

'He'd be out on his ear,' Ames interrupted. 'But I won't be. Is it O.K. if we use these, Captain?'

'You don't have much choice, Mr. Ames. You know where to plug them in?'

Ames grinned. 'If I didn't I'd be a pretty lousy engineer, wouldn't I?' He handed a headset to Trent-Jones who fiddled with the head band and swivel clips as he had seen Staunton do. 'Is Mr. Staunton here going to ride with us on the way down? Ames asked. 'Cause if he is, he can use the extra socket behind me.'

'I'd rather not,' Staunton replied before Huston could decide. 'Whatever happens, I know I'll be in just as good hands in the Lounge as I will up here. Besides, I think Dr. Osterton and Miss Rice might need some help with the boys if it gets as rough as you say it might.'

Huston nodded. 'Are those boys strapped in tight?'

Page looked across. 'Our Mr. Ames here has rebuilt the inside of that Lounge. I think we ought to send Pan Am a bill for all the work International's going to be faced with getting our Sky Lounge back into shape.'

'Maybe you'll find Pan Am sending us a bill, my son,' Huston replied. 'Mr. Amers's activities on board this flight aren't incumbent you know.'

'It was a free ticket,' Ames said, strapping himself into the forward observer's seat. 'And for the first time in six dozen trans-Atlantic flights I haven't been bored silly.'

Page looked heavenward. "We'll be sure to arrange something like this on every flight for you. That's if you're dying to fly that much.'

Alex Trent-Jones tried to familiarise himself with the location of the navigational systems on board. Beside him, on his left, and beside Ames were the observer's consoles which

166

monitored much of the information the Captain was getting from his instruments. Sitting where he was, he was slightly aft of Sturgess who sat on the opposite side of the cockpit. 'Just what are our orders, Captain? I mean, how can we help?'

'We're coming in on a PAR talkdown. We have to take a wide swing over London and make our approach on an extended centreline. We don't know just how our control surfaces will behave once we get below twenty thousand feet, and the Met report is as near to zero zero conditions as it comes. What you call a Cat. Three C.'

'In other words even the Autoland systems are out,' Trent-Jones said.

'We don't use Autoland,' Huston continued. 'We aren't fitted with any of that gear. Not many of the American airlines are – as I guess you know. But even if we had Autoland, the maximum landing conditions only go as low as Cat. Three B if my memory serves me right, and we aren't going to see the runway until our bogies are right on top of Two Eight's threshold.

'What I'd like you to do is to keep an eye on our approach and landing instruments. We'll be going in on a talkdown, but I'll be a lot happier if you can let me know what our approach looks like from the ILS instruments. We won't be on the beam all the way in so don't start yelling if those lines aren't meeting spot on, but if we're really out of line near flare out, scream your head off if I haven't already aborted.'

'You'll be hearing the talkdown on your headset,' Ames began. 'You can sort of combine what the Captain's being told with what you can see on the instruments.'

'Won't they hear me if I say anything with this headset on?' Trent-Jones asked, peering down at the thin grey microphone tube.

'The only time they'll hear us is when I press the transmit button on my stick – the same as Mr. Sturgess there. If you know we're talking to Approach Control or our Escort friend, then I wouldn't say anything. Only if it's an emergency. But we won't be doing much talking. Just listening – all the way down. You can swivel that mike out of the way if it bothers you.'

Trent-Jones fiddled with the mike. He lightly turned it in

its housing at the ear piece and it rotated back away from his face. 'I feel better that way.'

'Now as for you, Mr. Ames,' Huston began, 'my Flight Engineer is having problems with his fuel gauges for the starboard tanks. We don't know how much fuel is in Number Four and we don't know if the starboard reserve tank is transferring to Number Four. We just hope it is.'

'I gathered that when we first came in. None of your flight Engineer's readings made sense. So Number Four could cut out at any time and you'd be coming in on two. Does London know that?'

Huston hesitated. He looked at Page. 'No. No they don't. I figure they reckon our chances pretty slim as it is. No point in frightening them any worse.'

Ames knew damn well that wasn't the reason. If London knew there was every possibility that Number Four would cut out at any time, they would never bring a 747 in over London. It wouldn't matter a damn about the plane or the passengers. Risk and chance could be carried only so far, and Ames reckoned that already London was taking one hell of a risk in routing this plane's approach over the city. But he wasn't about to say anything – now or ever.

Huston hoped Ames felt that way because he knew Ames didn't believe the bit about frightening London for a moment. 'You're a trouble-shooter for Pan Am's jumbo's, Mr. Ames, which means you know just about everything there is to know about this particular aircraft. I'm going to give you a copy of the damage report sent to London by that Nimrod up there and you can read it while I talk to the passengers. Then you can read the Met report and see just what we're heading into. I don't want to know whether or not you think we stand a chance of making it. What you can do is give me some kind of professional prediction of what might happen and when. And if it does happen and I haven't already begun to take corrective action, then you yell your head off. O.K.?'

Ames took the reports from Page. It was perhaps that he wasn't scared of facing the odds that were against him, or because he had test flown too many aircraft that should have never left the ground, but in either case his reaction was as cool and calculating as Huston could have hoped. 'If I know you're doing something wrong, Captain, I won't waste my time giving you flight instructions. If I make a move for your controls, you just get the hell out of the way.' And in case Huston didn't believe him, Ames struck the release catch on his harness and wriggled free.

'Just one thing, Mr. Ames,' Huston replied coldly. 'Succeed or fail, *I* am the Captain. I don't want to turn our landing into a wrestling match.'

'Understood,' was Ames' reply before he began reading the reports.

Ames seemed to know what he was doing, Huston thought. At least he was confident. He'd let Ames have his way for awhile, but only so long as Ames remembered who was responsible for this ship.

'When they build airports, why the hell do they pick places like this?' Coburn was mumbling angrily. 'My idea of an airport is solid concrete. Just one big, flat level bed of concrete about three miles long and a mile wide. Because if they built airports like *that*, Mr. Wilks, we wouldn't be busting our asses trying to haul your PAR Caravans through all this water.'

'I didn't design Heathrow,' Wilks retorted. 'I only do what I'm paid to do. I didn't ask for this rain and I didn't ask for this jumbo. What I did ask for was your help.'

'I know, I know,' Coburn replied, cuffing him on the back. 'I didn't mean it personally. Just put it down to a hard day.'

From the gloom of the oncoming night, the rain and the swirling mists, Doug Parent emerged in a land rover, followed by several support vehicles from MT. When he had brought the rover into position, he flicked on the overhead spotlights and directed them towards the towing bar of the caravans. 'All over again, David?' he asked wearily as he stepped into the rain.

'Only this time quicker. Have you got the men to lay those steel plates in the area off Block Thirteen?'

'You don't half ask a lot,' Parent replied. 'We had to bloody well *steal* some mobile lights from Blake in order to *find* the plates we laid down off Block Eighty Seven. The mud's covered them all up. They're as slippery as a pig's ass. Simson had to be taken to the Medical Centre just a minute ago with a broken arm – one of those damn plates fell off the trailer and caught him right on the elbow. I should think it's bloody well shattered his arm to pieces.'

Coburn struggled to right himself against the cold and the wet. After all Simson had been through that afternoon, after the hours of concentration Simson suffered in the pouring rain – he had seen Simson nearly convulsing with shivers. And now this. Coburn shook his head and wished it might end. 'Who's with him?' he asked quietly.

'Kitchley. He nearly caught it, too. You couldn't tell the mud from the plates. His hand's cut up a bit, but he was well enough to drive Simson over. I expect they'll both be on their way to hospital soon.'

'Well, at least they'll be away from all this,' Coburn sighed. 'Let's get the ramps under those wheels and we'll pull the Caravans along with two tugs. Get the lads to lay some treads from here to the edge of the runway just so these caravans don't slosh around too much. By the time we get to Block Thirteen, they ought to have enough plates laid so we can position the trailers wherever Wilks wants them. He said to go easy on towing them 'cause of all the gear inside. Another 'nice and easy' towing job. I just hope we make it before that jumbo comes plowing into us.'

'You know about the extra emergency procedures the AGM's laid on?' Parent began. 'As soon as we get this equipment shifted to Block Thirteen, we have to move out most of our vehicles. No standbys. Everyone's to turn out. I've given the lads their instructions and we aren't going to have a second to spare once this job's done.'

'Naturally,' Coburn spat. 'Never is a bloody second around here. Well, we better get on with it.' He turned and shouted to his men, and for the first time in the five years Parent had worked with Coburn, he heard harshness in his voice.

'Coburn's crossing Two Eight now,' Ramaley said to Congdon. 'He said there's a lot of mud around, but that's about it. One of his sweepers is seeing to that so you might as well turn out for the jumbo alert.'

'Will do,' Congdon replied. 'Let's go, lads. We might as well get there first and get the best seats.'

'Very funny,' Vimr said, snatching his jacket from the hook. 'Are you taking Checker?'

'Yeah. you can have Ops One. Rowe can take Ops Two and Ted's out in Seagull now. The Tower can get him on RT.'

'It's going to be interesting if nothing else,' Vimr began, holding open the door for Congdon. 'I've never seen a bigger flap on.'

'Neither have I,' Congdon replied. 'I don't know who to pity more – all of us down here or those poor blokes coming in from up there.'

When the three land rovers from Ground Operations rolled out from the Ops Building, they were the first of the many emergency procedure vehicles that were to assemble. Up to a hundred miles away, other vehicles and emergency services were organising themselves into a standby readiness, while still more cars, ambulances and fire appliances began to turn out of their bases and head for Heathrow.

'Ladies and gentlemen, this is Captain Huston speaking. I know you will all be glad to hear we are about to begin our descent into London Heathrow Airport, and before I give you some information which will insure your safety and comfort during our descent and landing, I would like to thank you all for remaining as calm and co-operative as you have. You have probably heard various rumours going around about what has been happening up here and just to keep you in the picture, a successful operation has been performed on a thirteen year old boy who would have died from a ruptured appendix had he not received immediate help. We were lucky to have a very experienced surgeon on board who is with the boy now up here in the Sky Lounge, and he has assured me that the boy is in excellent shape. So despite our unfortunate incident some while back, we are not only in good enough condition to land safely at Heathrow, we can even hold ourselves steady enough to let a doctor operate. I tell you this because we all need re-assurance of some kind and also because some of you were thinking we were delivering a baby up here! So whoever had put their money on whether it was going to be a boy or a girl can split the difference.

'If this young boy was fortunate in having an experienced

171

surgeon on board, I am just about as lucky because I have two extra men with me in the cockpit. That's in addition to my First and Second Officers, of course. One of these men is a trouble-shooter from one of our competitors. But he knows all about these 747 Jumbo Jets and he's up here with the flight crew to give us whatever extra assistance we might require. It wasn't easy for me to let someone from a competing airline help manage my airplane, but I thought we could show him that we're every bit as good as his company and after we land I'll see if he won't admit it to you.'

Ames grinned. The Captain was playing it cool. There was no need to rush into blaring out emergency instructions to already nervous passengers. If the Captain had time to chat to the passengers in this cool unruffled tone, then Ames felt confident the passengers would accept Huston's emergency escape instructions as a matter of course.

'The other gentleman who is with me is very experienced in instrument landings and while we are getting some pretty special attention from the airport as it is, he will help the First Officer and myself get you down as smoothly and quickly as we can. So this is our back up team, and we couldn't have a better combination of skills to assure us of a safe descent and landing if I had picked them myself. And lastly, before I give you some extra tips for our approach to London, I should mention that the aircraft you've seen tailing us from time to time is our escort plane from the Royal Air Force. Captain Pilkerton is flying it, and he has been helping us along with advice on weather and what the conditions are like down below.

'At the present time we are over Ireland at an altitude of thirty three thousand feet. There's some pretty heavy cloud cover below us so I'm afraid we won't see Ireland on this trip. In a short while we'll be crossing the Irish Sea and coming over South Wales slightly to the south of Fishguard and Newport. We'll be descending at the rate of a thousand feet per minute once we've crossed the Welsh coast and it'll take us another twenty five minutes before we make our final approach into Heathrow. If any of you are concerned about friends and relatives waiting at the airport to meet you, I have been told that they are being given some very special treatment and are of course being kept informed of our progress. Once we are down on the ground at Heathrow, you'll also be pleased to know that Customs and Immigration have made special arrangements to get any formalities over with as quickly as possible.'

Captain Huston paused. It was time to prepare the passengers for all the possibilities that he hadn't mentioned. The possibilities that only he and four others knew existed. The single possibility that Flight One Two Four might never make Heathrow. 'I'd like to give you all some brief instructions now and I would ask that you pay extra careful attention to what I have to say. For the past half hour we have begun to experience some slight turbulence, but this turbulence will increase as we descend, due to the cloudy weather below. Due to the nature of our difficulties, I am therefore going to ask you to remove the life jackets from beneath your seats and to put them on. It is very important that you follow the directions which the cabin staff will give you shortly so please wait until I have finished before actually taking the jackets out. Once you have put your jackets on, I would ask you to remove any sharp objects from your pockets such as pens and pencils. Also, those of you who are wearing glasses should remove them and place them with your hand luggage. Finally, remove your shoes and loosen your clothing by undoing collar buttons, giving your belt an extra notch or two and so on. We are taking these precautions merely to ensure that your safety and comfort is guaranteed during our descent and *not* because we anticipate any danger to the aircraft.

'The cabin staff will gladly help you with any problems you might encounter while you are following these procedures, and they will also instruct you in the correct position to take when we are about to land. You might find the special emergency instruction sheet in the pocket in the seat in front of you helpful in reviewing what I've said, and please do not hesitate to ask the cabin staff for any extra help or advice.

'We will be commencing our descent shortly, so I shall leave it to our stewardesses to take over. I'll be talking to you from time to time as we make our final approach into London. Thank you all very much for listening to these instructions and I'd ask you now to pay close attention to your cabin staff.'

Page looked across to Huston and nodded. 'I am very glad to be sitting here at this moment and *not* downstairs. I hope your final words haven't had the effect I have nightmares about.'

'We'll soon hear how it went from the cabin crew,' Huston replied. 'As long as they keep the passengers busy and keep their minds off the idea of a crash, then we should get down O.K. Sometimes it helps if you're too scared to do anything but sit there and pray.'

'One Two Four, this is Escort. Ready to begin your descent?'

'Escort, I am commencing our descent to be at two five zero by Strumble. Keep an eye on us.'

'Roger, One Two Four. Descending to two five zero. Good luck.'

Page tuned to the approach frequency for London Airways. 'Area Control, good evening, This is Astral One Two Four. We are beginning our descent from flight level three zero to be at two five zero over Strumble. I understand we have a priority approach to be at Woodley at eight and we estimate our rate of descent at one thousand feet per minute.'

'Roger, One Two Four. Report crossing Strumble.'

'One Two Four. Report over Strumble.' Page repeated.

Huston closed his eyes for a brief moment. He opened them, shook his head, and turned to Page. 'Let's take her down together. Is everyone ready back there?'

Ames and Trent-Jones acknowledged. Ames was relaxed, reviewing the reports and juggling the cause and effect probabilities around in his mind. He never anticipated incidents but waited for something to happen. Then, and only then, did he react with the swiftness that his years of experience and snap judgements had disciplined into him. He was feeling out every tremor, every whine and groan, every hum from the three good engines, and waiting for the single sound that would indicate the plane was malfunctioning. Ames had become more a diagnostic machine, a computer capable of sensing the slightest change – the faintest deviation from the norm. He had programmed himself to compensate for the structural damage, and now all he could do was tune to the aircraft as the turbulence grew rougher and the first vicious shocks pummelled the weakened starboard wing.

Trent-Jones was no trouble-shooter. He was a simple man who was more accustomed to the complexities of flight instrumentation in experimental workshops, link trainers and the security of ground installations. He knew his theory, however, and he was experienced in putting it into physical practice. But never before in an emergency situation. Trent-Jones was frightened, and his palms were sweating, but he forced his concentration onto the instrument panels beside him and forward. The magnetic compass, true heading, VORTAC panel, Distance Measuring Equipment, artificial horizon, slope and glide path indicator: all the instruments which had anything to do with One Two Four's bearing Trent-Jones located and memorised so that he could keep a constant check on every fluctuation. He wasn't familiar with the layout of the 747 navigational gear, but it was similar to the 707, a bit more sophisticated, but in general the instruments gave him the same information he would expect to find on any commercial airliner.

There was silence in the cockpit. Sturgess was immersed in his console, sweeping his eyes across instruments which monitored every internal function of the aircraft. Page and Huston had eased the stick forward, each feeling for the slight but pronounced movement of the other. Their eyes also skimmed over instruments, air speed indicator, vertical speed, horizon, heading, and all the time fighting the forces that played against them: the drag from number three, the starboard control surfaces which refused to respond with the promptness to which pilot and co-pilot were accustomed, the rough air and the power reduction which Captain Huston still maintained in number one. Huston waited for the challenges ahead, the unexpected which would fight to send his aircraft plunging helpless into the sea below. Grimly and in total ignorance of all but his controls, Huston descended through thirty thousand feet and as the air grew heavier, so the battle to keep command of his aircraft grew harder.

There was something tempting about that 'Pull to Inflate' cord which the stewardesses had said to leave alone. Forbidden fruit, thought most of the passengers. Why the hell couldn't they pull it? Because they'd get stuck in the emergency exits. Because they'd be too fat. So don't touch it unless you find yourself bobbing around in the Irish Sea.

Sandra Gesner responded to the passenger call button in 69A. There was no life jacket under Jules Morehouse's seat. Nor was there a jacket in 85B and C. Susan O'Burns was told by Mr. and Mrs. Monaghan in 104E and F, centre aisle, that they had no jackets. Mary Stewart faced an angry Wilbur Cross because he, too, had no under-the-seat life preserver. It was the souvenir hunters again. The bright yellow jackets with day-glow red lettering in International's logo. Eight pounds sterling or twenty dollars each. With the two hundred and sixty one passengers on board, Mary Stewart wasn't too concerned. There were a hundred vacant seats under which were enough life jackets to hand round to those who found themselves without. But if the plane had been full. If more jackets were missing. The added panic – that extra margin of fear. She cursed beneath her breath as she smiled apologetically handing out extra jackets.

In the galley Julie Stark watched, her hands trembled on the counter. 'What is going to happen to us, Catheryn?'

'I'm frightened too, Julie,' murmured Catheryn Mayhill.

The plane lurched, bounced several times, and settled down again.

Tears had slipped down Julie's cheeks. 'How much can this thing take? You know the Captain wouldn't order emergency procedure unless he didn't think . . .'

'We're going to make it,' Catheryn pleaded. 'All of us. We've made it this far. Please, Julie, believe me we'll make it.'

Julie wiped her eyes. 'I'm sorry, Cathy – I'll be fine. Just give me a minute or two.'

Catheryn poured out a cup of coffee and added a small dash of scotch from one of the bonded bottles. 'Drink this down. There's just enough to flavour it. It'll help.'

Julie grasped the cup and sipped the black coffee.

'I mean we are over the Irish Sea and it is Irish coffee.'

Julie smiled. She took another small sip and poured the rest away. 'I've broken the rules enough already. Thanks. We better see what our holy ones are up to.'

At twenty minutes to nine, British Summer Time, One

Two Four was closing on Strumble with fifty minutes to go before reaching London. Bill Auer, Alan Manley and Mike Wise were in Approach Control in the room two floors below the Tower. Their instructions had been sent out, Air Traffic Control's to West Drayton and Wise's to all the services he had told Cohen to inform. Once Approach Control had picked up One Two Four on their thirty mile radar scanners, Auer, Manley and Wise would follow him in until he was reaching the talkdown stage of his descent at which time Auer had volunteered to take over the responsibility of bringing One Two Four onto the threshold of Two Eight Right.

The eerie glow from the radar screens revealed no air traffic. Every screen was blank as the sweeping arm circled again and again, waiting for the 747. The control room was strangely quiet as controllers spoke in hushed whispers rather than their firm commands to incoming aircraft. Manley felt out of place; for the first time in its history Heathrow had come to a total standstill, waiting patiently for a single aircraft.

In the Tower Ramaley and Anderson had stayed on past their shift. Meyer sat in front of his console, hypnotised by the distance-to-touchdown screens which were empty save for the monotonous repetition of the see-saw scanning motion. Clive Amery, still unhappy about the loss of power in Blake's section, watched the ground radar screen fill with the emergency vehicles Wise had called in. The northern perimeter was congested with vehicles and the only clean strip was the thin outline of two eight right, guarded at every point along its two mile length. In the distance the Heathrow beacon fought to penetrate the rain and mist, flashing out the letters LH in morse code which could be seen from sixty thousand feet on a clear night. Now, the usual bright green lights of the beacon were barely visible. The runway visual range was down to one hundred metres. From the tower, it was impossible to distinguish the threshold light on Two Eight. Only the rain, battering against the Tower windows, stirred the silence as Meyer waited for Auer to come up from below and end this hellish night.

The few staff from Travellers' Help waited in the restaurant below Aerodrome Control. They hadn't been in service long at

Heathrow, helping passengers with their problems whether they dealt with travelling difficulties, stolen money or whatever cropped up from day to day. The problems were as different as the passengers. And tonight there would be an onslaught of distressed travellers, all converging at once and probably all suffering from nervous shock. But there would be other assistance arriving any minute – medical aid and representatives from International Airlines. Between them, they would have to sort out the various problems that One Two Four's arrival would bring – if it arrived.

Malcolm Wilmet faced the pouring rain as he shivered against one of the three mobile passenger steps International had driven out into Block 13. He was as indistinguishable as the dozens of other men who either sheltered themselves in their vehicles, or braved the rain in readiness for what might be a long wait. Wilmet could just make out the flashing blue lights of the fire appliances to his right and left on the other side of the runway, and all around him flashed the yellow lights of the ground support vehicles from MT, Engineering, Ground Ops and Marshalling. There were lights up and down the edge of the runway, shimmering against the ceiling of rain and extending out of sight into the mist.

Congdon had found Coburn not long after he heard from the Tower that the PAR Caravans had been situated. Blake had also managed to single out the pair of them from the muddle of men and machines, and they sat together in Checker waiting for the Tower to radio that One Two Four was on radar at which time Coburn and Blake would return to their assigned positions.

'You can't tell one bloody car from the rest of them,' Blake had cursed when he found Checker. 'Looks like a fair ground not a ruddy emergency.'

'It's Manley's idea,' Congdon explained. 'He figures that if the Skipper of that jumbo can just get a visual fix on the runway while he's on talkdown, it'll make it a lot easier for him to hit the centreline and threshold together.'

'And if he falls apart when his wheels are down it'll make it a damn sight easier for him to plow all over us,' Blake replied. 'But if he does make a clean landing, I hope to God everyone remembers to switch off their overhead lights or there'll be confusion like you've never seen.'

Coburn had been thinking of all the water that was about, the water that had built up around the BranAir 707 and nearly resulted in Bartlett's death, the same water that had flooded the electrical circuits in Blake's section and swamped the PAR Caravans and the water that was pouring down all around them and building up on Two Eight Right. 'What're the chances of that thing aquaplaning?'

Blake frowned. 'You mean the jumbo? Well, what's the standing water like?'

'Thurnblad's been on it all evening,' Congdon replied, grinning. 'Nearly got run down by a Trident. It was one of those few times when the plane *didn't* aquaplane. Thurnblad says the standing water saved his life. I don't know about jumbo's though. I shouldn't think they'd be prone to aquaplaning with all that weight and eighteen wheels to settle down on.'

'He doesn't need wheels, mate,' Blake snickered. 'He needs pontoons from the looks of it. He could come in here with his undercarriage up and make a perfect water landing without hurting himself or the runway. The trouble is does *he* know that?'

'And if she does land safely – or otherwise – does anyone know exactly what we're supposed to do? I mean if we *all* start heading for that jumbo once she's down that pilot'll be so frightened he'll take off again.' Coburn wiped the condensation off the inside of the window and peered out.

'The word is if she can touchdown and come to a normal stop before shooting off the runway, then we begin to stand down. If anything else happens, then we can switch off our overheads and wait for further instructions – just like it says in the manual,' said Congdon. 'They've got it all worked out. What they haven't figured on is the mess it's going to be when the order comes to stand down. There'll be every vehicle Heathrow's got trying to find its way back home and calling up the Tower for directions. I bet a dozen of them get lost and we never hear of them again.'

'Suits me,' Blake grinned. 'How much longer do we have to sit out here?'

Coburn glanced at his watch. 'Not long. They're opening up Two Eight for departures at nine fifteen and if she isn't down by then, well, she just isn't coming in at all I reckon.'

Carol Dennison felt out of place amongst the people who sat nervously around the BOAC canteen waiting for news of Flight One Two Four. Normally, she would be home at her flat in London after solving the problems of Heathrow's fifty odd thousand employees. She was the one and only airport counsellor whose office was alongside the Chaplain's, and she was a compromise between the BAA and every other company at Heathrow. She was employed to see anyone who had a problem and who didn't want to see the welfare officers many of the companies employed themselves. Some of the smaller firms had no counsellor, and Carol Dennison filled this gap. Marriage problems, shift work problems, housing problems, job problems. But what did she do to encourage a few hundred people who were on the edge of their chairs with worry? She glanced around the canteen for Reverend Baxter, the Chaplain who had asked her to help. What was *he* doing? she wondered. How did *he* cope with this particular problem? But she guessed. The same way one helped with any problem. A bit of comfort and reassurance. Maybe a prayer or two.

Carol straightened herself, smiled down at a woman who was twisting a handkerchief around her fingers, and spoke to her. Soon she was speaking to a lot of people, and she was sharing the worry and fervent hope that One Two Four would make it down.

In the Press and Public Relations offices in Queen's Building, the corridor was jammed with reporters. Outside, two coaches waited to take them to the runway once the 747 had landed and the passengers were evacuated to safety. Milross was trying to make some kind of statement to the reporters who were nearest him, but with the shouting in the corridor, only a few caught his words. No sooner had he said something than a barrage of questions interrupted him. Somewhere behind him the telephone was ringing, and two of the other public relations officers tried to push their way through the newsmen to answer it.

Milross swore to himself and wished the ruddy plane would hurry up and do something. The heat and the smoke from dozens of cigarettes were oppressive, and he couldn't take much more of the greedy witch hunting the reporters were hitting him with. Who was to blame? Was it a bomb? Where's the International Representative? Is the jumbo really coming in over London? Why are all the emergency vehicles surrounding the airport? Why is the airport sealed off? Is the jumbo going to belly land? When can we go to the runway? Isn't the plane overdue? Has it crashed? Where was it flying over now? Could it have gone down? What condition is it in? Is it true it's being escorted in by the R.A.F.?

Andy Bennett, the first Press Officer to reach the phone, handed Milross a message which was nearly torn from his hands by the reporters. He unfolded the slip of paper, read the hastily scrawled note, and tried to make an anouncement.

'International Airlines Flight One Two Four has reported crossing the Welsh coast and is now descending to Heathrow. The Captain reports no trouble.'

There were perhaps four or five who heard the message.

'Give me a bit more from one,' Captain Huston began. 'Keep our airspeed steady.'

'Twenty thousand feet, Skipper,' Page reported.

The plane shuddered violently. Ames gripped the sides of his chair. 'Throttle back on number four or you'll lose that wing!'

'Fuel, Sturgess?' Huston shouted.

'No report on four, Sir.'

Huston's right hand slid the throttle back slightly and felt the added power.

'On course, Skipper,' Page said. 'Still at twenty thousand.'

'Push her down, Captain,' Ames advised. 'So far she's doing nicely.'

Huston's arms were beginning to ache and sweat trickled down his sides, staining his white shirt. 'It's like flying a goddam tank. Give me some flap on the port side, Dick. Feel her down.'

'Nineteen thousand five hundred,' Page announced, easing

the port flaps down enough to compensate for the drag from number three.

'If we don't straighten out this plane, we'll be flying in sideways,' Huston said coldly. 'There's no damn control over the starboard surfaces.'

The turbulence grew worse. And they were into cloud. A sudden updraught lurched the plane forward, bounced it down and lurched again.

Ames leant forward and fingered number four's throttle. 'O.K. to open her up – all the way?'

'Open number four,' Huston nodded. 'And pray there's fuel to keep it going.'

'Engine temperature in number four's rising, Skipper,' Sturgess called out. 'She's taking all the strain.'

'She'll goddam have to,' Huston replied. 'Christ knows what's going to happen when we drop our undercarriage.'

'Reduce your airspeed so you can test your bogies over Woodley,' Ames said, gripping his chair as another patch of rough air tossed the plane upwards.

'I wasn't figuring on dropping our gears until we're just about down,' Huston said.

'And you could spin this thing all over the runway if one of your bogies won't lock. Remember, you've still got pieces of something stuck in your . . .'

'We'll drop them over Woodley,' Huston sighed heavily. 'Anything so long as we get this thing on the deck.'

'She'll be very light now with all that fuel used up, so she's going to take a harder buffeting,' Ames began, leaning forward. 'But with the fuel gone out of your starboard wing, it'll take the extra strain off her.'

'Is that supposed to reassure me?'

'It might. But I was thinking . . .'

At a point somewhere near Chepstow One Two Four hit a heavy squall. The winds blasting in severe up and down draughts caught the 747 just as the overheat indicator on number four forced Huston to retard his single starboard engine. Within thirty seconds the aircraft had dropped from nineteen thousand feet to seventeen thousand, caught in a monstrous downwind current. With his harness unstrapped Ames never had a chance.

'One Two Four, this is Nimrod Escort. How do you read? Over.' Captain Pilkerton glanced across to his First Officer. 'International One Two Four, this is Nimrod Escort. How do you read? Over.'

'He's still on radar, Sir,' advised the First Officer.

'What's left of him maybe. It was bad enough for us. These squalls are going to rip that plane apart. One Two Four, this is Escort. Are you reading me? Over.' Captain Pilkerton gave One Two Four ten seconds to reply before he turned his frequency to one two eight decimal five. 'London Airways, this is Nimrod Escort Lima Zulu Bravo. We have encountered severe turbulence at nineteen thousand and are unable to contact International code-name Astral One Two Four. Are you receiving him?'

'Escort, this is London Airways. Negative. We have him on radar at seventeen and holding course. Advise you descend to eighteen thousand and reduce your airspeed to three seven five.'

'Three seven five to eighteen. Roger. Escort out.'

'Ladies and gentlemen,' began Mary Stewart over the address system, 'Please ensure that your seat belts are fastened securely. We are encountering some strong turbulence on our descent and it is important that you keep your seat belt securely fastened. Thank you.'

Mary turned to Lynn Almirall who was collecting dozens of plastic coffee cups which had cascaded onto the galley floor. 'That one was too close for comfort. I don't know about that wing, but this galley is going to fall apart if we do any more dives like *that*.'

'At least we're still in one piece,' said Lynn nervously. 'I wonder how they're taking it upstairs.'

Mary knew what she was thinking. 'You better go up and see. Maybe you better stay up there. I know there's the Doctor and another passenger in the Lounge. And you can check on the crew. We can handle things down here.'

'Thanks, Mary. Give me a buzz if you want me back.'

Sandra Gesner braced herself against the bucketing aircraft and struggled forward to find Mary Stewart.

'I'm serving coffee now if anyone wants it,' Mary said

jokingly, picking up the last of the cups. 'Or tea or milk.'

'Give me a double brandy,' Sandra panted. 'What the heck is going on? The passengers are ready to open the exits now they're so scared. Why don't we just make for the nearest patch of grass and try our luck?'

'That would suit me fine. And you've cut yourself. Here, let me.' Mary wiped a trickle of blood from the back of Sandra's arm. 'It's not too bad. Where the devil do they put the first aid boxes in these galleys?'

'Here,' Sandra replied. 'Above the food storage.'

'You won't bleed to death, but I'd get that seen to once we're down. Make a claim. It's about the only compensation you'll get out of this flight.'

Catheryn Mayhill appeared looking pale and worried, but keeping up appearances for the sake of the passengers.

'Another five minutes and the whole cabin staff will be packed into this galley,' Mary decided. 'What's your hang up?'

'Nothing so far. I just don't want to go through that again. One more and that's our luck run out. Right now the passengers are just about at breaking point. Two of them pulled those damn release valves on their life jackets as soon as we hit that rough patch. I've had to give them new jackets. All of them – they're clinging to those release cords.'

'What they don't realise, dearie,' Sandra announced, 'is that we are over land. Unless the Captain dumps us in some reservoir those life jackets aren't going to do much good.'

'It's a pacifier,' Mary replied smugly. 'If it gives them some kind of security, let them play with the things all they want.'

Bruce Ames knew what he was doing when he secured the seat belts into the wall panels and dados, both for Brodie and for Paul. He had added extra padding by shoving pillows between the belts and the boy's bodies and the sudden drop of two thousand feet had had little effect on either. Fortunately, both boys were still unconscious when the violent winds from the squall struck the plane and their bodies absorbed the shock harmlessly. Dr. Osterton had advised Roger Staunton to brace his neck with an extra pillow after they had strapped themselves in, and though Staunton felt far from comfortable, the precaution had prevented what could have been a near fatal whiplash when the aircraft plunged. Lynn Almirall found the four occupants of the Sky Lounge in good physical shape and both men were facing the situation as bravely as they could, but Osterton was visibly shaken.

'Your brother is fine, Miss Almirall,' Osterton said weakly. 'Mr. Ames did an excellent job of strapping the boys in. I should think he saved both their lives.'

Lynn sighed and tried to smile. She felt a surge of relief that overcame the fear of the bouncing aircraft and brutal shocks that were eager to tear the starboard wing from its spars. 'Thank God,' she whispered. 'Are you all right?'

'We're fine,' Staunton replied. 'But I'll be a lot happier when I know I'm on the ground. If you're going to see the Captain, ask him why he has to choose such a bumpy road to bring this thing in on, will you?'

Lynn knocked on the cockpit door. She was surprised that it wasn't opened in the few seconds it usually took. She knocked again. She heard someone fumbling with the door knob, then the door swung open and Trent-Jones faced her.

'Is everything all right?' she asked suspiciously.

'I'm afraid not,' Trent-Jones whispered. 'You had better come in.'

From the rear of the cockpit Lynn could see the outline of Bruce Ames strapped into the forward observer's seat. But his head hung limply forward, and there was no attentive character in his shoulders which she had seen to be erect and expectant.

'He's in a pretty bad way,' Trent-Jones explained. 'He wasn't strapped in when we had that rough patch. His head went straight into the circuit breaker panel above him. We don't know how serious it is.'

Lynn pushed forward to Ames' seat and knelt down. In the dim green glow from the instrument panel, the pallor in his face looked like death. She felt for his pulse: it was weak, but steady. His cheeks were cold and splotches of dried blood clung to his hair. 'Should I call Dr. Osterton forward?' she asked, leaning towards the Captain's seat.

Without turning, Huston shook his head. 'We could get another one of those draughts and then there'd be just one more to add to the list. How are the passengers?'

'No injuries if that's what you want to know,' Lynn replied coldly. 'But at least let me take Mr. Ames into the Lounge.'

'I'm sorry, Lynn, but he stays where he is. And you should be strapped in as well. There's no telling what we'll hit and next time it could easily be worse. Up here we're riding around in the most turbulent air you'll ever come across.'

Then from the corner of her eye she spotted Page. There was a white bandage wrapped around his forehead and an ugly red stain was growing. 'I'm getting Toni,' she announced firmly. 'It's one thing for you to fly this plane, but someone's got to see to it that whoever's flying it can continue to do so.'

Before Huston could countermand her, she had gone aft and pushed the galley call button. Juli Stark answered. 'Julie, it's Lynn. I'm in the cockpit. Send Toni up here, will you? No, nothing serious but just send Toni up. Hurry.'

'That could cost you your job, Miss Almirall,' Huston snapped coldly.

'And you could cost us all our lives, Captain,' she returned harshly. 'Look at him, that's your First Officer. He can hardly keep his head up. I don't know much about flying these planes, but I know it takes more than one man to land an airliner. For heaven's sake, see reason.'

Huston looked across at Page who was fighting the waves of dizziness and gripping the stick with every last bit of strength he could muster. He hadn't even heard what was being said. He was pulling out all the energy left in him to carry on flying.

'All right, Lynn,' Huston began slowly. 'I'm sorry. Do what you can and then get back to your seat. Be quick. We're dropping lower all the time and we could hit another bad one — maybe even worse.'

As if to prove it, the winds outside struck the jumbo with vehemence as though the storm considered the plane's presence an insult. The cockpit shook and Lynn gripped the back of Huston's seat. Page's head lolled around and Huston felt his arms carrying the full weight of the stick.

'He's passing out,' Huston snapped. 'Sturgess, strap him in your seat and take over. He'll never last out.'

Toni Rice knocked on the door. Trent-Jones who had unbuckled his harness to help Sturgess fumbled with the handle and let her in. Lynn lifted Page's left arm as Sturgess gently slipped him free of his straps and eased him clear of the controls. Trent-Jones grabbed Page under his arms and settled him into his own seat. The cockpit shook again and everyone grasped for the nearest hold.

'I'll do more good in the Flight Engineer's position than in that seat,' Trent-Jones called out. 'Is that all right with you, Captain?'

'Just don't touch anything. Sturgess will tell you what to do.' Huston turned to Sturgess. 'Get the feel of the stick, Peter. It's heavy. Your starboard controls are just as bad. Very little response. If you want her to do something, then you've got to overplay it, understand?'

'Roger, Skipper.'

Huston continued. 'I'm going to ease off on the stick to let you get the feel of it. Slowly – do you see? Heavy as a ton of bricks.'

'Christ, it's as if she were flying through a sea of muck. O.K., Skipper. I'm getting it. Just keep refreshing my memory.'

Huston went over the controls and instruments quickly, giving Sturgess one chance only to memorise the flight management of the aircraft. As he did so, Toni stood behind Page and slowly unwrapped the towel Trent-Jones had taken from the Captain's flight bag. Lynn knelt in front of him, gripping the edges of the seat in case the turbulence threw them once again.

'How'd it happen?' Toni asked loudly. 'What did he hit?'

'I don't know,' Huston called back. 'All I saw was the blood. It happened when we took that dive.'

Toni didn't stop to examine the wound. She ripped open the cellophane wrapper on a roll of gauze and folded part of the bandage into a pad which she tucked over the gash. Quickly, she wrapped the remaining gauze around his head and safety pinned the end. 'Hand me the kit, Lynn,' she said, holding Page's head upright. 'Put it on his lap. There's an ampule of ammonia in there somewhere. That's it. Now break it and wave it under his nose.'

'But if he's concussed . . .'

'He's got a plane to fly,' Toni said coldly. 'It may be concussion but I doubt it. His pulse is strong. Just do as I say.'

Page didn't respond at first. Slowly he weaved his head

away from the acrid smell before blinking his eyes. His head throbbed as he focused on the girl in front of him.

Huston's headset crackled. 'International One Two Four, this is Escort. Can you read me? Over.'

'One Two Four,' Huston snapped.

'Are you all right down there, Captain Huston? We've been trying to contact you for ten minutes.'

'We've had some trouble, Escort. We're all right now. Our frequency must have been joggled when we took that plunge. We've had two injuries in the cockpit, but we're still making for Heathrow.'

'Advise you contact London Airways immediately, Escort out.'

Huston checked his frequency selector. 'London Airways, this is Astral One Two Four.'

'Good evening, One Two Four. Report speed and heading.'

'Three five zero estimating Woodley at five seven.'

'Roger, One Two Four. Reduce your speed to two four zero when crossing Woodley. You should be at six thousand feet over Woodley to descend to four thousand at Ockham. Report crossing Woodley.'

'Two four zero over Woodley to be at four over Ockham. Report crossing Woodley. One Two Four,' said Huston.

Page rubbed his hands together, forcing the tingling sensation away from his fingers. His arms were limp and his legs felt like rubber. He breathed deeply, trying to gather strength. 'What's our situation, Skipper?'

'We're still in the clouds, Dick,' called Huston. 'About eight minutes to Woodley. How do you feel?'

'I'm alive. But my head isn't.'

'Think you can fly this thing again?'

'No, he can't,' Toni replied hotly. 'Not for another few minutes. If you push him now he'll only pass out on you again.'

'I didn't intend to push him, Miss Rice,' Huston said. 'All I want to know is if he can take over from Sturgess after we cross Woodley. I'll need Peter on the Engineer's console and I'll need Page up here with me. Can he or can't he still fly this thing?'

'I'll fly it, Skipper. Just give me time to catch my breath.

I've had worse cuts than this falling off roller skates.' Page began to remember. He looked up at Toni. 'How's Ames?'

'I don't know yet,' she replied. 'He's a lot worse than you, from the looks of him. Do you feel any better?'

'I'm fine,' Page said with a touch of impatience. 'Just let me know when we're over Woodley.'

Whether Page was concussed or not was debatable, but Ames was clearly hurt and there was no way to help him now. Whatever his injuries, he would have to wait until they reached Heathrow before he could get any effective treatment, and with the turbulence pushing the aircraft up to and beyond its limits, Huston ordered Toni Rice and Lynn Almirall back to the cabin. When they eventually reached Woodley, however, Trent-Jones promised to hold Ames as still as he could from his seat. Toni knew that if they didn't make it soon, neither would Ames.

Huston was cutting his air speed down to two hundred and forty knots. At this speed he called for additional life and began lowering his flaps. Number four had cooled down and whether she was going to overheat or co-operate, it was time to bring her power up. By now Huston knew the reserve tank alongside number four's was feeding in – otherwise he would have lost fuel for number four at least thirty minutes ago. And he had full use of his port engines. His indicated altitude showed him to be at six thousand feet, and his true altitude – his actual height above sea level – read eight thousand. He was twenty seconds before closing on Woodley.

'London Airways, One Two Four. Crossing Woodley.'

'Roger, One Two Four. Report crossing Ockham.'

'Report crossing Ockham. One Two Four.' Huston acknowledged.

'All right, Mr. Page, rest period is over. We'll be on our finals any time you're ready.'

Page carefully hoisted himself up and limped his way to the right hand seat. Sturgess returned to his console and Trent-Jones strapped himself in, leaving enough play in his harness to lean forward and hold Ames' head steady. He preferred this anyway, since he had a better view of the navigational instruments.

'Let's try our undercarriage,' Huston said slowly. 'Anytime now, Dick.'

Page reached for the lever which would drop the four bogies beneath the wings, fuselage, and the nose gear. Between the five gears, eighteen wheels would be resisting the onward motion of the aircraft. His head ached, but he dropped the lever and heard the rumblings below.

'Ladies and Gentlemen, this is Captain Huston. I have just tested our landing gear and we will be on our final approach into Heathrow in a few minutes. I would now ask that you ensure you are securely strapped in, that you have extinguished any cigarettes and that you are ready to assume the landing position your cabin staff have demonstrated. Once we have landed at Heathrow I must ask you to remain seated until we are sure that it is safe for you to disembark. Thank you.'

'What do our gears look like?' Sturgess called out.

'Undercarriage down and locked. No indication of trouble from our starboard bogies,' Page reported. 'Whatever was stuck in there's gone.'

'I should goddam think so after that dive we took,' Huston snapped, fighting the pressure on his stick. 'I never thought we'd pull out of that one. Not in a million years.'

'Nearly over Ockham, Skipper,' Page advised. 'Want me to call in?'

'I've got it,' Huston replied. 'One Two Four. Crossing Ockham at four.'

'Roger, One Two Four. Make your heading zero eight zero. Begin your descent to three thousand five hundred feet. We will advise you when to change your heading for your extended approach.'

Huston acknowledged. He had already lost five hundred feet soon after the added drag of his undercarriage cut his speed. 'Descent check, please.'

'Roger, descent check, Skipper,' Sturgess called back. He and Page now faced the final checking of all the aircraft systems for their descent. Between them, window heat, booster pumps, hydraulics, altimeter setting and cabin pressurisation, engine compressors, thrust valves, flow meters, and a score of other internal and outside functions were called out, checked, and reported. Despite the emergency approach of One Two Four, there could be no landing without checks on all systems so that Huston knew exactly what he had to work with.

Page first noticed the warning on his starboard main and wing bogies as the check was complete. He told Huston.

'Any ideas, Dick?' Huston asked as the dim red glow showed up beside the undercarriage release lever.

'Too much drag on the wing, Skipper. Those bogies could be the last straw as far as those spars are concerned. You've got number four trying to compensate for three which isn't helping the stress either. I'd pull up our bogies and leave them till the last second. It feels like it's going to get rougher all the way down.'

Huston nodded. 'I agree. Pull 'em up, Dick. Next time I call for those gears, you've got about three seconds to get 'em down otherwise we're going to belly flop.'

'One Two Four, this is Nimrod Escort. We are returning to base. You'll be closing for finals shortly so good luck. It's been a pleasure flying with you, Captain.'

'The pleasure's mine, Captain Pilkerton. I'll buy you a drink if we ever meet again. As long as it's on the ground.'

'Roger, One Two Four. Bon voyage.'

Huston wished he could have said more, said some kind of thanks that expressed what he really felt. But there wasn't time. It didn't matter. Captain Pilkerton knew only too well what was ahead for One Two Four.

'She's slipping, Captain,' Trent-Jones announced. 'Check your horizon.'

'Christ, she is,' Huston replied. His hand shot to the throttles and he juggled number four open. It was his only choice – to risk relying on his starboard controls to correct his altitude was suicide. If he didn't keep himself straight and level at this low air speed, the plane would drop. 'Keep your eye on number four, Peter,' Huston called out.

London Airways cut in. 'One Two Four, make your heading three zero zero to close on the centreline. Air speed two four zero. Maintain three thousand feet. Contact London Approach on one two one decimal two. Good luck.'

Auer wasn't happy with the way One Two Four was skidding around in the skies. The lower he got, the less control

Huston seemed to have over his plane. He was coming in at well over two hundred and fifty knots, and he'd have to close onto a heading that would give him a target of just three hundred feet of concrete – one hundred and fifty feet either side of the centreline. He'd be coming in fast to keep control of his aircraft, and that meant nailing it down on the threshold and not a foot further down the runway. Radar showed One Two Four swinging about the skies like a pendulum and when it seemed Huston was able to confine his swinging, he began bouncing up and down like a rubber ball. Before Auer could clear him to land, Huston would have to tighten that plane up. His approach would have to be limited to a margin of a few degrees – up or down. One degree too much on his glide slope and he'd either touch down on top of the localiser, or end up half way down two eight with no runway left to stop. If he kept swinging from right to left, his bogies would miss the runway by a few hundred feet and he'd end up plowing through the emergency appliances. And if at the very last moment he couldn't confine his plane to a three hundred foot wide threshold touch down, Auer knew the chances of aborting his landing were nil. To open up whatever power he had left in his engines would rip his starboard wing straight off. It was make or break all the way.

Mark Meyer had come down from the Tower and was sitting behind Auer. Though Auer was a Training Officer, Meyer had more experience in Precision Talkdowns. He could predict the way a stricken aircraft might behave once he saw it on the radar screen and he could judge just how much chance the pilot had of making an uneventful landing in spite of his troubles. Of course much depended on the Skipper and Meyer had had a brief talk with Huston over the RT. He made much of his judgement of a Captain by how he sounded on the airways – a voice told an experienced controller just about everything he wanted to know about a Captain. Some were pompous, demanding, over efficient. Others were less pompous, but still too officious. American pilots seemed the most relaxed and organised of the sixty three different airlines flying into Heathrow. TWA came out top in Meyer's book and he swore TWA had a special school for pilot training. Whether it was TWA's 707's or 747's, the perfect nose up attitude landings he witnessed every morning when the rush hour traffic was at its peak were never equalled by any other airline. TWA never left a spot of rubber on the runways, never bounced around with smoke billowing from over stressed tyres and never pulled the famous engage-thrust-reverse-before-touchdown stunt that one airline was famous for. Meyer thought this particular airline's landings looked like someone had dropped a giant rubber ball onto the runway and he wondered how those planes ever stayed in one piece. There were other good airline pilots, Meyer admitted from time to time, and there was the daredevil Spanish pilot who, in his words, 'took off by raising his landing gear'. The controllers called him Miguel and whenever it was Miguel's turn to roll, they stood glued to the take off sequence. Miguel wasn't off the runway before his gears were up, and his ascent procedure was about as unorthodox as the book allowed. His flaps were in before he was at two hundred feet and this caused him to drop back down to barely one hundred feet before he developed enough engine speed to gain height. It was lucky that Miguel only flew cargo.

Huston's voice was typical of American commercial pilots. In spite of the dangers that faced him, Huston came over the RT in a calm co-operative monotone that didn't reveal the slightest hint of trouble on board. He was quick in his acknowledgements, equally quick in his decisions and in Meyer's opinion, capable of bringing the 747 down. But he would have had more confidence in the next few minutes if it was TWA up there. Meyer stared at the radar screen and waited. Behind him stood Manley and Wise.

The Precision Approach Radar had picked up One Two Four eleven miles from touchdown. Auer peered at the radar screen and took a deep breath, 'One Two Four this is your talk-down director. Maintain three thousand feet. You're closing on the centreline from the left. Your heading is two eight zero. Continue heading two eight zero. Check your wheels are down and locked.'

'One Two Four. Holding our wheels up until final possible moment. Please advise absolute minimum to lower undercarriage,' Huston snapped as quickly as he could. There was no time for explanations. Both he and Auer knew it.

'Roger One Two Four. Will advise maximum allowance.

Heading two eight zero. Turn left five degrees. Make your heading two seven five. Ten miles from touchdown. You're a little too high. Stand by to lose height. Maintain heading two seven five. You're off your heading. Heading two seven five. Begin your descent now to maintain three degrees glide path. Two seven five is your heading. On the centreline. Heading two seven five. Eight miles from touchdown.'

'You're below glide path,' Trent-Jones called nervously. 'Bring her up, Captain.'

'Damn it to hell, it's like a bull-dozer,' Huston swore.

'That's better,' said Trent-Jones no less reassured by the corrected heading. 'Now bring her back on course.'

The low level turbulence was pushing One Two Four up when she should be down. When she was down, the winds teased her and jostled her up. As soon as Huston had his aircraft on the correct heading, the crosswinds pushed her away.

Auer looked over to Meyer. Meyer shook his head. 'You'll never get him down, he's bobbing around up there like a cork. It's suicide.'

'Seven and a half miles from touchdown,' Auer persisted. 'Make your heading two seven five. I say again. Make your heading two seven five. You're coming in a little low. Bring your plane up to maintain three degrees glidepath. Turn slightly left now two degrees. Heading two seven five. You're nicely on the glidepath. Not too high. Settling down onto the glide path. Seven miles from touchdown. You're swinging around a bit much. Try to hold your heading steady. You're back onto two seven five. Maintain your glidepath. Six and a half miles from touchdown. Turn right three degrees. Heading two seven five. Turn left one degree. Your heading is two seven five. Two seven five is your heading. Nose up to maintain your glidepath. Try to confine yourself to the glidepath. Heading two seven five. Six miles from touchdown. Try to cut your airspeed to around one five zero.'

'Page, order the passengers to assume crash position for landing,' Huston snapped.

Trent-Jones was shaking his head unconsciously. There

wasn't a hope of making a decent approach. The plane was swinging one way or the other. It was being jolted upwards or down. They might as well try to land on a needle: the threshold could be five hundred feet wide and Huston would have trouble hitting it. He wanted to close his eyes and wait for the end but he tightened his jaw muscles into a painful grimace and kept his eyes glued to the instruments.

'Overheat number four, Skipper,' Sturgess shouted. 'She's ready to burn.'

'Throttle back, Dick,' Huston answered. 'Keep her running. Let me know if she gets any worse.'

'Five and a half miles from touchdown. One Two Four you're off the centreline. Turn left eight degrees. Make your heading two seven five. Turn left four degrees. Nose up to maintain your glidepath. Turn left two degrees. You're on the centreline. You're moving off the centreline. Turn right three degrees. Five miles from touchdown. Continue to reduce airspeed.'

'Any more of this and I'm hitting the crash button,' Meyer said coldly. 'He's going to scatter himself all over the bloody airport. It's murder if you keep this up, Bill.'

Auer ignored this. Meyer might as well have been ten miles away. Meyer realised Auer wouldn't stop and he pushed himself away from the desk and stood above the crash alert table.

'Four miles from touchdown. Turn left two degrees. Your heading is two seven five. Two seven five is your heading. You're coming in low, One Two Four. You are below the glidepath. Left of centreline. Make your heading two seven five. Nose up to maintain three degrees glidepath. Three and a half miles from touchdown. Advise you lower your undercarriage. Check wheels down and locked.'

Huston was ready for this one. As Page hit the undercarriage lever, the pilot opened number four and his port engines, at the same time giving himself as much flap as he dared. He had to compensate for the drag without boosting his air speed or losing lift. But with his airspeed still pushing two hundred knots, he also knew he'd have to cut back to no more than one hundred and forty knots before he was 'over the hedge' and onto the runway.

'Three miles from touchdown. You're on the centreline.

Heading two seven five. Maintain your glidepath. Clear to land Two Eight Right. Surface wind one two zero at twenty-three knots. You're still on the centreline. You're settling down nicely. Two and one half miles from touchdown. You're looking good, One Two Four. Heading two seven five. Maintain your glidepath. You're slightly to the right of centreline. Turn left two degrees. Still a bit fast – reduce your airspeed. Your heading is two seven five. Two miles from touchdown. Check your company minima.'

Huston smiled grimly. His company minima – that was a laugh! His company minima would have told him he was a dead duck two hours ago. He was over-riding about everything there was to over-ride.

'One and half miles to touchdown. You're a little high. Settle down on your glidepath. Your heading is two seven five. Reduce your airspeed to one four zero. You're on the centreline now. You're settling down nicely. One mile from touchdown. You're slightly high. You're coming in high. Heading two seven five. You're still too high, One Two Four. Correct your height. One half mile from touchdown. Your heading is two seven five. Centreline and glidepath. Coming up to touchdown. Talkdown complete. Out.' One Two Four was out of radar contact. There was nothing more Auer could do.

At less than a quarter mile from touchdown, when the bogies of One Two Four skimmed over the buildings in front of Two Eight Right, Captain Huston was losing all control of his aircraft. His control surfaces were useless at the retarded airspeed. Number four was ready to burst into flames. He still hadn't seen the runway. Trent-Jones was calling for attitude corrections. Sturgess was calling out a fire warning in number four. Page was lost in a flurry of final landing adjustments. Huston was caught between skimming his instruments or peering out for the threshold. And then in one blinding, thudding horrendous moment, One Two Four's fate had been decided.

'Ladies and Gentlemen, this is Captain Huston. On behalf of International Airlines, I'd like to welcome you to London's Heathrow Airport. I must ask that you all remain seated until we are ready to deplane and if any of you are anxious to get your feet on the ground I expect that the passenger ramps and coaches will be ready for you shortly. You needn't worry about all the vehicles you see surrounding the aircraft as these are here merely as a precaution. I'd like to thank you on behalf of our flight crew and cabin staff and offer my sincere apologies for the difficulties we have encountered during the flight. I think we're all pretty happy to be back down again.'

Huston wiped the sweat from his forehead and sighed deeply. His hands hung limply over the stick and he rested his head on the back of his seat.

'That's the first sea landing I've ever made,' Page began. 'And I hope it's the last.'

'I don't know,' Huston replied, sitting himself upright. 'If it wasn't for all that water, I doubt we would have managed to bring this thing to a stop much before that localiser out there.'

'You can thank whoever it is that handles these miracles that we didn't slide all over the airfield.' Sturgess lifted his head. 'Skipper, I never thought we'd do it.'

Huston grinned wearily and looked over his seat. 'There were times, Mr. Sturgess, that I had my doubts. Remind me to write a letter to Boeing sometime and tell them I think they build a pretty good airplane.'

Page looked out of the starboard window and watched the Fire Service pouring several thousand cubic feet of carbon dioxide into number four. He was tired, and he wanted to fall asleep right there.

Mary Stewart appeared from the Sky Lounge. Her face was still pale, but she was smiling. 'Captain Huston, the ramps are in position. We are ready to deplane.'

'Have the ambulance men come on board?' Huston asked.

'Both boys have been taken off the aircraft. They're coming up for Mr. Ames now.'

'Then you may inform the passengers that they may leave the aircraft,' replied Huston.

'And don't forget to thank them for flying International,' Page grinned.

London Tower released the order for all emergency vehicles to stand down. Slowly and in mild confusion, over three hundred vehicles from the Fire Service, Mechanical Transport,

Engineering, Marshalling, Ground Operations and the BAA Constabulary moved off through the driving rain. Two ambulances, their bright blue lights piercing the dismal night, shot off Runway Two Eight Right and headed for Hillingdon Hospital.

In the grey light shrouding Heathrow Airport the massive bulk of the 747 dwarfed the surrounding vehicles. Huston leaned back in the pilot's seat checking off the instruments.

'Thank God,' he murmured to Page, 'we made it!'

ACKNOWLEDGEMENTS

This novel was written – in its entirety – at London's Heathrow Airport. Weeks of research among the numerous Sections under the British Airports Authority and Air Traffic Control only served to scratch the surface of this vast airport which can only be likened to a small city. The Sections which live and operate within this city – from Mechanical Transport to the Medical Centre to Aerodrome Control – are communities unto themselves but all linked together to form the basis of this international airport. There is unquestionably a feeling of loyalty and all pervading sense of camaraderie amongst all of the fifty odd thousand employees who keep Heathrow running night and day in all weathers throughout the year. In a book of this size, or one several times its length, one could never hope to adequately portray the life of this airport. It is a microcosm – a society separated from the boundaries of Hayes, Hillingdon, Staines and Feltham by the fifteen mile perimeter road which encircles Heathrow. There are scandalous affairs, deeds of great courage, political skulduggery, hopeless bureaucracy and intense co-operation mixed into this society which every day welcomes or bids farewell to thousands of travellers who never once consider the massive labour force required to keep Heathrow ticking over.

In this book I have created a number of incidents which introduce as many of the peripheral activities of Heathrow Airport as is possible without losing the reader in the social and political structures of the airport. It is more a tale of adventure, of heroics on the ground and in the air, and however possible or impossible the events in this story may seem to the reader, the majority of events that have been depicted have at one time or another actually occurred. For reasons of security, or at my discretion, I have sometimes altered certain aspects of an incident, but the underlying truth is there. Most of the employees at Heathrow will recognise the background of these events and while some will no doubt feel my representation of life at the airport has been overdone, I earnestly hope that the majority will appreciate the enormous difficulties an author faces in trying to portray the complexities of such a place in such a way that is both fair and realistic – for at Heathrow the truth of incidents and activities is many times harder to believe than fiction.

I am naturally indebted to far too many people to mention individually, but I have listed those men and women who have made considerable efforts to develop, criticise and authenticate all that concerns Heathrow. In particular I must express my sincere thanks to Robin Baxendale and the Reverend Ben Lewers who each in their own way made my work at Heathrow an exciting, interesting experience and who ingrained in me an innmense respect for the task these men and women face each day. Also, Pan American World Airways – 'The World's Most Experineced Airline' – proved to be the world's most co-operative airline and through the patience and skill of their employees I now feel competent enough to take a Boeing 747 to pieces, reassemble it and fly it to any point on the globe. Fortunately, my confidence will never have to be put to the test and I shall stick to flying aircraft whose only means of propulsion is that single whirling propeller for I have yet to satisfy my left hand bosses that I am capable of keeping it revolving.

Finally, I wish to make it perfectly clear to the reader that the pit covers mentioned in the story will no longer pose a threat to aircraft at Heathrow. The British Airports Authority is re-surfacing the twelve thousand foot main runways this year and the days when pit covers chipped, slipped or collapsed will be gone when the asphalt surfacing replaces the traditional concrete. As one who has had the good fortune to fly to many airports around the world, I shall always look forward to returning to Heathrow which I know from personal experience is the safest, kindest and most advanced airport anywhere. There will always be room for improvements as the pace of aviation increases in both size and technical sophistication, and it is reassuring to know that Heathrow is not afraid to meet the challenges and expectations that tomorrow's giant aircraft and supersonic jets will bring.

To each of the fifty thousand employees, to the sixty-three

airlines, the plane spotting enthusiasts and the Directors of Heathrow Airport go my thanks and sincere good wishes.

The following individuals, companies and airlines have spent many patient hours assisting with the compilation and editing of this book. I sincerely hope that what has been written here serves as some token of thanks for their enduring and invaluable efforts.

At London Heathrow Airport

The British Airports Authority, especially: –
  R. Baxendale and D. S. Harvey: Press and Public Relations
  R. J. B. Cann: Operations
  C. J. Churchill and M. C. Churchill: Executive Officers, Roads Administration
  A. R. W. Duff: Manager, Roads Administration
  J. P. Durrant: Manager, Manoeuvring Areas
  A. I. Johnson: Deputy Chief Meteorological Officer
  A. J. Kemsley, M.B.K.S.: Photographic Officer
  (Miss) O. M. A. King: Principal Nursing Officer
  The Reverend B. H. Lewers: Airport Chaplain
  I. A. MacGregor: Deputy Fire Officer
  J. Tough: Mechanical Transport
  (Miss) Diana Whitaker: Heathrow Counselling Service
  Ground Operations Unit: Senior Assistants: R. Bye, J. Fisher, G. Frost, D. Lane, D. Sims. Assistants: E. Hall, P. Phipps, R. Mattingley, T. Tew and Percy.

Air Traffic Control, especially: –
  Basil A. Turner: Chief Officer, Civil Aviation Authority, N.A.T.C.S.
  Richard Stokes: A.T.C. Training Officer
  A.T.C. Officers: B. A. Buckingham, D. Bush, I. MacKay, R. Plant, R. Randall and I. Saunders.

Pan American World Airways: –
  R. F. Batten: Technical Training
  F. J. Hermitage: Purchasing Supervisor
  David McKellow: Assistant Purchasing Supervisor.
  Henry Maskell: Hangar Maintenance Supervisor

British Overseas Airways Corporation: —
  T. E. Scott-Chard, Reference Officer
  A. Pickersgill, Senior Special Visits Officer

British European Airways: —
  Malcolm Parr, Public Relations

General Advisers on Civil Aviation

  Adams Aviation (Avionics)
  Amplivox Ltd. – Racal Group Services
  Boeing Aircraft Corporation
  Counsel Ltd.
  Decca Systems Ltd. (H. H. B. Capes, D.B.A., A.Ae.S.,
  F.R.S.A., M.I.P.R.)
  Marconi-Elliot Avionic Systems Ltd.
  Plessey Radar (Parker PR Ltd.)
  Smiths Industries – Aviation Division
  VHF Supplies

Textual references used in the writing of this book have included: —
  'The World's Great Air Mysteries,' Michael Hardwick
    (Odhams, 1970)
  'The Jet Age,' William Gunston (Arthur Barker, 1971)
  'The Boeing 707,' Barry Schiff (Arco Publishing Inc., 1967)
  'Boeing 747 Jumbo Jet,' B. Tomkins and J. Lucas (Airline
    Publications, 1971)
  '747 In Service – Economic Considerations,' George Bouvet
    (Boeing, 1970)
  '747,' Boeing Corporation, 1970
  'The Language of Aviation,' W. S. Barry (Chatto & Windus,
    1969)
  'The British Airports Authority – Reports and Accounts,
    1970–71'
  'London's Heathrow Airport,' M. G. Housego, M.B.E. (Jar-
    rold Colour Publications)
  'Interavia SA,' Geneva, Switzerland, 1972
  Southern England and Wales (NW50/5½) Aeronautical
    Chart (August, 1971) Conical Orthomorphic Projection

Orthomorphic Projection – Ordinance Survey – Crown
   copyright
International Aeradio Flight Guide London S.I.D.'s

My thanks and recognition to the thousands of men and
women who keep air traffic moving swiftly, competently and
safely, both in the air and on the ground; and to London
Heathrow Airport which deserves far more justice than I can
present here.

A Selection of Popular Fiction from Sphere

A Selection of Historical Fiction from Sphere

THE GAME OF KINGS	Dorothy Dunnett	40p
QUEENS' PLAY	Dorothy Dunnett	40p
THE DISORDERLY KNIGHTS	Dorothy Dunnett	60p
THE BLACK PLANTAGENET	Pamela Bennetts	30p
BORGIA PRINCE	Pamela Bennetts	35p
THE BORGIA BULL	Pamela Bennetts	35p
KATHERINE OF ARAGON	Julia Hamilton	30p
ANNE OF CLEVES	Julia Hamilton	30p
ANNE BOLEYN	Margaret Heys	30p
JANE SEYMOUR	Frances Clark	30p
KATHERINE HOWARD	Jessica Smith	30p
KATHERINE PARR	Jean Evans	30p

The above six titles are also available in an attractive slipcase at £1·80

A Selection of Westerns from Sphere

by Zane Grey

THE SHEPHERD OF GUADELOUPE	25p
THE LONE STAR RANGER	25p
THE DRIFT FENCE	25p
PRAIRIE GOLD	25p
NEVADA	25p
THIEVES' CANYON	25p
RIDERS OF VENGEANCE	30p
WILD FIRE	30p

POCKET MONEY	J. P. S. Brown	45p
JUNIOR BONNER	Paul Fairman	30p
GHOST DANCE	John Norman	40p
BITTER GRASS	T. V. Olsen	25p
SOLDIER BLUE	T. V. Olsen	30p
EYE OF THE WOLF	T. V. Olsen	30p
KILL ANGEL	Frederick H. Christian	30p
SEND ANGEL	Frederick H. Christian	30p

A Selection of Science Fiction from Sphere

All Sphere Books are available at your bookshop or
newsagent, or can be ordered from the following address:

Sphere Books, Cash Sales Department,
P.O. Box 11, Falmouth, Cornwall.

Please send cheque or postal order (no currency), and allow
7p per copy to cover the cost of postage and packing
in U.K. or overseas.